SNAP

SNAP

A NOVEL

Susin Nielsen

HarperCollins*Publishers*Ltd

Snap
Copyright © 2025 by Susin Nielsen.
All rights reserved.

Published by HarperCollins Publishers Ltd

First edition

No part of this book may be used or reproduced in any manner whatsoever
without written permission.

Without limiting the author's and publisher's exclusive rights,
any unauthorized use of this publication to train generative artificial
intelligence (AI) technologies is expressly prohibited.

HarperCollins books may be purchased for educational, business,
or sales promotional use through our Special Markets Department.

HarperCollins Publishers Ltd
Bay Adelaide Centre, East Tower
22 Adelaide Street West, 41st Floor
Toronto, Ontario, Canada
M5H 4E3

www.harpercollins.ca

Library and Archives Canada Cataloguing in Publication

Title: Snap : a novel / Susin Nielsen.
Names: Nielsen-Fernlund, Susin, 1964- author.
Description: First edition.
Identifiers: Canadiana 2025014316X | ISBN 9781443473286 (softcover)
Subjects: LCGFT: Novels.
Classification: LCC PS8577.I37 S637 2025 | DDC C813/.54—dc23

Printed and bound in the United States of America

25 26 27 28 29 LBC 5 4 3 2 1

To my husband, who puts up with me

Crime

Frances hurried down the empty corridor, tote bag and purse slung over one shoulder. The school was a brand-new build but already a number of the purple lockers had been vandalized. *F.U. Dylan*, declared one; *Marcy is a hoe*, declared another. Normally Frances would have delighted in this spelling error—Marcy is a garden tool—but today it barely registered. She was almost at the doors. They made a familiar metallic *clang* as she thrust them open.

She breathed in the chilly January air, a welcome contrast to the low-grade funk inside. It was a scent that permeated every middle school she'd ever visited, the blend of body odour (there were always children who'd hit puberty overnight, before anyone could talk to them about deodorant), cheap and overpowering colognes (children who were fully aware puberty had hit and used desperate measures to mask their treacherous new smells), forgotten lunches, gym kits mouldering in lockers, and cafeteria french-fry grease.

Her heart pounded wildly. There was a ringing in her ears. She glanced over her shoulder, suddenly worried that someone might be following her; the pear-shaped principal, for example, who'd said to her, "So, you're an author, eh? Can't say I've heard of your books."

There was no one. She was alone. It was dead quiet. Perhaps eerily so.

Except for the ringing in her ears, which was getting worse.

I think I have done a very bad thing.

She pushed a lock of damp grey hair behind her ear. Damp because the school library had been grossly overheated; damp because at fifty-five she was in full-on menopause and her body ambushed her multiple times a day from the inside out, bathing her in layers of sweat. She zipped up her impractical black leather jacket, chosen because she'd thought it would help her look cool, more relatable; ditto the slightly flared jeans and the short black boots with a modest heel that wouldn't exacerbate her fallen arches.

Oh, Frances, listen to yourself. You are a deluded idiot. She walked briskly to Belinda the Beemer, named by her daughter when the car was fresh off the lot over ten years ago, when Daisy still thought her mother could do no wrong. She fumbled for her keys and climbed inside.

One more glance back at the school. White brick facade, earthquake-proof. Still dead quiet. No one chasing her down. *Perhaps I'm making a mountain out of a molehill.* Her heart rate started to slow. She punched in home on her GPS, which reminded her that it likely wouldn't be her home much longer, and that made her start to cry, which made her hate herself because *how many tears can one person shed, I am so sick of crying!* Which only made her cry more.

Siobhan—her name for the voice she'd selected on Google Maps—spoke to her in a soothing Irish accent. "Head north on Rupert Street." Frances knew the way home, but Siobhan's voice was a calming presence, a bit of much-needed company. For that reason, she put on Google Maps whenever she used the car these days, even on a run to the grocery store.

"It should be okay, Siobhan, don't you think?" Talking to Siobhan was a relatively new thing. Probably not a healthy thing, but no one else was around to hear, so what did it matter? *If a tree falls in the forest and all that?* "Do you think I can still cash the cheque?" The librarian had handed her an envelope with her payment before she'd started her presentation, and it was tucked away in Frances's purse. "I got well over halfway through."

"In three hundred metres, turn left," Siobhan replied.

"Agreed," said Frances. "I'll deposit it."

Traffic was terrible. The drive, from East Vancouver to Kitsilano, took close to an hour. But in that time, Frances—with the help of Siobhan's soothing, measured voice—managed to calm herself down. She concluded that, on the balance of probabilities, nothing would come of this; in fact, in the not-too-distant future, it might even be a funny story to tell at dinner parties.

But as she pulled onto her tree-lined street, an image popped into her head.

The girl in the crop top.

Familiar heat started to rise from within. She rolled down Belinda's windows, trying to stave off the worst of it, but it was too late. Sweat sprung from every one of her pores, and within the span of a minute, her blouse was soaked through. A rivulet meandered its way down between her butt cheeks.

The girl in the crop top was twelve or thirteen, fully developed. Frances had only noticed her because she was revealing *so much flesh*. She'd had a motherly urge to pull the girl aside and beg her to cover up, to tell her that in spite of how mature she might feel, she was nowhere near ready for a certain type of creepy male gaze. But then she'd heard Daisy's voice, telling her she was a second-wave feminist (like that was a bad thing) and grossly out of touch, and that all women, even young women, had the right to bodily autonomy. So she'd kept her mouth shut.

But when Frances—*oh god*—did what she did, the girl in the crop top had been near the front of the room. Frances could picture her now, eyes wide, laughing. Holding her phone aloft.

Recording everything.

"You have arrived," said Siobhan.

Frances managed to park the car. She turned off the ignition and clutched her stomach. "Siobhan," she said. "I think I'm fucked."

"Yup. You are," Siobhan replied.

Or at least, that's what Frances heard.

Beloved Children's Author Under Investigation for Assault

Kerry Silver, *Vancouver Post*

Frances Partridge, fifty-five-year-old children's author of the best-selling *Phoebe Unknown* trilogy and other award-winning middle-grade novels, is under investigation for allegedly assaulting a minor.

The incident occurred during a presentation given by Ms. Partridge at Harwood Middle School. Says a student who recorded the incident on her phone, "This kid was talking a lot and not paying attention, and she kept asking him to be quiet, and he just, you know, ignored her. And then suddenly she grabbed him by his collar and pulled him up and started shaking him and shouting, like, an inch from his face, telling him to shut the *eff* up, and she was so tired of this crap except she didn't say eff or crap— then she let him go and grabbed her stuff and walked out."

When asked for comment the school's principal, Jim Davidson, said, "We value the safety of our students above all else. Immediately after the incident occurred, we informed the student's parents and called the police. As you can imagine, we are shocked and saddened by this turn of events, especially since the perpetrator is someone whose work is so beloved by so many children. Although personally I have not read any of her books."

The student uploaded the video to YouTube, where it currently sits at 157,000 views.

Geraint wished he'd worn a warmer jacket over his black Adidas track suit. He was shivering with cold and his legs were getting numb, but he didn't dare stand up and stretch. Instead he tried shifting his weight to bring some of the feeling back. Thankfully Ron's neighbours spent half the year in Maui, so there was no one home to see a hulking, hairy six-foot-four man in his early forties squatting on their front lawn and peering through the shrubbery in the late January dusk. In fact, a lot of the homes in the leafy, old-money Shaughnessy neighbourhood were devoid of life: a combination of offshore owners and wealthy retirees who wintered in warmer climes.

He glanced through the box cedars towards Ron's house. It had been built to stand out, a monstrous, Spanish-style villa with loads of columns and statuary. He remembered when Ron was having it built three years ago; the neighbours, at least the ones who were in residence, raised a holy stink. It was an eyesore, they said. It didn't fit with the neighbourhood, they said. Ron had revelled in the controversy. As a crowning *screw you* he'd had a large, phallic-looking fountain installed on the front lawn, the water spurting out of a tiny hole in the tip. Ron had sworn that it was *not* a massive erect penis, and that only filthy-minded people would see it that way. But he'd said it with a smirk.

Ron loved flaunting his newfound wealth, and Geraint had never begrudged him that, even though, as Ron's number two, he hadn't had a raise in five years. There were now eleven Quicky Mufflers in and around the Lower Mainland, and Geraint had finally saved up enough to give Ron a cheque for the down payment on number twelve, which Ron had cashed just last week.

It started to drizzle. The neighbourhood was now completely dark; just a few streetlamps, placed far apart, and the odd window lit from within. Geraint looked at his watch, an old Seiko that had belonged to his drunken pa, may he rest in peace. It was almost half past five. He hoped Ron would come home soon. Geraint really needed to pee, and while he could probably get away with doing it right here, against the neighbours' shrubs, it felt disrespectful; what had they ever done to him? Nothing, that's what. No, he would hold it for a while longer.

He heard Ron's Lamborghini Huracan before he saw it. He'd never quite understood the logic—surely a very expensive car should also be very quiet—but Ron had told him, "Oh, Geraint, my fat friend. The point is to be seen *and* heard."

The banana-yellow car pulled into the driveway. Fear suddenly clenched Geraint's stomach. *What if Ron wasn't alone?*

The doors to the Huracan opened upwards, Batman-style. Ron extricated himself from the car with some difficulty. Geraint breathed a sigh of relief to see he was by himself. He watched as Ron disappeared inside the house, whistling cheerfully as he went.

Whistling! After what happened today!

Rage swept over him again. He stood, his knees cracking with the effort. A light went on in the back of the house. That meant Ron was in his massive kitchen, with its La Cornue range and cookware, the name of which meant exactly nothing to Geraint except that he knew one pot cost more than all of Geraint and Darlene's appliances put together, and the reason he knew this was because Ron had told him repeatedly.

Another light went on, also in the back of the house. Ron had moved into his den, or "man cave" as he delighted in calling it, with its movie theatre–style seats and industrial-sized popcorn machine. Geraint had sat in those movie theatre chairs more than once, had eaten buckets of popcorn more than once, because Ron had not only been his boss, he had been his *friend*. Or so Geraint had thought until approximately two forty-five this afternoon.

A small sob caught in his throat.

Geraint waited a few more minutes. Then he lifted his long legs over the box cedars and headed up Ron's driveway, stopping in front of the Lamborghini. He pulled a can of spray paint out of his satchel and got to work, careful not to touch the car in case it sounded the alarm.

Then he unzipped his fly and peed for what felt like minutes into the fountain.

When he was done he felt not better, exactly, but just a tiny bit lighter, even as big salty tears rolled down his face. He knew he'd be the obvious suspect, but he'd watched enough police procedurals on TV to know the cops couldn't charge you with a crime unless they had solid proof, and he'd been careful. He'd left nothing behind. He hadn't touched anything.

You're stealthy, like Cary Grant in To Catch a Thief! he told himself as he headed back down the driveway, the smallest of smiles on his face—completely unaware that three different surveillance cameras had been trained on him the entire time.

P arker walked at a good clip, practically skipping past two of the set dec guys who carried an enormous boar's head between them. It was, she knew, destined for the Great Hall, where they'd be filming later in the day. She did a mental search for their names from the pages-long crew list she'd been studying at night—Rob and Ali? She wasn't confident that she was right, so gave them a smile and a wave instead. *I can't believe it takes so many people to make a TV show!*

All morning they'd been shooting in Lady Charlotte's bedchamber. Parker had been stationed on set to help Analise Olsen— aka Lady Charlotte—get out of her historically inaccurate heels and into her UGGs between set-ups, and to deal with any other wardrobe issues that might arise. Even though they'd been shooting the same two pages of dialogue between Charlotte and her young lover, Darian, for well over an hour, Parker never felt the slightest bit bored. In fact she'd been inadvertently humming Pharrell Williams's "Happy" ever since she'd started two weeks ago, and it was getting on people's nerves.

This was her first union gig. She was one of three on-set costumers, the most junior of the trio, still learning the ropes, still trying to get used to the long hours. Her legs were tired in a way they'd never been before, her lower back sore in a way that made her feel like she was seventy instead of twenty-three. She was still figuring out how to deal with actors who were sometimes short with her because she hadn't learned their patterns and preferences yet. *Am I allowed to make eye contact with this one? Does this one like chit-chat or prefer quiet?* Analise, she had discovered, preferred quiet, so Parker did her best to curb what her mom, Sharon, referred to as her "periodic verbal diarrhea."

The job was a dream come true, and the cherry on top was that she was a fan of the show. *Knights of the Castle,* now shooting its sixth season, was among her and Sharon's all-time favourites. It was a thrill, getting to read the scripts and know what was going to happen before the rest of the world. Her mom was always pressing for spoilers on their bimonthly phone calls, but it was in Parker's contract that she couldn't breathe a word, and Parker honoured that, much to her mom's chagrin and to Parker's secret delight. It was the first time in her life that she had something special and precious and private that belonged only to her. Even her diaries hadn't been sacred because her mom believed "there should be no secrets between mothers and daughters," which meant that Parker had known way too much about Sharon's tumultuous love life and Sharon had known way too much about Parker's non-existent one.

She arrived at the studio doors and waited for them to cut. Her mind drifted to the mean girls she'd gone to school with in Penticton, a central BC town that was as pretty as it was suffocating. Arabella, her worst tormentor, had made fun of her red hair, her freckles, and her clothes, because the only place she and Sharon could afford to shop was Value Village. But even then Parker had been drawing her own designs in notebook after notebook, and sewing some of them on Sharon's ancient Singer. One day she'd gathered up the courage to wear one of her creations to school, an up-cycled skirt that was half plaid, half polka dot. Arabella had teased her mercilessly until Melody, an impossibly cool girl in the grade above them, had declared it "awesome" and asked if she could buy it. Not only had the teasing stopped, but Parker developed a sweet side-hustle from that day on, charging good money for custom-made pieces.

Parker knew from social media that Arabella was still in Penticton. She had two kids already and lived in a trailer park with her lunkhead high school boyfriend, Dwayne. *I hope she's happy*, she thought to herself. Almost meaning it.

The bell rang and the red light went off, which meant it was safe to step outside. The daylight hurt her eyes after the dark of the studio. It was an unusually beautiful January day, not a cloud in the sky. She felt a frisson of excitement; she couldn't believe she'd been summoned to *his* trailer. Sebastian Trevor, star of *Knights of the Castle*, with a long list of stellar credits before this. He was George Clooney famous and still strikingly handsome for an old guy. Parker had seen him from a distance on set, and a couple of times she could have sworn he'd looked right at her and smiled. But she was nearsighted, so it might have just been wishful thinking.

Oh my god, Sharon would poop herself if she knew I was about to meet him face to face! Her mom had swooned over Sebastian for years.

Parker couldn't resist; she took her phone from her fanny pack and dialed Sharon, even though it was long-distance.

"*Hola, mi hija*," Sharon said. She and her latest boyfriend, Tad, were currently wintering in San Miguel de Allende, living on the cheap in a camper van and taking art classes—part of her mother's ongoing quest to find her "strange jewels" hidden within (Sharon was a big fan of Elizabeth Gilbert).

"*Hola*, Mom." Saying "Mom" still didn't roll off Parker's tongue. Sharon had forbidden her from calling her that for years, claiming it made her feel too old. But when she'd turned forty last year, a switch had flipped and suddenly she insisted Parker use the word. "Guess where I'm going."

"*No sé.*"

"Sir Godfrey's trailer."

A small gasp. "Sebastian Trevor's trailer? No."

"Yes! He needs help with his costume, and he asked for me by name! Well—not by name. He asked for the freckle-faced girl from wardrobe."

"Did I ever tell you I wanted to be an actress till I got knocked up?"

"Yes. You have. Many times—"

"I'd have been good, too. What are you wearing?"

"What am I—my Peruvian sweater and my bedazzled jeans."

"At work?"

"It's a film set, we all dress super casual. Alexei said I looked great."

"Okay, well—just remember to smile. But not your awkward smile. And make sure you don't do your horse laugh."

"I've gotta run," she whispered. She'd arrived outside Sebastian's trailer.

"Call me back when you're done and tell me everything. Oh, and tell him your mother is hot—"

Parker hung up. She secured her phone in her fanny pack, suddenly nervous. Before she knocked, she pulled her ponytail holder out and let her thick red hair cascade around her shoulders, because her mom was always telling her it was her best feature. "Mr. Trevor? Parker Poplawski from wardrobe."

"Step up," he said in his beautiful upper-class English accent.

Parker entered. Wow. Sebastian's trailer was bigger than any of the others, with its own little bedroom, even. A huge bouquet of flowers sat on a built-in table, along with a bottle of champagne, his script, and a cudgel—a prop for his upcoming scene.

The door to the bedroom was partially closed. "Make yourself comfortable, I'll be out in just a moment." Parker took in the other few items in the trailer: A photo of his almost-age-appropriate, stunning wife. A Kindle. A worn Aran sweater.

The bedroom door swung open and Sebastian emerged, wearing

a bathrobe. He gave her a big smile, showing off glaringly white teeth.

Parker felt just the smallest hint of disappointment on seeing him up close for the first time. He was even older than he looked onscreen, and he'd clearly had work done. He looked a bit . . . waxy. "You're new, aren't you?"

"Yes, sir."

"I caught a glimpse of you on set the other day. Pam, correct?"

He almost knows my name! "Parker. Parker Poplawski. My mom named me after her favourite indie actor, Parker Posey, but Parker Posey rolls off the tongue a lot easier than Parker Poplawski—" *Verbal diarrhea alert! Stop!* "I understand you need help with your wardrobe?"

"I do. It's the codpiece." He held it out to her. "If you could just help me strap it on, I'd be grateful."

The smallest tingle of concern wormed its way up Parker's spine. *Hasn't he had to put this on a million times?*

He stepped closer. "You're very beautiful, Parker, do you know that?"

She didn't know that. Her mom had always told her she was "just north of pretty." So she was torn between feeling flattered and feeling uncomfortable. "I could talk you through putting it on."

"I prefer a hands-on approach." His robe slipped open, and Parker noted with alarm that he was naked underneath.

"I . . . I'm sorry, I'm not comfortable doing that—"

Suddenly his hands were on her shoulders and he pressed down, pushing her onto her knees. He was surprisingly strong for an old dude. She was frozen with fear. Her eyes were now in line with his groin, and she had a perfect view of his semi-erect penis obtruding towards her and, worse, his inordinately enormous balls, which hung like a couple of rotting, wrinkly Kiwi fruits.

Parker unfroze. She started to flail, but his hands had gripped her head, drawing it forward. "Now, now, take it easy, we're just having a little fun, Pandora—" Her hand found the cudgel on the table. It was papier mâché, but still weighty. She swung it as hard as she could between his legs.

"Aaaagh!" He released her head as he doubled over. Parker dropped the cudgel and ran out of the trailer, down the metal stairs, back into the cold sunlight.

She glanced around. One of the drivers was standing by his truck having a smoke, but beyond that, she could see no one.

Her breathing was rapid and shallow. Her mind was fuzzy. Without thinking, she ran towards the crew parking lot and found the ancient Honda Civic that she and Alexei shared and climbed inside. Her phone buzzed.

Well??? What's he like?

Her phone buzzed again. And again.

Did you tell him about me?

Did you smile?

I want a full report!!

Hands shaking, she started the car and peeled out of the parking lot.

Punishment

1

Frances stood at the kitchen counter, waiting for the kettle to boil. She wore the flannel pajamas her kids had given her at least a decade ago: baby blue with a multitude of cartoon cat faces, and for the past year, anyway, a rather large tear in the crotch. She tugged up the pants, which hung loosely around her waist. Her left eyelid twitched uncontrollably.

It was 7:30 a.m., and the first signs of daylight were just starting to appear in the sky. January, always the dreariest month of the year. In the kitchen, however, the lights were blazing and it felt warm and cozy. Oh, how she loved this room, with its butter-yellow walls and blue and white accent tiling around the countertops. Daisy said it was out of date—"It's like being at an IKEA"—but since Daisy also thought her mother was out of date, Frances figured she and her kitchen suited each other perfectly.

The Arts and Crafts house was small by modern-day Vancouver standards, but it was just eight blocks from the ocean and had a decent backyard, where Frances had slowly created a beautiful garden oasis. They'd bought it twenty-four years ago during a brief slump in Vancouver's real estate market, trading up from a duplex. It had been a fixer-upper—code word for dump—but over the next ten years she and Jeremy had renovated it room by room, largely with their own labour and sweat, keeping many of the original features (the wainscotting, the hardwood floors with custom inlays). They'd turned it into their forever home.

Now it was another thing she'd probably have to give up.

Mr. Pickles—who had the physique of a giant meatball on four toothpick-like legs—rubbed against her and meowed incessantly until Frances poured kibble into his bowl. He wolfed it down as the kettle started to whistle. She poured water into the French press and yawned loudly.

She hadn't slept a wink. Every time she'd started drifting off, she'd seen herself grabbing a twelve-year-old boy by his shirt collar. Shouting at him, inches from his face. *That was me. I did that.* It was impossible to compute.

Then again, everything about her life these days was impossible to compute. The last six months had been like a waking nightmare, and the only thing that kept her going, the thing her friends kept repeating to her like a mantra, was that it would eventually get better. Instead, as of yesterday, it had gotten a hell of a lot worse. Until this point, she'd been able to plant the blame for her newly minted shit-show of a life at someone else's feet, but now—now *she* was the villain, and a rather infamous one at that. At 4 a.m. she'd done the thing she knew she shouldn't and punched in her name on You-Tube. The video—titled "Children's Author Goes Batshit!"—was up to over three hundred thousand views.

She scooped up the cat (the trick was bending at the knees and engaging her core) and kissed his big orange head. "You still love me, right, Mr. Pickles?"

"Merp," he replied.

The police had arrived on her doorstep just a few hours after she'd returned home. There were two of them: an older woman, Frances's vintage, and a younger man. The guy had been gruff, but the woman, number 2461 according to a Velcro strip on her chest, had been kind. So when she'd asked Frances if she would be willing to come to the station and give a voluntary statement, Frances had done just that.

Alone with the policewoman, who introduced herself as Constable Vargas, Frances had tried to explain the confluence of events that had led to, as she referred to it, "the unfortunate incident." She'd told the constable why the day had started out on a sour note before she'd even left the house. Then she'd told her about the school, describing the chaos, the fact that there were twice as many kids as she'd agreed to and only two teachers in the room, who stood at the back throughout her entire presentation in a flirtatious tête-à-tête. Then the boy, the boy who would *not shut up*. Who chatted with his friends. Who yawned and belched loudly. When she'd asked him to be quiet, he'd stared at her while whispering to his friends, and they'd all cracked up. Midway through her presentation she'd felt something moist hit her forehead, then her neck, and realized with a jolt of disgust that the same boy was lobbing *spitballs* at her through a cafeteria straw. And *laughing*. That was when she'd snapped. "He was just so . . . cavalierly *mean*," she told the constable.

"Oh, honey," Vargas had said, and for a moment Frances thought they were bonding. "That's nothing. Try doing my job for a day." *But you're a cop*, Frances wanted to say. *I'm a writer. I'm not used to casual cruelty, except maybe on Goodreads.*

Then the constable had played the crop-top girl's video on a large TV screen.

"That's not me," Frances pleaded. "It's not who I am."

Vargas hit play again. "Just so we're clear. It is very much you."

Then she'd been fingerprinted and formally charged with assault. Only then did it sink in that she was truly up shit creek.

The moment she was back in her car she called Jules Osomo. Jules was one of the top criminal defence lawyers in town, and also her best friend.

"Frances, you *never* should have given a voluntary statement!" said Jules. "Did they read you your Charter rights?"

"Yes."

"Meaning, they told you you had a right to a lawyer?"

"Yes."

"Then *why didn't you call me immediately?*"

"Because I've never needed a criminal defence lawyer before!" wailed Frances. "Besides, what difference could it possibly have made? I did it. There is video evidence to prove I did it."

"It could have made all the difference," Jules said. "Right, from this moment forward, *I am your lawyer.*"

"But I can't afford you—"

"Oh, for fuck's sake. Do I need to say it? I'm not charging you, you silly twat. Now listen carefully: you say nothing to anyone from here on in without my say-so, got it?"

"Yes, Jules," Frances had replied. "Thank you, Jules." It gave her a strange bit of comfort to be bossed around by her fierce and competent friend.

This morning, though, she was a jangly ball of nerves. Even Mr. Pickles, who lay like a dead weight in her arms, limbs splayed, couldn't comfort her.

Just as she pushed the French press down, she heard noises. They were coming from the basement.

A door opened. Closed. *Oh god.* There were footsteps on the stairs. They were getting closer. Closer.

"Help me, Mr. Pickles," she whispered.

Moments later, Frances's beautiful, passionate, and exceedingly frustrating twenty-two-year-old daughter stepped into the room.

"Do you have any idea how humiliating this is for me, Mother?" Daisy wore her old UBC sweatshirt and a pair of boy's boxer shorts. Her eyes were puffy from crying and lack of sleep, her brown bob matted and dishevelled. Her expression was pinched and down-turned. (Daisy's expression was often pinched and downturned, but this morning it was particularly so.)

"I'm guessing less humiliating than it is for me." Frances had agonized over how to tell her daughter what had happened, but she needn't have bothered; Daisy's current boyfriend, Rolfe—or was it Paolo?—had shown her the video the night before.

Daisy had graduated a year and a half earlier with a Bachelor of Arts from the University of British Columbia. Frances and Jeremy had been supportive—Frances had a BA from the same university, after all, and they believed in learning for learning's sake. But Frances had gone to school in a different era, one where the world was a BA grad's oyster. Daisy had been spinning her wheels ever since, living in the basement, doing short-term jobs for a temp agency and complaining that there were no jobs to fit her skills.

"*What* skills?" Jeremy had asked Frances one night when the two of them were home alone, settling in for a night of Netflix. "A deep understanding of the symbolism in Japanese cinema?"

"Don't forget her expertise in the waves of feminist thought," Frances had shot back. It had been the secret ingredient in their marriage, the ability to make each other laugh, especially in the face of their daughter's mercurial mood swings and tendency to blame all of her problems, from a missed bus to a pimple on her face, on her parents.

Daisy had always been more challenging than her kid brother, Max, but when she'd started university even the most innocuous of conversations with her had become a minefield. One wrong step and you'd be blasted to smithereens.

"You're such a racist!" Daisy told her mom one evening when Frances, trying to remember James Earl Jones's name, had said Tommy Lee Jones instead.

Or the time Frances had dared to say, "Hey guys, what do you want for dinner?" and Daisy had hissed, "*Folx*. I'm not a *guy*!"

Or the time Jeremy had asked her, "Your roommate Alex, where is she from?"

"Why would you automatically assume Alex's pronouns are she/her? God, you are such a gender conformist!" Alex, it turned out, *did* use the pronouns she/her, but that wasn't Daisy's point. Her point was that her father, from his position of privilege as a cisgender white man, had just *assumed* that and was therefore part of a grave societal problem. "Honestly, you two need to go to a re-education camp!"

"Do you think they taught her about Maoist China in school?" Frances had asked Jeremy over a glass of wine that night.

"If they did, she probably took Mao's side."

Frances had laughed so hard she'd snorted Chardonnay up her nose.

But back then Daisy had been manageable because they were still a family. Max still lived at home; he could poke gentle fun at his sister in a way Frances and Jeremy couldn't, and tensions would ease. Then a year ago, Max had announced he was dropping out of first-year engineering and going travelling instead. Three months later he'd landed in Sydney, where he quickly fell in love with the climate, the surfing, and a girl. He'd found work under the table at a local pub and showed no signs of coming home any time soon.

But Frances had still had Jeremy. It was still two against one. Then Jeremy had left, too, and hence any buffer. Sometimes, when Daisy was lecturing her mother about her white privilege, Frances wanted to shout, "You are the *epitome* of white privilege! My single parent mother raised me on her nurse's salary. I had to work three jobs to pay my way through university. You had a fat RESP and live rent-free in our granny suite!" But she never did because she was Dr. Frankenstein, after all. She—along with Jeremy—had created this monster. And right now, she felt guiltily relieved that her monster hadn't left the nest. To have endured the past six months here, alone . . . the thought was unbearable.

Frances poured Daisy a coffee in the Reading Is Sexy mug. Frances used the I Like Big Books and I Cannot Lie mug. They were just two of the many gifts she had received over the years from grateful librarians and teachers.

Another wave of dread washed over her. *How many of them have seen the video?* A large part of her yearly income came from school visits. Would anyone invite her now? Would they even be allowed to invite her if she wound up with a criminal record?

Frances gripped the countertop. She tried to focus on her daughter, who was scrolling through her phone. "My friends have been texting me all morning. Oh my god, Jared reposted the video and tagged me. What an asshole! He is blocked!" She picked up her coffee mug and blew on it. "Why did you do it, Mom?"

"The kid was obnoxious."

"So? You've dealt with tons of obnoxious kids before."

"True. But this one took the cake. He was laughing at me. Lobbing *spitballs* at me. And also . . ." Frances hesitated. She wasn't sure she should burden her daughter with the other reason. Daisy had already had a front-row seat to her parents' break-up.

"Also what?"

"I realized that morning it was our twenty-fifth wedding anniversary."

Daisy's face crumpled. "Oh, Mom." She threw her arms around Frances and held her tight. They stayed like that for a while, Frances willing herself not to cry.

When her daughter wasn't criticizing every last detail of her mother's appearance, her laugh, her choice of words, her opinions, her very existence—she was a wonderful human being.

* * *

Frances made them a quick breakfast of porridge and fruit, then she and Daisy moved into the living room and sank down onto the sectional couch. Frances opened her laptop to begin their Zoom call with Max. It was the middle of the night in Sydney, but Max worked a late shift at the bar on Thursdays, so they caught him in the wee hours of Friday morning before he went to bed. "Please, Daisy," she said before she pressed start, "can we not tell your brother about this yet?"

"He's not a kid anymore, Mom."

"I know." *But he's still my sweet baby boy.*

Daisy sighed. "Fine."

Frances admitted Max from the virtual waiting room. The moment his tanned face appeared, he burst out laughing. "Mom, holy shit! I knew you were bad-ass, but—you were like She-Hulk!"

"How did you—"

"Bailey sent me the video. And Arpad. And Vijay." Three of Max's closest friends in Vancouver. "You're also trending on social media. Hashtag *AuthorLosesHerShit*. You're famous."

"I think you mean *infamous*," said Daisy, opening one of her many apps. She and Max took turns reading some of the comments aloud:

I'm a retired teacher and I wanted to do this about a million times during my career. But news flash: I didn't.

Kids have zero respect for authority figures these days, he got what he deserved. #BringBackCorporalPunishment

Ugh, guess I'm gonna have to bring all my "Phoebe Unknown" books to the dumpster.

I LOVE the "Phoebe Unknown" trilogy. Can Frances Partridge still be my problematic fave?

Ha-ha badass old broad!

It's called a power imbalance and that crazy lady totally took advantage. #WhitePrivilegeGoneWild

I don't care what that kid did, he did not deserve to be woman-handled by that entitled old lady. #WhitePrivilegeGoneWild

"That white privilege hashtag is really trending—" Daisy started.

"Okay, okay, that's enough, thank you very much," Frances interrupted, wondering what it said about her that it was the frequent use of the word *old* that stung the most. "I'm glad you're able to have a bit of fun at my expense."

Max grew serious. "Mom, it'll be okay. Honest. In a few days, everyone will have moved on to the next thing."

Bless him, thought Frances. Max had always been a sweet, happy boy, tolerant and forgiving and generous with his affection. His good cheer was infectious. Where Daisy had perfected her scowl by the age of two, Max had perfected his ear-to-ear grin. He seldom lost his temper, even when he was a teenager; he was just genetically easy-going, a glass-half-full kind of guy. He had a way of lifting her mood, and for a split second she felt just a tiny bit better.

Until Daisy brought her crashing back down to reality.

"People may move on, but our mother could still wind up with a criminal record. She will be a pariah in the world of children's literature."

Frances took a deep breath. The coffee had worked its way

through her system, and she was desperate for the loo. "You two get caught up. Back in a jiff."

Mr. Pickles followed her to the bathroom like he always did and sat watching her do her business. They'd grown used to this disconcerting habit of his over the years.

Frances wondered if she should ask Max if he'd spoken to his father yet, then decided against it. He was a grown-up, twenty-one, even if she would always think of him as her baby. Max was furious with Jeremy, and while she knew it spoke ill of her, a small part of her was pleased by that. Frances knew that Daisy spoke to her dad; she was trying to maintain some form of relationship with him, because what would it say about her identity as an ally if she didn't?

Frances washed her hands and hoisted Mr. Pickles into her arms. As she approached the living room, she overheard her daughter. "I envy you. I wish I was thousands of miles away, too."

"I'm sorry, Daze. I wish I was there to help carry the load."

"No you don't. And I'm glad you're not. It's no fun being under the same roof with her right now."

"No one's forcing you to stay. You could move."

"I wish. I can't afford it. And even if I could . . . I couldn't leave her alone. She's just so *sad*."

"I want to kill Dad."

"Yeah. Me too, sometimes."

"You don't think she'd ever . . . ?"

"I don't think so. But I honestly don't know."

Frances felt her eyes prickle. *No*, she told herself. *Don't you dare.* She coughed loudly, announcing her return. The three of them wrapped up their call a few minutes later. Daisy gave her mom another hug, then headed downstairs to shower and get ready for her latest temp job at an insurance firm.

Frances had just started clearing away their breakfast things when her phone rang. "Call from: Asshole," the bland AI voice said.

Frances closed her eyes. She knew what this meant. He'd seen the video, too. She let it ring.

Once she was sure Daisy had left for work, she went back upstairs. She crawled into bed and pulled the duvet over her head.

Everyone she loved had either left her or wanted to leave.

But she was still right here.

2

Parker let herself into the tiny one-bedroom apartment she and Alexei shared in Vancouver's Sunset neighbourhood, an ethnically diverse area full of low-rise apartments and single-family homes. Their place was on the third floor of a rather ugly pink stucco four-storey building, but it was close to all the shops on Fraser Street and Parker loved it, even if it often smelled skunky thanks to their pot-smoking downstairs neighbour. Alexei wouldn't be home for a few more hours. It felt strange to be here at 2 p.m. on a Friday, like she was playing hooky from school.

She pulled off her purple Converse high-tops, put them on their tiny wooden shoe rack, and made her way into the tiny kitchen, where she made herself a mug of tea. She carried it into their tiny living room and sat on the tiny red loveseat, which someone had left in a nearby alley even though it was in almost perfect condition. She and Alexei had carried it the three blocks home, stopping when they got tired. Parker had added some colourful throw pillows and flipped one of the cushions to hide one unsightly stain and voila! Now they had a comfy and attractive place to watch TV.

She spent the rest of the day watching *Friends* reruns and blocking what had happened with Sebastian Trevor from her mind. At one point her phone rang and she saw it was Wanda, the costume designer. She willed herself to pick it up, but her hand had other ideas. So instead she waited five minutes and sent her boss a text.

So sorry! Bad flu. Barfing. Worried I was contagious so came home.

Wanda texted back a terse message.

Sorry you're sick. But you can't just leave without telling anyone.

First and final warning.

On her sixth episode of *Friends*, Parker started wondering how she'd explain what had happened to Alexei. The two of them had met less than a year ago; she was taking fashion design courses by day and working at a coffee shop by night. Sweet Alexei, with his perfect, compact body, bushy eyebrows, gorgeous hazel eyes, and wavy brown hair, had come in every night and ordered a flat white. Then he would sit for hours doing what looked like homework. Her manager finally sent Parker over to talk to him. "I'm sorry, but my boss says if you want to stay longer than an hour, you have to buy more stuff." So Alexei had ordered a stale croissant. An hour later he'd ordered a day-old cookie. After a few nights like this, she'd started bringing him his hourly treats without being asked, switching it up so he could try their entire roster of baked goods. He'd told her he was getting his last few credits towards becoming a CPA while working full-time at a large accounting firm downtown.

One week later she'd boldly formed a large heart on the top of his flat white and asked in a quavering voice if he'd like to go on a proper date.

Three months after that, they'd moved in together. Parker felt like she'd won the lottery. But what amazed her even more was that Alexei seemed to think *he* had won the lottery, too. With her! Horsey-laughed, north-of-pretty Parker!

At five thirty she heard his key in the lock. His bushy eyebrows shot up in pleasant surprise when he saw her in the living room. "Well, hi! I thought you were shooting till late."

Parker had rehearsed how to tell him the story, and she launched into it now, trying her best to make it sound comical, leaving out the worst bits. She didn't tell him Sebastian had pushed her to her knees. She did tell him about his wrinkly and enormous balls, and about whacking him with the papier mâché cudgel. But all in all, she tried to make it sound like it was a misguided come-on from an aging actor.

Alexei didn't think there was anything funny about it. He was furious on her behalf. He wanted to drive to the set of *Knights of the Castle* and punch Sebastian's lights out, but that was unrealistic for so many reasons. First of all, Alexei was just a couple of inches taller than Parker, and Parker was only five foot four. And more to the point, Alexei had never thrown a punch in his life. He was a lover, not a fighter. Also, she was worried he could wind up being charged with assault.

"But he's the one who assaulted you!"

"I'm fine, Alexei, really. It wasn't a big deal. He got it worse than me."

Besides, there was the not-insignificant fact that Sebastian was a world-famous actor held in high esteem. No one would believe that someone like him—he could sleep with supermodels if he wanted to!—would have gone after someone like her. And a darker thought arose: Had she sent him signals? Maybe he'd noticed her staring at him on set, and believed he was doing her some sort of favour. Also—she cringed at the memory—she'd taken out her ponytail holder just before stepping into his trailer, because she thought she looked prettier with her hair down. She knew you weren't supposed to blame the victim, but now that, technically speaking, she *was* the victim, it was easy to blame herself. She just wanted to forget the whole thing.

Before she and Alexei went to bed that night in their tiny bedroom, she had made her decision: she would simply show up for work on Monday and make it her policy to never, ever be alone with Sebastian Trevor. She picked up her latest notebook, a purple sparkly number that Alexei had bought for her, and flipped to a blank page.

YOU'RE GOING TO BE FINE!!!!! she wrote in all caps. *A BAD DAY DOESN'T MAKE A BAD LIFE!!!!!* Parker had read a lot about manifesting and using the power of her mind to will her desires into existence. So surely, with that many exclamation points and a whole lot of positive thinking, she could make the words on the page come true.

3

Geraint woke to the sounds of heavy metal music. It was bleeding through the paper-thin walls of his apart-hotel in the West End, where he'd spent the last two nights. He lay with his head on the lumpy pillow, listening. Was it Whitesnake? He loved Whitesnake. He'd taken Darlene to see them in concert a few years ago, but they'd left halfway through because Darlene said their music was giving her a headache.

Darlene. Darlene, Darlene.

Yes, he was quite certain now, it was Whitesnake's "Give Me All Your Love." Which was truly ironic, since Darlene had definitely not given him all of her love. Or, after their conversation two nights ago, possibly any love at all.

A sob caught in his throat. He rolled onto his side, slipping into the well in the middle of the bed because the mattress was old, and the springs had long since given out. He gave up on sleep and hoisted himself, with some effort, out of the well and out of the bed. He put on yesterday's track suit; he'd only packed a small suitcase, so his options were limited.

He immediately picked up his phone from the chipped night-stand and checked for messages. Nothing. *Just give it time. Darlene will reach out,* he told himself. He peed in the circa 1970s bathroom, with its pink toilet, bathtub, and sink. Even the simple act of peeing was fraught, since it brought him back to a certain fountain in a very different part of town just two nights earlier. Then he headed to the sparsely stocked kitchen to make himself a pot of coffee.

The place smelled vaguely of stale smoke (even though at least three little plastic No Smoking signs were placed strategically around the apartment), cabbage (though he'd never once cooked cabbage in his time here), and mildew. Everything was beige, except for the black leather (or was it leatherette?) couch and chairs and the carpeting, which was a swirling design in brown and dark green, perfect for hiding stains. A few bland pastel prints of mountains hung crookedly on the walls.

He opened the dust-caked slatted blinds on the kitchen window and found himself looking directly across the alley into another window. An elderly, unshaved man in a stained undershirt was brushing his teeth. Geraint gave him a small grin and a wave. The old man gave him the finger and snapped his blinds shut. In his vulnerable state, the gesture stung more than he knew it should. He'd only felt this way once before in his life, when he was seven years old and his parents had moved the family to Canada from Cardiff, Wales. It was a loneliness so profound and so deep that he could feel in his bones.

Geraint poured himself a cup of coffee. He was still in partial shock at the sudden turn his life had taken. Just a few days ago, his life had been—in his view, at least—utterly perfect. He'd had a job he loved, a wife he loved, and a son he adored more than life itself.

His son. Just thinking of his little boy made Geraint feel like he'd been punched in the nuts. He collapsed onto the leather (leatherette?) couch. What would his boy be thinking, waking up for the second morning in a row without his dad in the house? What had Darlene told him? His heart started pounding against the walls of his chest, and he had to force himself to take some deep breaths. *It will all be okay. Darlene will come to her senses. You'll be back in the house in no time. And at least I got away with what I did at Ron's.*

He was just trying to figure out how to fill the void that was Saturday, without his family and without his carpentry tools, when there was a knock at the door.

Geraint leapt from the couch and lumbered to the door. "Darlene," he said as he flung it open.

It wasn't Darlene. It was two police officers. When they brought Geraint to the station, they played him the security footage from Ron Neumann's cameras—all five minutes and thirteen seconds of it.

A full three minutes and six seconds of which was Geraint's never-ending pee.

4

She was at a gala dinner, a publishing event of some sort, seated at a table near the front, dressed to the nines in an actual ball gown. *How odd*, she thought, *I didn't even know I owned a ball gown.* A woman sat down next to her.

It was Judy Blume.

Judy Blume! One of her literary heroines! Frances felt giddy with excitement. She and Judy fell into conversation. Judy was warm and attentive, and seemed genuinely interested when Frances told her about her own body of work: nine middle-grade novels (three of which comprised the *Phoebe Unknown* trilogy) and five picture books. Judy had even heard of *Phoebe Unknown*, and Frances thought she might faint. This was the best night ever. "It must be so gratifying, knowing your books will live on for generations to come," she said to Judy.

"It's certainly not what I set out to do," Judy responded, "but it is rather lovely."

"Do you think my work will have anywhere near that sort of longevity, Ms. Blume?"

Judy guffawed. She actually *guffawed*. "Oh, heavens, no, dear." She burst into peals of laughter. "Hey, Christopher!" Judy turned to the man next to her. It was another of Frances's idols, Christopher Paul Curtis. "She asked me if her books would have *longevity*!" Christopher burst out laughing, too. They were mocking her!

Frances's face fell. "Why are you being so mean, Judy Blu—"

Suddenly Judy grabbed her napkin and shoved it over Frances's mouth and nose, pressing down hard. She couldn't breathe—

Frances woke to find Mr. Pickles lying on top of her face, pawing her scalp with his sharp claws, meowing for food. It was Saturday morning, after nine o'clock; she'd slept in. In spite of being the only occupant of the king-sized bed, she still slept on the right-hand side, never deviating. Even after six months she would, when in that wonderful state between wake and sleep, reach out a hand to search for Jeremy's warm, naked body beside hers.

She could hear the pitter-patter of rain on the windows and felt no inclination to leave her warm duvet cocoon. Instead, she rolled to her side and picked up her phone from the bedside table.

Two more missed calls from Asshole, one from her writer friend Norah, four from unknown numbers, possibly scammers. Or worse, press.

And two from Jacqueline Ainsworth.

Jacqueline was calling her on a weekend.

Her heart pounding, she hit redial.

Jacqueline picked up after the first ring. "Frances, my dear. I thought you were avoiding me."

Frances did her best to sound bright-eyed and cheery. "You? Never."

"How are you?" Jacqueline was British, well into her seventies. She sounded like Judi Dench if Judi had smoked a pack a day for the better part of her life. Just hearing her voice was a balm to Frances's soul.

"Been better."

"Yes."

"I take it you . . ."

"Oh, darling, of course."

"I just snapped. Everything became too much."

"You don't need to explain, Frances. It's been your *annus horribilis*."

Hearing the kindness in Jacqueline's voice made Frances want to weep. "You have my word, I'll be back in fighting form by the time the new book launches in the fall." Her latest novel was a somewhat shameless attempt to try to reinvent her earlier success with the *Phoebe Unknown* trilogy; it followed a secondary character from those books. The heavy lifting was long since done; it just awaited one final, minor copy edit.

There was a long pause. "About that."

No. No, no. Frances shut her eyes. "Jacqueline. Please."

"The video . . ."

"Will be a thing of the past in a few weeks, my son swears it will."

"The story's international, my dear. You had a mention in the *Guardian*. In *Der Spiegel* and *Le Monde*."

"If only my books got that much attention," she said, trying to inject a bit of levity. Jacqueline did not say a word.

"Maybe it will boost sales," Frances continued. "You know what they say, any publicity is—"

"You assaulted a minor," Jacqueline interrupted. "Beloved children's author."

"Yes, but I have a very good lawyer. This may all go away."

"The video won't . . ." A pause. "You understand my predicament, my dear."

A wave of nausea swept over Frances. She loved Jacqueline. Jacqueline was the best children's book editor and publisher, not just in Canada but in North America. She knew how to draw the best out of her writers, and she treated each of them with kindness, tough love, and respect. "Jacqueline, please. We've been together for, what? Twenty years?"

"Twenty-three."

"Don't dump me. I couldn't handle it."

"I'm not dumping you! Look"—she lowered her voice—"if it were up to me, I'd just publish the book, public opinion be damned. But it's not just up to me anymore."

"But you're Jacqueline Ainsworth! You are Ainsworth Books!"

"Not anymore, I'm not. I'm surrounded by young up-and-comers who walk the halls with barely concealed knives. They would love to have an excuse to put me out to pasture." Jacqueline took a deep breath. "I'm not saying never, Frances. I'm just saying not in the fall."

"The rest of my advance doesn't get paid until publication."

"I'm afraid not. But sales of your old titles are still brisk, especially for *Phoebe Unknown*, and quite honestly, I don't think that will change very much at all. J.K. Rowling is forever at the centre of a social media shitstorm, and it hasn't affected her sales one bit."

"J.K. Rowling is one of the best-selling authors of all time. She could sell no more books from here on in and still bathe in champagne for the rest of her days."

There was a pause. "Do you need money? Because I could lend you some—"

"No, no. I'll be fine." For a while at least. For a year or two. My mother always taught me to save for a rainy day."

"Good for your mother. And of course, because Jeremy earns more money than you, he will have to pay spousal support."

"I suppose so. He still hasn't started divorce proceedings."

"Why ever not?"

"Apparently he wants to talk first."

"Oh, for heaven's sake." They were both quiet for a long time. Frances might have thought Jacqueline had hung up if she couldn't hear her breathing. "I'm truly sorry for your troubles, Frances. But as we Brits like to say, Chin up, old girl. This, too, shall pass. I'll call in a few weeks to check in."

Then she was gone.

Frances thought about just staying in bed, but Mr. Pickles's incessant meowing put an end to that. Reluctantly she threw back the duvet. Oh, how she hated Saturdays; the only day worse was Sunday. Come to think of it, Mondays weren't great, either.

Until six months ago she'd been extremely diligent about structuring her days. Monday to Friday she had a strict routine, making herself write at least five pages a day. She'd always scoffed at artists who said they needed to wait for the muse to strike. Writing had been her *career*, her life. Brutally hard, even after all these years, but those moments—oh, those moments when she pushed through the weeds to see a path forward, when a piece of dialogue sang, when she suddenly had a revelation about one of her characters, when she wrote a sentence that lifted off the page—there was nothing like it. She had always loved sinking into an imaginary world, bringing characters and their stories to life. It was what had given her days meaning and purpose.

But ever since Jeremy had moved out, her brain was in a constant fog-like state. She'd tried more than once to sit in front of her computer and write something, *anything*, but it was like she'd forgotten how.

And now she wasn't even sure she had a publisher anymore.

She stripped out of her pajamas, catching sight of herself in the mirror. She was thinner than she'd been in decades; eating was still an effort. She wished she could enjoy this slimmed-down version, but all she could see were her sallow cheeks, the increasingly wrinkly skin around her elbows, her wide hips, her knees . . . What was it with aging knees? They looked like they belonged on an elephant. Until she'd turned fifty, she'd never understood the title of Nora Ephron's book of essays, *I Feel Bad About My Neck*. Now she felt bad about her neck and every other part of her body. Worst of all, she had jowls when she frowned, and these days she frowned a lot.

She had a long shower and willed herself not to look at her body again as she pulled on a pair of old black tights and a large navy sweater that reached just past her thighs—her uniform these days. She brushed her grey hair back into a ponytail. In the kitchen she made breakfast, leaving enough for Daisy, who wouldn't be up for at least another hour. She read the *New York Times* on her iPad and did Wordle, which was far less fun when she wasn't competing with Jeremy to see who could get the word first. She got to "genius" on Spelling Bee. She clipped Mr. Pickles's claws, and it was a toss-up which of them hated it more. She spent an hour cleaning some of the grouting around the tiles in the bathroom.

Finally, at eleven thirty, she put on her boots and coat in the foyer and reached for the door handle.

Then froze. She hadn't left the house since the video was released. The couple to the east, the Sihotas, were lovely people with two young children. They'd always been friendly; she and Jeremy had once looked after a four-year-old Meera when Amita and Nabil had to race a two-year-old Rishi to hospital because he'd wedged a gherkin up his nose. In the months since Jeremy had left they had been so kind, dropping off meals on a regular basis. Had they seen the video? Would they think she was a monster? To the west was seventy-something Cheryl Underwood, a widow for as long as they'd known her. Their family used to joke that her husband had probably killed himself just to get away from her. Frances felt guilty about that tasteless, macabre joke now. But Cheryl was a constant low-grade annoyance, sticking her nose where it didn't belong, offering unsolicited parenting advice when the kids were little, complaining about the noise when Daisy and Max were playing in the yard. If she'd seen the video, Frances would never hear the end of it.

She grabbed a striped scarf and wrapped it around her head, babushka-style. She opened the door and almost tripped over a container. It was homemade butter chicken with a card attached: a child's drawing of Mr. Pickles. The likeness was uncanny.

With love from Amita and Nabil
(and Meera and Rishi, too!)

Frances knew this wasn't just any butter chicken or any card. It meant they'd seen the video and they'd decided to be kind to her anyway. She blinked back tears as she put the container into the fridge, then headed outside.

"Frances! Hello, Frances!" Even though it was still drizzling, Cheryl Underwood was kneeling in her garden, sporting a rain poncho, gardening knee pads, and a bright yellow sou'wester hat. She started to stand, which took some time because, as the entire neighbourhood knew since Cheryl talked about it incessantly, she had bad knees.

Frances pretended not to hear. She dove into the driver's seat of Belinda the Beemer and pulled away from the curb. Cheryl got tinier and tinier in the rear-view mirror.

"I believe Cordelia is waiting for the bus," said Jamal, Frances's favourite nurse at Shady Pines. She searched his face for any signs that he'd watched, or heard about, the video, but all she saw was his usual kind smile. Either he legitimately hadn't seen it or he had an excellent poker face. Both options were equally plausible.

Frances headed across the courtyard, past a coffee shop and a beauty salon, and found her mother sitting patiently on a bench next to a large Bus Stop sign. She had on her favourite black winter coat. A small bag was at her feet. Cordelia was a beautiful woman, even at eighty. Almost regal, with her perfect posture and gorgeous silvery-white hair. Frances hadn't had the same luck when she'd stopped dyeing hers. Hers was salt and pepper: distinguished on men, an invisibility cloak on women.

Her mom's face lit up when she saw her. "Franny, hello."

Frances smiled, relieved; so far, her mom always knew who she was. "Hi, Mom." She sat beside her on the bench.

Cordelia gazed at her. "Dear girl, you have got to take better care of yourself. You look frightful." Alzheimer's had turned her formerly tactful mother into an imparter of harsh truths. "What do I always say? You're never too busy to put on lipstick before you leave the house."

Frances found an old lipstick in her purse and did her best to apply some without aid of a mirror. "Where are you headed?"

"I told them I thought it was time for me to go home."

"Ah. Well, since I came all this way, shall we go to the lounge and have some tea? Perhaps you can catch a later bus."

"Of course."

Cordelia had been at Shady Pines for just over a year. Her decline had started earlier than that, but for a long time, they all—Cordelia included—tried to ignore the signs, passing off her increasing forgetfulness as a typical by-product of aging. "I mean, I also misplace my keys all the time," Frances would say to Jeremy. But when they started finding Cordelia's keys in the fridge—and worse, when Cordelia couldn't remember what the keys were for—they knew it was time to get her tested. Even after the devastating diagnosis, her mom was able to stay at home for a while longer. A home-care nurse slept over four nights a week and Frances slept over on the other three. But after Cordelia was found by a neighbour, wandering the streets in bare feet and a housecoat during a rainstorm, lost, agitated, and almost hypothermic, Frances and Jeremy had made the tough decision that her mother could no longer live independently.

They did their research and landed on Shady Pines, a memory care home in Burnaby that was set on a number of acres of land. Frances had had a vague idea what memory care meant, but the first time she'd found her mother at the fake bus stop, she'd been upset. "It's part of our philosophy," Jamal had explained. "A patient isn't going to get better because we keep correcting them. They just get more distressed. So if they say they want to go home, we let them go to the bus stop. After a while they forget why they're there, or they get distracted by something else and head back to their rooms."

"It's deceitful," Frances had said.

"Perhaps," said Jamal. "But isn't it also kind?"

For the first few months, Frances had hated coming here, and not just because of the bus stop. No matter how quaint and charming they'd tried to make it, the care home still smelled faintly of urine and other bodily fluids. When patients were no longer able to perform certain tasks, or became violent, they were moved to another wing that was a lot less charming.

Also—and this was the part Frances was deeply ashamed of—she hadn't liked coming because there were so many other things she'd rather do with her time. Visits to Shady Pines took at least two hours door to door—an hour to drive there and back, an hour to visit. That was time that could be spent working on her novel, or going to a yoga class with Jules, or gardening, or watching back-to-back episodes of *Love Is Blind* with Jeremy while judging the contestants. Almost anything at all was more fun than visiting her mom, because those visits were always tinged with sadness. It was painful to watch her vibrant, fiercely intelligent, and independent mother slowly disappear.

But then Jeremy had left, and Cordelia became practically the only family she had in town aside from Daisy—and, unlike Daisy, Cordelia was usually happy to see her. Now her visits to Shady Pines were a lifeline.

As they walked back to her room, Cordelia asked, "Where's Jeremy? Is he watching the children?"

"Yes," Frances said, because she'd learned to engage in her own deceptions, too. She'd told her mother that Jeremy had left her, but it hadn't stuck. And if she was honest, there was something rather soothing about being able to pretend, for a few afternoons a week, that she and Jeremy were perfectly fine.

They arrived at Cordelia's room, which was small but pleasant. Frances and Jeremy had brought a small Persian carpet from Cordelia's house, and lots of her artwork hung on the walls. "Just let me pop to the loo, then we can go to the lounge for tea and a biscuit."

"Take your time," said Frances.

While Cordelia was in the washroom, Frances unpacked her

mom's bag: in it was a clean pair of underwear, a toothbrush, a roll of toilet paper, one sock, and a decorative gourd.

The lounge was a big, cheerful room full of mismatched furniture and a large-screen TV. Cordelia ordered tea from one of the kitchen staff. A few of the residents were watching the local news.

Suddenly Frances heard, "Local children's author Frances Partridge is facing criminal charges after a video allegedly showing her assaulting a young boy went viral." Cordelia's eyes darted up to the screen.

Frances leapt up, trying to find the remote as she heard her own voice onscreen. "How many times did I ask you politely to shut the *bleep* up?" Cordelia stared at the TV, transfixed. Frances finally found the remote and switched the channel.

Cordelia turned to look at Frances, eyes wide as saucers. "Goodness gracious, dear girl. Imagine if that had been you!"

5

Frances drove along Grandview Highway towards Kitsilano, stopping along the way at Bosa Foods to pick up some of her favourite Italian food staples. She had no plans for the evening, seldom did these days unless Jules and Carmen invited her over (which they did with generous frequency), so she tried to cheer herself up with the thought of making herself a simple pasta dinner with salad.

She drove past Ontario Street.

I can eat in front of the TV, watch something with Idris Elba in it.

She drove past Manitoba Street.

Open a nice bottle of Italian red.

Columbia Street.

"Siobhan," she said, "don't let me do it."

There was a break in the eastbound traffic. She swung hard left, onto Yukon Street. "Recalculating," said Siobhan.

Frances pulled the car over at Yukon and 21st.

It was a cottage-style home, all on one level. Painted sky blue. There were lights on inside.

Frances opened her glove compartment and took out a small pair of binoculars. She peered through them, focusing on the window on the main floor.

Jeremy entered the living room.

He looked good. Relaxed. He wore slim-fitting jeans and a polo shirt. Kelly had probably made him ditch his high-waisted, ill-fitting dad jeans.

Then Kelly entered the living room, too. Frances's stomach lurched as she watched them kiss. She needed wine. But first she needed air. She could feel another hot flash coming on. She dropped the binoculars in her lap and unrolled the window. The cold air was an immediate relief. Grabbing the binoculars again, she brought them to her eyes and adjusted the focus.

Jeremy and Kelly were standing at the window, peering out into the night.

Directly at her.

Her heart stopped beating. *It's okay. They can't see you, it's too dark out here*, she told herself as she watched Jeremy pull out his phone.

A moment later her own phone rang. "Call from: Asshole."

Frances tossed down the binoculars, put the car into drive, and squealed away.

They'd met during karaoke night at a campus bar thirty years ago.

Frances quickly discovered just how minimal her vocal range was and sang Boy George songs for the rest of the night. Jeremy's voice was even worse than hers, but he sang Bowie and Springsteen and Byrne with such conviction, such joy—he knew his voice was terrible *and he didn't care*. Frances was immediately smitten by his unassuming self-confidence (that and the fact that he was adorably handsome with his floppy mop of brown hair and his lanky, un-muscular frame). Between songs they sat next to each other. He told her he was from Medicine Hat. She told him she was born and raised just down the hill. They lived in the same residence at UBC, although until that night their paths had never crossed. Jeremy wanted to be a lawyer. She confessed that when she wasn't going to English, history, or psychology classes, or working at one of her three jobs, she loved to write. She told him her dream was to make a living as a writer, which seemed an impossible and somewhat arrogant goal. She'd never told anyone before, but after knowing Jeremy for only three hours, she'd felt comfortable telling him. They both got loaded on cheap, cloyingly sweet white wine and went back to her dorm room for unmemorable sex.

Come to think of it, the sex had never been the highlight of their three decades together. But she'd never had complaints, and she hadn't thought he did, either, because their bond was based on so much more. They were very physical; always hugging, kissing, cuddling. Daisy and Max would fake-barf at the sight as they got older. In so many ways, they were two peas in a pod. They both loved travel and Christopher Guest movies and anything French. They loved to host dinner parties and shout out the answers to *Jeopardy!* together. She got him into swimming and word games; he got her into hiking and tried to get her into Sudoku, with little success. And oh, how they'd laughed! If Frances was in a mood, Jeremy would invariably break into a Monty Python funny walk, and he'd keep at it until she'd forgotten whatever had upset her.

Best of all, he believed in her. He believed she could make a living as a writer. (She believed he could make a living as a lawyer, too, but that wasn't as much of a stretch.)

They lifted each other up. They made each other better people.

And then, six months ago, over bowls of *cacio e pepe* at their favourite neighbourhood restaurant, just half a year shy of their twenty-fifth wedding anniversary, Frances had said, "I think the hot water heater is on the fritz."

And Jeremy had said, "I'm leaving."

"Are you not feeling well? I can ask for the bill."

"No. I'm leaving you. I'm sorry. I . . . I've met someone."

At first Frances had just stared at him, unable to comprehend.

Then she'd projectile-vomited her *cacio e pepe* all over the table and all over his lap.

I'm leaving you. I'm sorry. I've met someone. With those few words, the world as she knew it collapsed. Everything she'd believed to be true and stable and sure vanished in an instant, gone to her forever.

(And her favourite restaurant was gone to her forever, too, because it was hard to come back from that.)

6

Parker and Alexei went about their normal weekend. They made a vat of lentil soup. They played Dungeons & Dragons at their local game shop like they did every Saturday afternoon, which bled into Saturday night. On Sunday afternoon they drove out to Surrey, where Alexei's parents lived, and feasted on boisterous conversation and Mrs. Papadopoulos's moussaka.

In alone moments, Alexei would try to convince Parker to tell her union rep and the producers exactly what had happened. Parker would agree, then ten minutes later she'd renege; it went like that all weekend long. The thought of rehashing events, no doubt to a room full of men, made her nauseous. Yes, #MeToo had made a difference, but how much? And who were they going to believe? The girl with exactly two weeks' experience under her belt, who'd ruined more than one take with her incessant humming? Or a famous, Academy Award–winning actor whose very presence was the reason the show was shooting its sixth season and employing hundreds of people every year and making the network gobs of money? No, she finally decided: The best plan of action was no plan of action at all. Just show up for work like nothing had happened.

But when Monday morning rolled around, Parker couldn't make herself walk out the door. She told Alexei they had a late call time so he wouldn't worry, and after he left for work she sat on their loveseat, trying to talk herself into getting her butt in gear.

When Wanda sent her an irritated text a half-hour after their 8 a.m. call time, Parker didn't respond.

An hour after that, the line producer called and left her a message: she was being replaced.

Then, around noon, her phone rang again. It was a lawyer who said he represented Sebastian Trevor. His name was Rodney Wagner, from Bernstein and Wagner, which meant nothing to Parker. He said he wanted to meet with her. "Do I need a lawyer?" she asked.

"No, no, not at all. This is nothing bad, Ms. Poplawski. Quite the opposite, in fact."

Later on, Parker kicked herself for having had only one other question: "Will *he* be there?"

"No."

So she agreed to meet. She agonized over what to wear; she didn't own anything business-like. Eventually she settled on a retro double-breasted navy suit jacket with shoulder pads that she'd found thrifting, and a pair of basic black trousers with ballet flats.

She took a bus downtown, then walked the last ten minutes to the gleaming glass office tower. In the elevator she rode partway up with a woman who looked a lot like one of her favourite children's authors, but older and more haggard, so Parker figured she was mistaken.

Bernstein and Wagner was on the very top floor. The elevator doors opened right into their reception area. Parker stated her name, and almost immediately a young, impeccably dressed woman swept in and shook her hand warmly. "You must be Parker. It's a pleasure to meet you. Cool suit jacket! Follow me."

Parker, feeling completely off-kilter, followed her into a light-filled boardroom. The young woman offered her coffee, water, juice. Parker settled on water. A moment later Rodney Wagner entered, wearing what Parker knew was a very expensive bespoke suit. He got right to the point. "Sebastian is upset that you and he had a misunderstanding," he began, his tone brusque. "An honest mistake, of course"—the young woman nodded vigorously—"but Mr. Trevor would never intentionally inflict harm, and he's asked me to offer you compensation for any confusion you might have experienced. I advised him against it, but . . ."

"It's just the kind of decent guy Sebastian is," said the young woman somewhat robotically, and later Parker would wonder if her lines had been rehearsed, if Rodney Wagner knew it would help to have a youthful female presence in the room.

"He recognizes that it's best for both of you if you find employment on another show." Again, it was only later that Parker would wonder: Had the line producer called to tell her she was being replaced at Wanda's request—or Sebastian's? "He wants to be sure you have enough to tide you over while you look for another job." The lawyer slid a cheque across the table. Parker flipped it over.

It was for a hundred thousand dollars.

A hundred thousand dollars. More money than Parker could even contemplate. More money than her mom had made in two years as an esthetician in Penticton.

"It's all yours," said Rodney. "All we ask is that you sign this paperwork."

"What kind of paperwork?"

"A non-disclosure agreement," said the young woman as she inched the paperwork towards Parker. "It's a big name for what's really just an agreement not to discuss this with anyone."

Parker looked at the pages-long document. The words swam on the page. "Can I take it away and read it over?" The money and the paperwork combined were making her head spin. She needed to discuss it with Alexei.

"Unfortunately, no. The offer is only valid if you sign here, now." The two of them gazed steadily at her. She felt beads of sweat break out on her upper lip.

A hundred thousand dollars. It was a lot of money. It would give her time to find another job without feeling stressed. She and Alexei could finally trade in their ancient Honda Civic and buy the 2015 Mazda they'd been eyeing, and that would use a mere fraction of the cash. And, she suddenly thought with a flutter of excitement, maybe she could treat herself to the Pfaff Passport sewing machine she'd been coveting since forever. She could buy Alexei a proper leather briefcase, maybe even something nice for her mom, and even if she did all that she'd be able to put most of the money into RSPs and maybe even invest some of it. She'd already decided she wasn't going to tell anyone; at least this way, something good might come out of it.

She signed.

When she told Alexei that night, he looked ashen. "This feels really wrong, Parker. They bought your silence." They sat beside each other on the red loveseat. Her stomach clenched.

"Okay, if you want to see it that way. But I wasn't going to say anything anyway, and this way we're a hundred thousand dollars richer!"

"But it's blood money—"

She raised a hand to stop him. "It's done, okay?" Her voice was tight. "It's done." He nodded. Took her hand. Said nothing, because the last thing Alexei wanted to do was make his spectacular girlfriend feel worse. Even if he spectacularly disagreed.

She put her head on his shoulder. "This is more money than I'd have made on the entire season of the show. And I'll get another job." She sounded convincing, even to her own ears.

"Of course you will."

"Maybe this is a blessing disguised as a curse. That's what my mom used to say about me."

"Your mom called you a curse?" Alexei looked dismayed. He hadn't met Sharon in person, but Parker sensed that the stories she'd told him made his head spin.

"Yeah, but as a joke. She was seventeen when she got pregnant, so for a while I probably did feel like a curse. But then she said I was ultimately a blessing. Maybe this is kind of the same thing. Maybe we just made lemonade out of lemons."

For a short while, it really did feel as if a weight had been lifted off her shoulders. Things almost returned to normal. They traded in the Honda for the Mazda. She ordered her Pfaff Passport. She bought her mom an Apple watch with a pink strap and a form-fitting top from Forever 21 because it was Sharon's favourite place to shop, and tucked them away for her birthday in the summer. She bedazzled a jean jacket she'd found at a thrift shop. She got called in to work on another TV show.

But when one of the actors put a hand on her arm to get her attention and ask where his blazer was, she growled, "*Get your filthy hands off me.*"

She was sent home. The work calls stopped.

Then, about two weeks after she'd cashed the cheque, she went to the Pacific Centre mall to find a briefcase for Alexei. That is where The Thing happened.

And Parker Poplawski's whole world unravelled.

7

Good news. I've managed to get the Crown to agree to divert your matter before laying a charge."

Frances let out a sigh of relief. She sat across from Jules in a posh boardroom in a posh downtown law firm. Her friend wore a striking yellow power suit that managed to be stylish, sexy, and intimidating all at once. No matter how much effort Frances put into her appearance—and she had put some effort in today, wearing a grey wool skirt and a navy blouse—she always felt frumpy compared to Jules. But because Jules was who she was—down-to-earth, blunt, caring, and exceptionally salty—Frances never felt "lesser than" when she was with her.

They'd met in prenatal yoga classes twenty-three years ago, exchanging nothing more than pleasantries until one day, during happy baby pose, Frances farted. Some of the other women had looked at her with barely disguised revulsion. Frances was mortified.

Jules was on the mat next to hers. She caught Frances's gaze—and farted, too.

The room went deathly quiet, then Frances and Jules had both burst out laughing.

After class, they'd walked together to a nearby café. "It was a solidarity toot," Jules explained. "What did the teacher expect, making us do happy baby? It's asking for trouble even when you don't have an alien being pressing down on your colon."

"I laughed so hard I peed a little on my yoga mat," Frances confessed.

She liked Jules even more when she ordered a big, sticky cinnamon bun at the café. Frances ordered one, too. A gaggle of the other expectant moms were at a nearby table, eating acai bowls, and a few of them gave Jules and Frances disapproving looks. "Righteous bitches," said Jules. "As if my kid's going to be born with one eye if I eat processed sugar once in a while."

From that moment on, the two of them were inseparable, and when Frances and Jeremy met Jules's wife, Carmen, the four of them became inseparable. Gabriela was born just a few weeks before Daisy. The four of them rode the parenting roller coaster ride together, had countless meals together, even holidayed together.

But in a million years Frances never thought she'd need Jules in a professional capacity. Jules represented accused rapists. Murderers. Gang members.

And now, her.

"That *is* good news," Frances said now. "So that's it? It's over?"

Jules arched a perfectly threaded eyebrow. "Where did you get that idea?"

"You just said you got the charge diverted—"

"Diverted. Not disappeared. You're a wordsmith, you should know the difference." Jules's assistant entered and placed espressos and biscuits in front of them. Jules waited until he was gone before she continued. "Crown counsel has agreed to not lay the charge *at this time*. She's referred you to alternative measures instead."

"Alternative measures?"

"It means you'll be assigned a diversion officer." Seeing Frances's blank look, she added, "Think probation officer, except you're not on probation."

"A probation officer?"

"Together you'll craft your program."

"My program?" Frances, in trying to process what Jules was tossing her way, kept repeating her words back to her.

"It will most likely involve a written apology to the boy and his family."

"I can do that. I'd *like* to do that."

"You'll probably have to agree to a certain number of hours of community service, maybe twenty to thirty."

"Fine."

"And you'll almost certainly have to attend anger management classes."

Frances paused. "But I'm not an angry person."

"Francy-Pants. You shook a twelve-year-old boy and called him a turd biscuit. I'm not saying it wasn't justified, but in the eyes of the law, you committed assault. Which usually happens when someone is not just angry, but in a rage."

Frances closed her eyes. Opened them. "If I agree to all this, will the charges be dropped?"

Jules tapped a perfectly manicured nail on the glass table. "You have to complete the program first. If the Crown is satisfied, you'll never *be* charged, you won't have a record . . . The slate will be wiped clean."

"And if I don't complete the program—"

"The charge will go ahead, and we will have to deal with it in *actual* court. Unlike your diversion program, this will all be public, and it will be much worse for you. We'll either have to work out a deal with the Crown if you decide to plead guilty, or we'll have to go to trial. And with that video, even with me as your lawyer—I don't love your chances."

Frances nodded, trying to absorb it all. "How long will this program take?"

"It will likely be more onerous than normal, because the incident was so high profile and it involved a minor. I'd guess around three to six months. It will take up a fair chunk of your time."

Frances gave her a rueful smile. "I have nothing *but* time." As she'd feared, her upcoming week of school visits, at three different schools, had been cancelled. The emails had come in late Sunday night. One had been apologetic and kind in tone; two had been perfunctory and cold.

"You'll get a call from probation pretty soon to set up an interview with your diversion officer. As long as you don't get The Sarge, you'll be fine."

"Who's The Sarge?"

"Carol Jansen. Everyone calls her The Sarge behind her back because she oozes this strict military vibe. Little bull terrier of a woman. Even I find her terrifying. But never fear, I'll work my magic."

A few exhausted tears coursed down Frances's face as the reality of her situation started to sink in.

Jules reached over and squeezed her hand. "This is the best possible outcome, Francy-Pants."

"I know. And I am eternally grateful, Jules. Thank you."

Jules looked at her watch. "Four o'clock. Which means in Calgary it's five o'clock. Calgary cocktail hour?" She stood, all five feet, nine inches of her, and walked to a bar fridge in the corner of the room. "I put a bottle of pinot gris in here just in case." She poured them each a glass of wine to the rim. Then she kicked off her shoes and put her feet on the boardroom table, just like she was the bad-ass star of a TV law series. "Want to come for dinner tonight? Carmen's cooking."

"Will there be more wine?"

"Is that a rhetorical question?"

"Then yes. I'd love to."

Jules raised her glass. "You'll get through this. And you'll come out the other side stronger than ever." They clinked glasses. Frances gulped a third of her wine in one go.

When Jeremy left, Jules and Carmen had sided with her. It made Frances feel a tiny bit better knowing that her soon-to-be ex-husband had lost something of significance, too.

8

He had no neck.

Or at least, Frances could not make out where his head ended and his neck began. The difference in girth and width between the two was negligible. And he was enormous, well over six feet, and wide, not exactly fat (that was another word that would earn a five-minute lecture from Daisy)—just *big*, a big forty-something man wearing a green Adidas track suit, squished into a high-schooler's desk. If he stood, he would surely take the desk with him. And he was hairy, *sweet Jesus*, you could make a fur stole from what sprouted out of his arms alone. He was like a sasquatch, trying to pass for human simply by putting on a pair of sweatpants. She could not stop staring.

Until she realized he was staring right back at her, a stupid grin on his face, showing off a mouthful of crooked teeth. She quickly looked away.

There were seven of them in the classroom, which was on the second floor of an east side secondary school. No matter their ethnicity, under the harsh fluorescent lighting every single one of them looked pallid, pasty, and slightly green. Of the seven there was only one other woman. She was young, around Daisy's age, a rather odd-looking duck with a mass of fiery red hair, oodles of freckles, and a multicoloured tent-dress that appeared to be made out of multiple swatches of fabric. The rest were men. Frances was hardly surprised. *Probably a bunch of wife beaters*, she thought. With the exception of Grinny McGrinnerson—who, Frances could see out of her peripheral vision, was still staring at her—nobody made eye contact. Everyone looked like they wanted to be anywhere but here. No surprise there, either.

Frances had had her meeting with the diversion officer a week earlier. Jules had worked her magic and gotten her assigned to a fellow named Doug Bachman. "He has a soft spot for women. Just play up your remorse. Make sure you acknowledge responsibility. Cry a little if you can. And I know I shouldn't say this because it's the twenty-first century, but it wouldn't hurt to undo one more button your blouse. He'll craft you a program you could practically do in your sleep."

So Frances had made her way to the drab 1970s government building near the courthouse and walked up the stairs to the fifth floor. It housed rows of identical rabbit-warren offices. She'd waited. And waited. She'd worn her favourite blouse, a silk creamy number that showed off a bit of cleavage, and prayed she wouldn't have a hot flash. She'd even put on makeup and blow-dried her hair.

Half an hour after her appointed time, a squat, unsmiling woman with a bowl haircut, beige trousers, and a white polo shirt had approached with a clipboard. "Frances Partridge?"

"Yes."

"Come with me." Frances saw her badge: Carol Jansen.

The Sarge.

"Um, I'm sorry, I'm supposed to be seeing Doug Bachman?"

"Doug's off sick."

"I can wait until he's well again—" Carol's look shut Frances up. She stood and followed.

Carol led her into one of the rabbit warrens and told her in a flat, bored voice what the list of requirements was. It was everything Jules had told her to expect: an apology letter, community service, anger management classes. "And I'd suggest you pay the boy's family one thousand dollars as restitution for the property you destroyed."

"I didn't destroy any property."

"They claim his iPhone got smashed during the scuffle. Also that you ruined his expensive sneakers."

Frances snorted. "That is bullshit."

The Sarge stared at her, her mouth a thin, humourless line. "Is it *bullshit* that you assaulted a twelve-year-old boy, Ms. Partridge?"

Frances answered with a meek no. Then she did the thing she did when she got nervous: she vocalized her thoughts. Jeremy had teased her about her compulsion to say things out loud that would have been better kept to herself. "Although I would argue that *assault* is a strong word. Perhaps because I'm a writer I feel there could be more nuanced language around what I did, like, 'I *upbraided* a twelve-year-old,' or 'I *admonished* a twelve-year-old—'"

"You manhandled him."

"My daughter would insist that I *womanhandled* him. Or *personhandled* him."

"Are you finding this amusing, Ms. Partridge?"

"No. Not even remotely."

"Good. Because if you can't take ownership for your crime—and it *was* a crime, Ms. Partridge—perhaps the alternative measures program is not for you."

Whoosh. Her internal organs suddenly ignited. She knew that in under ten seconds, she'd be dripping with sweat. "I'm sorry. I do take ownership." Droplets of perspiration slowly coursed between her breasts. She knew her face looked like a sweaty beet. "I'm sorry. I'm having a hot flash—"

"Do you take ownership?"

"I do. I really do. You have my word."

The Sarge handed her a box of Kleenex, a small gesture of

compassion. Then she glanced at her computer. "Let's discuss your community service."

Frances tried to discreetly wipe a Kleenex between her breasts, and another across her face. "Yes. Of course. I was told about twenty to thirty hours."

"I'm recommending sixty." She stared at Frances, as if daring her to utter a word, then handed her a piece of paper. "Here's a list of possible assignments. Rank them in order of preference." Frances scanned the list and did as she was told.

On her way out she said, "Thank you, Sarge—I mean Ms. Jansen." *Damn it!* She scurried away, making a wrong turn in her haste. It took her a full five minutes to find the elevators.

Jules was right; the woman was terrifying.

Now, as she absent-mindedly studied the graffiti carved into her desk—*JM loves YR. BLM. Mr. D sucks ass*—a thin wisp of a man, the opposite of terrifying, entered the room. Frances guessed he was around thirty. He put his scuffed briefcase down on the teacher's desk. His cheap brown suit hung loosely on his frame. His eyes, along with his Adam's apple, were exceptionally large. "Good evening," he said. "My name is Dennis, and I'll be your instructor for the next eight weeks. Confession: this is the first time I've ever taught this class. Actually, this is the first time I've taught, period—so go easy on me, okay?" He tittered nervously. No one cracked a smile. "We'll be covering a lot of ground, and remember, we all have a common goal." He spoke slowly, articulating every word, like he was speaking to a room full of kindergartners. "We are all here to learn skills to manage our"—he picked up a piece of chalk and wrote ANGER in big letters on the chalkboard. "Let's say it together, shall we? *Anger.*"

No one said it.

"Okay, again, on the count of three: one, two, three, *anger*."

A few of them muttered it this time; the young girl said it quite loudly, then immediately looked embarrassed for it and stared down at her sparkly purple notebook.

"Come on, now, you can do better than that."

"ANGER!" shouted the bald man at the back. Angrily.

Dennis tittered again. "What is anger? That's what I'd like us to explore tonight. And please remember, we are in a safe space."

Frances snorted loudly.

Dennis blinked. "Sorry, you are . . . ?" He glanced at his class list.

"Frances." Out of her peripheral vision Frances saw the young girl's head swivel towards her.

"Frances, is there something you'd like to say?"

"This is an anger management class. I could be surrounded by violent offenders right now. Quite honestly, *safe* is not a word that comes to mind, no offence to anyone else."

"None taken," said the bald man, crossing his arms across his barrel chest.

"Rest assured, violent offenders have their own programs. Beyond that, *why* anyone is here is not our business."

"Except we all know why she's here, don't we?" said Grinny McGrinnerson, looking at Frances. Two of the other men nodded and smiled. "*How many times did I ask you to shut the eff*—except you didn't say *eff*—*up, you little turd biscuit*." Good god, he was quoting her.

"Why don't *you* shut the fuck up," Frances blurted, and Grinny's eyes grew wide in shock.

Dennis blinked rapidly. "Okay, maybe we can turn this into a teachable moment. How many of you would say Frances managed her anger well just now?" Frances half-raised her hand, hoping others might follow. No one did. "How many of you would say she overreacted?"

Four people put up their hands, including Grinny. Frances noted with some satisfaction that the bald man and the young girl had abstained.

"What might have been a better way to deal with—I'm sorry, what's your name?" Dennis asked Grinny.

"Geraint."

"What would have been a better way for Frances to deal with Geraint's somewhat insensitive comment?"

A scrawny man with tattoo sleeves spoke up. "She could've said something like, *When you talk about me like that, it hurts my feelings.*"

"Very good. And you are . . . ?"

"Wayson." Wayson smiled, pleased with himself. "I heard that line on a rerun of *Full House.*"

"I didn't mean to hurt anyone's feelings," Geraint said. "I was trying to break the ice. I mean, we've *all* done something that's landed us here." He looked at Frances with a stricken expression. "I'm truly sorry. I didn't mean to offend. I just meant, yours was very public. Over a million views as of yesterday."

Frances saw the young girl whip out her phone and start typing.

"If it's any consolation," Geraint continued, "it's very entertaining. You're very entertaining."

"Okay, I'm out." Frances grabbed her purse and stood up.

"If you leave," said Dennis, "I have to inform your diversion officer."

Frances sat.

"Okay, let's start with the question. What is anger—"

Suddenly Frances could hear her own voice, but tinnier. "*How many times did I ask you politely to shut the *bleep!* up, you little turd biscuit?! You need to learn to respect your elders!*" She pivoted in her desk. The young girl was staring at her phone, her mouth agape, watching Frances's video. The others immediately leapt up and gathered around her desk.

"Now, now," said Dennis as he scurried towards them, "this isn't the time for watching videos, we have a lot of material to cover . . ." But the moment he saw the action on the screen, his words petered out and he watched, too.

The class was two hours. It felt like five. Frances swore she saw the minute hand on the clock move backward at one point. Even though they hadn't been obligated to tell anyone why they were there, the bald guy, Byron, told them (rather proudly, Frances thought) he'd punched his boss in the nose after said boss had threatened to fire him for insubordination (news flash: Byron was then fired for insubordination). The scrawny guy with the tattoo sleeves, Wayson, let them all know he'd smashed an old lady's windshield with a tire iron after she'd cut him off in traffic. (Wayson, at least, seemed full of remorse.) When Dennis talked—and talked—about anger and its positives and negatives as an emotion, Frances felt like she was in a surreal episode of *Sesame Street*.

When the clock finally struck 9 p.m. Dennis said, "Next week we'll discuss triggers. What *triggers* your anger? That's your homework. Make a list. I'm a big believer in lists." Frances was already out of her seat when he said, "Oops, I almost forgot. I have your community service assignments from your diversion officers."

He took forever to find the paperwork in his briefcase. "Ah, here we are. Jimmy and Roy, you'll be at the Greater Vancouver Food Bank. Byron and Wayson . . . you'll be working at the Gospel Mission soup kitchen. Frances, Geraint, and Parker . . . the three of you will be doing roadside sanitation."

Roadside sanitation. That sounded an awful lot like—

"Garbage picking?" asked the young girl, whose name, Frances now knew, was Parker.

"Perhaps you ranked it in your top three?"

"It was my last choice," said Frances.

"Mine too," said Parker.

"Ditto," said Geraint.

Dennis glanced down at his paperwork. "Ah. I see you all have The Sarge—*ahem*, Ms. Jansen." Dennis gave them a pitying look. "Try to look on the bright side: all that fresh air and exercise! Better still, the three of you will get to spend a *lot* of time together. Who knows, perhaps you'll become fast friends!" Dennis smiled at them.

They did not smile back.

In fact, Dennis—who'd already seen a lot of unhappy faces in his short career—thought he had never seen such a miserable-looking trio in his entire life.

9

P arker bolted out of the classroom ahead of the others, clutching her sparkly purple notebook under her orange faux fur coat. The corridors were empty except for a lone janitor who sang out of tune as she washed the floors. Parker ran down the main stairs and out the front doors, gulping in the crisp night air.

As she headed to the parking lot, her inner monologue was going a mile a minute. *I just spent two hours in a room with someone who smashed an old lady's windshield with a tire iron. And a dude who looks like every Bad Guy Number Two in every action picture I've ever seen. And one of my all-time favourite authors, who went postal on a kid!!*

That particular tidbit really took the cake. Parker loved the *Phoebe Unknown* series, had reread her dog-eared copies countless times. The books had been an escape from her sometimes less-than-idyllic childhood, especially during the years Sharon dated Abelard, an aging, angry Buddhist who constantly yelled at Parker for "fucking with his inner tranquility." *But holy moly, that video! Does this mean I have to throw out the books? Or can I love the art but not the artist?*

Then the irony walloped her like a mallet to the head, and she started to laugh. *What Frances Partridge did is nothing compared to what you did, you dork!*

She reached the Blood Money Mazda and slipped into the driver's side. She was so tired. Not because she was busy—she'd never had so much time on her hands in her entire life. Who knew the crush of boredom could be so exhausting? And she was having trouble sleeping, which was truly out of character; Alexei liked to joke that she could sleep through the apocalypse.

The truth was, she was having trouble with a lot of things lately, things that used to come easily to her. Number one, sleeping. Number two, eating. Parker loved eating! Sharon used to complain that she ate like a linebacker. "You're going to eat us out of house and home," she'd say, and Parker would joke, "I think you mean out of trailer and trailer park," which Sharon did not appreciate. Normally she could eat two portions of Alexei's mom's moussaka when they went for Sunday dinners. Now she had to force herself to get even one portion down.

Number three, reading. Parker was a voracious reader; she could easily devour a book a week. The librarians at her local branch knew her by name. But now she couldn't concentrate on the words. If she got through two pages of a novel and actually retained what she'd read, it was a good day.

Number four, being kind. Sharon used to caution her that there was a fine line between being kind and being a pushover, but it was in Parker's nature to assume the best in people. Lately, though, she'd been impatient and short with everyone from the bank teller who'd wanted to put a hold on her massive silence-buying payout to the police who'd questioned her after The Thing at the mall. She'd even been short with Alexei once or twice. Alexei, who was her rock star. He was only trying to be there for her, to help her in any way he could. But one night when they'd been eating tuna casserole at their tiny Formica table, he'd said, "Time heals all wounds," and she'd wanted to stab her fork into his eye. Because in this case time was making everything worse, giving her ample opportunity to play everything back in her mind at all hours of the day and night, to question her every decision, her every move.

Parker still couldn't believe what a mess she'd made of things. Her encounter with Sebastian Trevor, the man who'd been one of her favourite actors until he most definitely wasn't, had been the match that lit a fuse inside her, a fuse she hadn't even known existed.

And now she'd been charged with assault—*assault!*—after what happened at the mall. How was this even possible? How had she gone from living her best life to sitting in a high school classroom with criminals?

Parker stared out the windshield. She told herself firmly she would get through this. She said it out loud: "I will get through this!" Just for good measure, she took out her purple notebook and wrote it down: *I will get through this!!!!! What doesn't kill you, makes you stronger!!!!!*

But then she thought about having to do sixty hours of garbage picking with the big hairy man and the crazy author lady, and she burst into tears.

10

"ou've been swimming again," said Norah as she, Frances, and Maryam found a table at Storm City Coffee on Broadway the next day.

"How can you tell?" asked Frances.

"Your hair's a bit damp. You smell like chlorine. And I can see the outline of your goggles." Norah's latest project was a series of middle-grade mystery novels, so she was in detective mode.

"It's so good you've kept that up," added Maryam.

When Jeremy left, Frances had stopped doing many things. Cleaning the house. Writing. Showering. Moderating her drinking. But the one thing she'd managed to stick to was her swimming. At least two mornings a week, she forced herself to go to the Vancouver Aquatic Centre. She'd never been a sporty person— she'd always been picked last for school teams—but when she was in the pool, her anxiety vanished. It was the one thing that stood between her and a total breakdown, she was sure of it. This morning she'd gone in spite of a wicked hangover; after arriving home from anger management she'd done that thing again, where she opened a bottle of wine, promising herself she'd only have one glass, and then drank the entire bottle while watching back-to-back episodes of *Only Murders in the Building*.

"Was The Turtle there?" Norah asked.

"Oh yes." Over the years Frances had regaled Norah and Maryam with stories of The Turtle, an older man who lumbered through the water like a brick with arms and legs, taking up the entire lane thanks to his flailing limbs. This wouldn't matter if he swam in the slow lane. But, like many men his age—or perhaps just like many men, period—his ego wouldn't let him associate himself with the word *slow*. So he always picked the medium lane, where Frances swam. "I passed him probably ten times. He hit me twice with his flailing arm. When I was getting out of the pool he said, *Someone was in a hurry today.*"

"I hope you said, *Well, it certainly wasn't you*," Norah tittered. Like most writers, she was good at coming up with sharp comebacks, but only after the fact and never, ever to someone's face.

The women—all around the same age, give or take five years—had become fast friends a decade ago after doing a panel together at Vancouver's Bookapalooza, an authors' festival for kids that drew big audiences and brisk sales. They'd been meeting for coffee once a week ever since—commiserating about writer's block, editorial notes, and the state of the publishing industry (always dire), and, of course, gossiping about other writers. Writing was a solitary and often lonely pursuit, and these weekly get-togethers were a lifeline.

Norah leaned forward in her seat. Her long greyish-blonde hair was tucked into a trapper's hat with flaps over the ears, and she still had her long sheepskin coat and sunglasses on. Norah's style tended towards "homeless Stevie Nicks"—her term—at the best of times, but Frances thought this was a bit odd, even for her. "Enough about The Turtle. How are you doing?"

Frances gave them the broad strokes, ending with: "Jacqueline's postponing publication."

Norah gasped. Maryam clutched her throat with her perfectly manicured hand. (Unlike Frances and Norah, Maryam put on makeup and dressed as if she was going to the office every single weekday, even if her office was just down the hall from her bedroom.)

"She says it's not forever."

"No, of course not," said Norah, but Frances saw her shoot Maryam a worried look across the table.

Maryam leaned in closer and lowered her voice. "If you ask me, that little shit deserved it."

Norah nodded. "I guarantee children's authors everywhere are cheering you. Just, you know, not in public."

"I even posted something on social media, supporting you," said Maryam.

"You did?"

"Then I deleted it. Sorry, Frances."

Frances was used to this by now: the words of support, the outrage, followed by, "Of course, I can't say anything *publicly*, you understand." And she did understand. She'd seen what had happened to the few authors who'd defended her on social media. Tina Vaziri, a revered children's author, had written:

I know Frances Partridge. She's a good person going through a bad time. She needs our forgiveness, not our ridicule or hate.

The backlash had been swift and furious.

So if I'm going through a rough time, it's okay to beat my kid?? My partner??

Guess I've gotta get rid of all *your* books now too . . .

Privileged white women banding together! Bunch of Karens!

The last one really got up Frances's nose because a) Tina wasn't even white, b) she knew a few great women named Karen who didn't deserve to have their birth name served up as a simplistic symbol for all that was bad about white privilege, and c) it all felt inherently misogynistic because there no male equivalent.

At any rate, it was all too much for Tina to handle, and a mere forty-eight hours later she deleted her statement and posted:

I see now the harm my words have caused. There is no excuse for violence, end of story.

She'd called Frances afterwards in tears. "I'm sorry. But my publisher was pressuring me, my agent was pressuring me . . ." Frances had found herself in the awkward position of having to comfort Tina, instead of the other way around. But she felt not a shred of ill will towards her. The world of publishing was insular and small. If you were to become tainted, for any reason—whether by deed or association—it could mean the difference between managing to scrape together a living or not.

Therefore she simply said to Maryam, "Defending me right now would be career suicide. If the shoe were on the other foot, I'd only support you in private, too." Maryam looked relieved. "But enough of my woes. How are your latest manuscripts going?" Norah and Maryam filled her in on where they were at: Norah was almost done a first draft of her third book in the mystery series, and Maryam, who was a fabulous illustrator as well as an author, was in the final copy edit of a picture book. Frances tried her best to stay engaged and interested, but it was hard. Even if she *could* write, no one would dare to consider working with her right now.

Perhaps sensing her mood, Maryam changed the subject. "Do you have plans for the rest of the day?"

"I have my first community service shift in half an hour."

"Doing what?"

"Roadside sanitation."

"That sounds an awful lot like—"

Frances nodded. "Picking up trash."

Maryam looked aghast, but Norah tried to look on the bright side. "David Sedaris picks up trash around his home in the UK. Voluntarily! They named a garbage truck in his honour."

"Something to aspire to," joked Frances. She noticed that Norah's upper lip was glistening with sweat. "Norah, for heaven's sake, take off your hat and coat," said Frances. "It's steaming in here."

"Is it? I hadn't noticed."

"We can see actual beads of perspiration on your face," said Maryam.

Norah stared down at her coffee. "I'm fine."

Suddenly Frances understood. "You're worried about being seen with me."

"That's ridiculous." But she made no move to take off her hat or her glasses.

Frances drained her coffee. "Let me make it easy for you." She stood.

"Just take your hat off, Norah," urged Maryam.

"It's fine," said Frances. "I have to be at Locarno Beach in fifteen minutes anyway."

Maryam looked alarmed. "But—that's practically your neighbourhood."

"So?"

Maryam lowered her voice. "You may see people you know. While you're in a *chain gang*."

"It's not a chain gang." But her heart started to race. How could she not have thought of this?

Norah's jaw set. Boldly, she pulled off her trapper's hat and sunglasses, blinking in the sudden light like a gopher poking its head out of the ground. She handed them to Frances. "Here. You need these more than I do."

For Norah, it was a selfless act of bravery.

Ten minutes later Frances pulled into a parking spot at Locarno Beach. She stepped out of Belinda the Beemer wearing Norah's hat.

It was one of those rare sunny winter days in Vancouver. White-caps pushed their way around the large tankers that were anchored in English Bay, and the snow-capped North Shore mountains were in full view. She stood quietly for a moment, trying to appreciate the view . . .

"Frances, hello! Over here! Hellooooo!" Geraint lumbered towards her, ruining the quiet and the view. He was like Bigfoot. Bigfoot in another Adidas track suit, red this time. He let out a bark of laughter when he got closer, revealing his jumbled Austin Powers–like teeth. He pointed a meaty hand at her hat.

"Ha ha! Look at you, all incognito."

"Yes, well. My house isn't that far from here."

The girl named Parker sat nearby at a picnic table, hunched over, humming to herself, wearing a ratty-looking wool coat and a pair of old red Vancouver Olympics 2010 mittens. She gave them a small wave but didn't move to join them.

A white pickup truck with a green decal stating BC Corrections pulled up beside them. Carol Jansen opened the cab door and hopped down gracelessly; the drop was long for short legs. "Hello, Carol, beautiful day," Geraint began.

"Your gear." She handed them each a retractable pole with a claw at the end. "Trash pickers . . . garbage bags . . . maps of your route . . . safety vests. I'll meet you back here in three hours."

"I didn't realize this was part of your job description," said Frances.

"It isn't. But I pride myself on being thorough. I like to make sure no one's slacking off." She gazed hard at Frances when she said this. Then she abruptly turned on her thick shot-putter legs and hoisted herself, equally gracelessly, back into the truck and drove away.

Geraint gave a low whistle. "She does not like you."

"If I'm remembering correctly, we all had garbage picking down as our last choice. So maybe she doesn't like any of us."

Geraint held up the map so they could all study it. "Looks like we're heading due west, along the beach and up the hill."

"Let's get this over with." They started to walk. Frances was acutely aware of the looks they were receiving from passersby and she kept her head lowered, terrified that at any minute someone she knew would walk past.

"I made a list of conversation starters for us," said Geraint. "You know, ice-breaker-type questions like, *Cat person or dog person*. Parker, would you like to go first?"

"Oh! Um, no, thank you?" She pulled out a pair of hot-pink headphones from an iridescent gold backpack and planted them over her ears.

Geraint's expression drooped. But just for a moment. He turned to Frances. "Looks like it's just you and me, then. Cat person or dog person?"

Frances suppressed a sigh. This was going to be the longest three hours of her life.

And also: cat person, *obviously*.

11

What would you rather: Parachute from a plane or go spelunking? What would you rather: Eat sheep's brain or bull's testicles? What would you rather: Spend a month stranded on a desert island or a month in a submarine?" Frances mimicked Geraint as she and Jules did their weekend run/walk through the Endowment Lands, the emphasis still very much on walk. "His mouth never stopped moving." Rain was pelting down, and the needles on the towering Douglas firs on either side of the mucky trail glistened with raindrops. "In an illustrated children's dictionary, they could put his picture beside *oaf.* Or *lummox.* Or *galoot.*"

"I can't wait to meet him." Frances knew from experience that Jules was serious.

"You will never meet him. There is no universe in which you will ever need to meet him."

Jules's watch beeped. They started running again, which was more of a plod. A group of young runners flew past. "Show-offs," Jules shouted after them. Then the two of them grew quiet, their breathing laboured. Frances tried to dodge a large mud puddle. Failed.

"Surely . . . it's been . . . a minute," huffed Frances, just as Jules's watch beeped. They slowed to a walk. "The young woman—Parker—she was no help at all. Hardly said a word to us."

"Come now, Frances, she's practically a kid. She's probably terrified."

"Fair point. She can't be any older than Daisy."

"Do you know why they're in anger management?"

Frances shook her head. "No clue. And get this, I have to pick up trash again tomorrow. On a Sunday! Oh, and Daisy told me I smelled like garbage juice last night, and that was after I'd had a shower."

"Ah, daughters. Gabriela told me on Zoom the other day that my up-do looked like a giant poo emoji." Gabriela was spending a year in Kenya, where Jules's father lived, working for a UN agency. *Beep.* "Time to run again." It was the final minute, and Jules started to sprint. Frances struggled to keep up but soon fell far behind.

Finally, *beep.* Frances stumbled up to Jules, who somehow still looked poised and gorgeous in her head-to-toe Lululemon gear, and put her hands on her knees, trying to catch her breath.

"Your tights have a hole in the bum," said Jules.

Frances tugged her equally tattered sweatshirt down. "What are you and Carmen up to tonight? That movie's playing at the Fifth Avenue—the one with Cate Blanchett."

"We can't tonight, sorry." Frances's heart sank. Every night was difficult, but Saturday nights were the worst. Jules linked arms with her as they left the forest. "Use the evening to write your apology letter instead. I want to read it over before we submit it to Carol Jansen."

Frances sighed. "Fine."

"Good." Jules took a deep breath. "Now, Francy-Pants, on another note. I know it's only been six months—"

"No."

"You have no idea what I was about to say."

"I'm not ready to date."

"I could help you set up a fabulous profile on a dating app or two."

"Ugh, no."

"I met Carmen on a dating app."

"Yes, when you were thirty. And also, Carmen's a woman. Men my age want to date women who are half their age plus seven years."

"Not all of them."

"Or they're still single for a reason. That's what Jeanette always says." Jeanette was a mutual friend, divorced for ten years, who frequently regaled them with her dating horror stories. "Remember that one guy? Goes into his room to change into something more comfortable . . ."

"I know, I know, and comes back wearing nothing but an adult diaper."

"And says in a baby voice, *Mommy change me? I make doody.*"

"But that guy was an anomaly."

"Was he? What if he's the norm?"

"He isn't."

"You don't know that!"

"I do know that eventually you have to get back out there."

Frances stopped by Jules's car, a brand-new silver Audi A8. "No. Not yet. Maybe not ever." Her voice caught. "Jeremy lied to me for decades. I don't think I'll ever be able to trust anyone ever again."

Jules gazed at Frances for an uncomfortably long moment. "Do you think, just maybe, you are being a tad melodramatic?"

"No, I do not think I'm being melodramatic!" Frances realized she was sounding, well, melodramatic. A woman walking a Pomeranian gave them a wide berth.

Jules took a deep breath. "All right. Jeremy ruined your life. Jeremy is a piece of shit."

Frances smiled, pleased. "That's more like it." They got into the car.

"And you will mope and wallow for the rest of your life, slowly turning into Miss Havisham, sitting in your mouldy wedding dress next to your insect-infested wedding cake."

"Okay, okay, that's enough."

Jules started the engine and peeled away.

Frances was ravenous when she got home. She made a beeline for the kitchen, then stopped in her tracks, dismayed.

It looked like a hurricane had hit. Hurricane Daisy, to be precise. She'd made one of her elaborate breakfasts again. She did this now and then, never thinking to make enough for her mother, and certainly never thinking to clean up.

The perpetrator flew into the kitchen, past Frances, dressed for work in an H&M skirt and simple white blouse. "The temp agency called, a company that's open on Saturdays needs a warm body. Pays double." She dropped her empty coffee mug into the sink.

"You know you have a kitchen in your suite."

Daisy looked at her like she was an idiot. "But all the food's up here."

"And we've talked about cleaning up after yourself—"

"Mom," Daisy huffed. "Some of us have jobs." Then she breezed out of the kitchen.

Frances took a deep breath. She knew she should leave the mess for Daisy to deal with when she got home. But she also knew it would invade her thoughts all day, like a virus. So she cleaned up the kitchen. Then she got out the Dyson. It had been weeks since she'd vacuumed the house because vacuuming—along with most of the cooking, dusting, toilet unclogging, bill and tax paying, gutter cleaning, and other general household maintenance—had been Jeremy's job.

She vacuumed the Berber rug in the living room, then carried the Dyson upstairs, vacuuming Max's old room, her office (which used to be Daisy's room before she moved to the granny suite), and the primary bedroom. She pushed the cleaner head under the bed. Something got stuck in the nozzle.

It was one of Jeremy's socks.

Jeremy's socks had been one of her biggest pet peeves throughout their marriage. He had left them everywhere: in the foyer, on the couch, even on the kitchen counter.

She recognized this one; it was part of a pair she'd given him the Christmas before. Black with electric blue stripes, merino wool, made in Italy. They jazzed up his suits in a subtle way.

She sniffed the sock.

This was the hardest part. Even after all these months, memories like this lay in wait, ready to ambush her. Last week Starship's "We Built This City" had come on the radio and Frances had turned to Jeremy so they could sing their own lyrics—"We built this city on sausage rolls"—only to be reminded for the umpteenth time that he wasn't here. It was like being stabbed in the heart with tiny little daggers, multiple times a day.

She turned off the Dyson and lay on the bed, immobile, cradling Jeremy's lone, smelly sock.

Cordelia gave her daughter the once-over when Frances entered her room at Shady Pines a few hours later. Frances was wearing her old black sweater over her favourite pair of old black tights again. No makeup. "Oh, Franny, you look a sight."

Frances ignored the comment. "How's your day been?"

"Your stepfather is late again." Frances had never known her birth father; Cordelia had raised Frances on her own, which, once Frances had children, gave her an even deeper appreciation for her mother. When Frances was in university, Cordelia had started dating Harvey. They'd married a year later. He was warm, exceptionally bright, and very funny. Best of all, he'd adored Cordelia. They'd had a fabulous twenty-three years together until he keeled over from a brain aneurism ten years ago.

But Frances played along. "Harvey has many great qualities, but we both know promptness isn't one of them."

Cordelia laughed. "So true."

Because it was raining, they decided to stay in Cordelia's room. They watched some cat videos on Frances's phone, which was a favourite activity for both of them. Then Frances pulled a photo album at random off the shelf. Cordelia enjoyed looking through them; her memory for past events was still surprisingly strong. The two of them settled on the floral loveseat. "Oh, I like these ones," said Cordelia. The album spanned the nine months of Frances's pregnancy with Daisy.

They flipped the page. A younger, and infinitely happier, Frances and Jeremy beamed up at them. Jeremy's hand on her belly in one; Jeremy's arms wrapped around her in another. Cordelia pointed at him. "He visits me sometimes."

Frances knew this wasn't true. After he'd moved out, Frances had asked him to stay away from Shady Pines (okay, she'd shouted it drunkenly on the phone one night). She'd told him her mom would find the situation too confusing (and she might have added that Cordelia was *her* mother, not Jeremy's, so he could "back the fuck off"). But all she said was, "That's nice."

Frances turned the page. "Oh, I'd forgotten about these." It was a spread of photos of Frances and Jules in profile, arms covering their bare breasts, their huge, pregnant bellies touching. It had been their ode to Demi Moore's *Vanity Fair* cover. They had their heads thrown back, laughing. God, they'd been young and beautiful, Frances thought.

"Who is that person?" asked Cordelia.

"That's Jules Osomo. My best friend."

"Have I met her?"

"Many times. Do you mind if I take one of these to give to her? I don't think she has any."

"Of course."

Frances carefully slid out one of the photos. Later, when Cordelia went to the washroom, Frances slid out all the photos of Jeremy, too, and stuffed them into her purse.

She told herself that if her mom was going to forget people anyway, there was no harm in nudging her towards forgetting him.

When Cordelia asked if she'd like to stay for dinner, Frances said yes because what else did she have to do? Daisy was staying at Paolo's—or had she moved on to Kwame?—and even if she wasn't, Frances would never try to rope her into hanging out with her maudlin mother on a Saturday night. She did have a few strands of dignity left. Plus, it was chicken pot pie night, and the kitchen made a really good chicken pot pie.

She drove home along Grandview Highway. As she neared Commercial Drive, the lively East Vancouver neighbourhood that Jules and Carmen called home, she spontaneously turned onto their street; she could drop the photo in their mailbox.

She parked outside their purple-painted heritage home. The house was ablaze in light. As she climbed the steps to the front porch, she could hear music and voices. Frances felt a twinge of jealousy, even though she knew Jules and Carmen had loads of friend groups, and not all of those friend groups included her. She reminded herself that she was grateful to be in their friendship orbit, period. She dropped the photo into their mailbox, just as the door swung open. Jeremy stood before her.

He blinked. "I—I thought you were Mahshid and Reza."
Mahshid and Reza. Mahshid and Reza were *her* friends first,
not his.

Jules appeared behind him, carrying two drinks. "Here's your
martini—" She locked eyes with Frances. Silence for a moment,
then: "Jeremy, why don't you go back inside."

Jeremy took no persuading. He grabbed his martini and hurried back into the house. Frances saw, in the kitchen, Shonda and
Raj. These were the couples she and Jeremy and Jules and Carmen had spent countless Saturday nights with, taking turns hosting potluck dinners.

"I can explain," said Jules.

And there was Kelly. Holding a cocktail, laughing at something
Shonda or Raj had said.

"It was Carmen's idea. She doesn't want to take sides."

There were footsteps behind her. Mahshid and Reza. "Hi-hi,
sorry we're late—Frances!" Mahshid's eyebrows shot up, but she
quickly masked her surprise. "So good to see you."

"I was just leaving."

Frances hurried down the stairs and across the street to her
car, picturing their collective pitying gaze as she went. She could
just imagine the conversations they'd have. *Poor Frances, she's a
mess. Poor Frances, she looks like a bag lady. Poor Frances, she's falling
apart.* Jeremy's car was parked directly in front of hers. How had
she not noticed it? *Because in a million years I never expected to
see Jeremy here. Because loads of people drive black Teslas in this city.*
Frances started her car. In her distress she put it into drive instead
of reverse, and accidentally bumped Jeremy's car.

She reversed again. Put the car into drive.

The second and third times were not bumps. And they were
definitely not accidents.

~~To Whom It May Concern:~~

Dear Boy,

First of all, I'm sorry I can't call you by your name, but I've been told that because you're a minor they won't give me that information, and also there seems to be a very misguided concern that I could stalk you or hurt you further if I knew your identity, which is ridiculous and frankly hurtful. Hence the reason this letter is getting off to an impersonal start. Maybe I will refer to you as Liam, if that's okay. Based on your age and demographic background, it gives me about a twenty-five percent chance of being right.

I am deeply sorry for what happened, Liam. I never should have grabbed you, or shaken you, or sworn at you. I know you'll have to take my word for it, but I've never done anything like that in my life—I have two grown children of my own who can attest to that. (Well, Daisy may remember the time she wriggled away from me when she was two years old and ran onto the road. Luckily the cars stopped in time, otherwise she would have been killed. Afterwards I hugged her close and spanked her three times. It's called adrenaline, Liam. Trust me, you'll understand all of this when you're a parent yourself.)

While there is no excuse for my behaviour, I do want to give you some context. My husband left me for someone else, after almost twenty-five years of marriage. You probably can't even fathom that number since you have been on this earth for less than half of that. On the day of my presentation, I realized it was our twenty-fifth wedding anniversary, and I felt enormously sad. Because you see, I truly believed my marriage was good—no, great. And I wasn't alone in thinking this. All our friends thought so, too. So to say I was blindsided is an understatement. (On that note, I hope you don't mind me asking, but do your parents seem happy together? You probably don't think about it much—why would you, you still think the adults in your life exist only to serve you. But just FYI, Liam, while they may *appear* to be happy, appearances can be deceiving. I'd suggest keeping an eye on them. Now that I think about it, the fact that you deliberately blathered through my entire presentation with little to no regard for my feelings, and lobbed spitballs no less, makes me wonder if you're seeking attention because you aren't getting enough at home. And you may not be getting enough attention at home because your parents are in the midst of a marital crisis. This is just a theory, of course. I could be totally wrong.)

(Then again, I could be right.)

But back to my explanation. While I was giving my presentation, I confess that my mind was somewhere else. While I was telling you all about how I became a writer, and why I started writing the *Phoebe Unknown* books, my inner voice was telling me that I will probably spend my remaining years alone. Meaning I'll probably die alone. Oh, and I'll probably never have sex again, which is a gut punch because I'm only fifty-five. To you this must sound positively ancient, like I have one foot in the grave. But Liam, I have a lot of good years left and I am still a sexual person with sexual desires!

Then I started wondering if my friends would stop inviting me to dinner parties, because singletons mess up seating arrangements, and also all the other couples either a) pity you because you're the only person without a plus one or b) resent the very idea of you because you're a reminder of what could happen to them if they're not vigilant. And if you think I'm exaggerating, why *just this very night* I discovered that *my best friend* did not invite me to her dinner party because it was "couples only," but guess who she did invite? My ex-husband, that's who! And his new partner! Forget the hell this asshole put me through; he and his new tart fit in so much better with their seating plan! I mean, come on, Liam, where is the fairness in that??

But I digress. As I was having all of those thoughts, my feelings of sadness were replaced by feelings of rage towards my ex. Because Liam, he lied to me for years, and even you, at age twelve, know that lying is something you shouldn't do, especially not to someone you're supposed to love. And there you were, being a disruptive little shit. And I snapped.

So, let me reiterate: I'm genuinely sorry. It won't happen again. (Well, it really won't happen again, because your classmate filmed the whole thing. So, no more school visits for me, which is honestly quite devastating because it was a decent chunk of my yearly income, so— way to make me unemployable, Liam!)

I should probably disclose that I've had an entire bottle of wine tonight, all by myself. I am experiencing a lot of pain right now and alcohol, while never the answer in the long run, does temporarily dull said pain. Please don't tell your parents I said that.

I hope you and your family are well. I would love to send you a box set of the *Phoebe Unknown* books if you would like that. Perhaps you'll be pleasantly surprised and enjoy the read. Perhaps you'll wish you'd kept your mouth shut so you could have heard what I had to say—who knows, you might have even learned something.

Best wishes to you,
Frances Partridge

12

". . . Someone will give you a million dollars, and all you have to do is lie in a bathtub full of earwigs for five minutes. Do you do it?"

She had endured two hours and forty-eight minutes of this. Almost three full hours of listening to more of Geraint's inane questions, and worse, listening to him with a rip-roaring hangover. When she'd got home from her humiliation on Jules's front porch, she'd poured herself a strong gin and tonic before moving on to a bottle of wine. Jules had called and texted repeatedly, but Frances had ignored her. The other details of her evening were fuzzy, but she remembered writing her apology letter and stumbling out under cover of darkness in her cat pajamas to mail it to Jules's law firm.

The calls had started up again early this morning, not just from Jules but from Jeremy, too. He'd left two long-winded messages. "Frances, I'm sorry about what happened. I'm sorry you're having such a rough time, I really am. But you can't just *hit my car*. Your car must have damage, too. Let's deal with this like adults, okay?" *As if.* Right after she listened to his message, she'd parked Belinda the Beemer—with her damaged fender and broken headlight—in the garage, away from prying eyes. Then she'd called her local repair shop and booked their earliest available appointment in a few days' time.

Only then did she listen to his second message: "I think it's time to get the process started. But I really think we should talk first. Please. *Talk to me, Frances.*"

But Frances didn't want to talk. Because talking would lead to filing for divorce, and filing for divorce would set in motion months and maybe years of dealing with lawyers, squabbling over assets, household items, *money.* Aside from a few great years with the *Phoebe Unknown* trilogy, Frances had always been a mid-list author, well reviewed but with modest sales; Jeremy had always made more than her. Truth be told, he'd been the reason she was able to be a full-time writer; his steady income had meant they could weather her ebbs and flows.

And of course, there was the matter of the house. The thought of losing it as well was too much for her to bear. She'd rather stay in limbo.

A gust of wind almost took the trapper's hat off her head. She buttoned the flaps beneath her chin. They were back down at the beach again, and the weather had taken a turn for the worse. It was cold and drizzly, the North Shore mountains now barely visible through the low-hanging clouds. She and Parker (who walked at least twenty paces behind them at all times in her big pink headphones and her sodden wool coat, which gave her the appearance of a drowning pink-eared rat) each carried a full bag of trash; Geraint carried two.

Aside from affirming that Geraint a) owned at least three track suits in different colours (today he wore a very old blue one under a long, worn raincoat) and b) was well and truly an idiot, the other thing she'd learned in her now almost six hours of community service was that human beings were legitimately disgusting. The things people tossed! She'd picked up three—*three!*—dirty diapers, seven used condoms, two used tampons, a few used needles, and—number one on the vile list—a large coffee tin full of human feces.

"Frances?" Geraint asked. "Do you do it?" This was something else she'd learned: if she didn't answer, he would just persist, like a toddler asking *why*.

"No."

"What if they were cockroaches instead of earwigs?"

"Still no."

"Okay, doodlebugs—"

"*No*, Geraint. No to any kind of bug, and to any kind of act where I would be deliberately debasing myself for someone else's amusement."

"Even for a million dollars?"

"Yes. My dignity is more important than money."

Geraint gazed at her, in her trapper's hat, safety vest, old jeans, old MEC raincoat, galoshes, and work gloves (because after just one day they had learned to wear only things that were destined for the trash bin when this was all over) and raised an eyebrow. "No offence, Frances, but between this outfit and your video, I think you'd score very low on the dignity-meter right now."

Frances gazed back at him in his worn blue track suit, stained flasher-beige raincoat, and pompommed toque and said, "Hello, Pot. My name's Kettle." Geraint gave her a mystified look in return.

They dropped their sticky, overflowing garbage bags in a pile at a designated spot at the side of the road, where city workers would pick them up later. "I'd do it if it was a bathtub full of doodlebugs," continued Geraint, even though Frances hadn't asked. "They'd all just roll into balls the moment I got in, anyway. Although I suppose I'd squish a lot of them, and the *crunch* sound might be unbearable. I could wear noise-cancelling headphones, maybe. Parker could lend me hers! Still, though, all that unnecessary death." Geraint used his claw to pick up an abandoned pair of reading glasses; one of the arms was snapped in two. Frances watched in horror as he pocketed them. "What? Just needs a little super glue. They're one-point-fives, exactly my strength!" He chuckled. "Guess this is my lucky day."

Frances shook her head in disbelief. "Has anyone ever told you your relentless good cheer is annoying?"

"Oh, sure. My wife. On a daily basis."

So he was married. Frances had assumed he was single because who would tolerate him? But then, she and Jules had observed over the years that loads of intolerable men were married, while loads of terrific women were not.

Ugh. Jules. Jules had been Frances's outlet for all of her worst, immature, bitter, hate-filled rants against Jeremy. And all the while, she'd been fraternizing with the enemy. The betrayal cut her to the quick.

Geraint raised his meaty hands up for a double high-five. "Well done, everyone. Six hours down. Only fifty-four to go." Parker—who had removed her headphones now that they were done—looked like she might cry. Geraint's hands hung, high-five-less, in mid-air. He lowered them, looking rather deflated. "Either of you need a lift?" He indicated an old forest-green Subaru nearby.

"Would you mind dropping me at the 99 bus stop on Broadway?" asked Parker. "My boyfriend has the car today."

"Frances?"

Frances didn't want to spend another second with Geraint, but she hadn't dared take her bashed-up car out of the garage, and after three hours of walking and carrying garbage, her feet and back were killing her. "I could use a lift to Broadway, too."

"Here's a thought," said Geraint. "I could drive you both up to Broadway and before you carry on home, we could get a quick pint at the Wolf and Hound. My treat." He looked at the two of them, his big brown eyes full of hope.

Parker turned to Frances. "I'm in if you are," she said, which was not at all what Frances had expected.

She opened her mouth to say no. Then she thought about the evening ahead. The prospect of yet another night with no one but Mr. Pickles for company filled her with anticipatory dread.

"Fine," she said. "One beer."

Because hair of the dog and all that.

"I think I smell like rancid butter," said Parker as they settled into a cozy table at the back of the pub. They'd ditched the safety vests and gloves in Geraint's car but were otherwise still in their garbage-picking clothes.

Geraint leaned forward and sniffed the air. "I don't smell anything."

"You wouldn't, though, would you?" said Frances. "We'd be the last people to smell it because it's permeated our olfactory systems."

A harried server dropped three pints of Guinness in front of them. Geraint raised his glass. "Cheers." They drank. "Ha ha, you both have foam moustaches," he said with glee. "Do I have one, too?"

"You do!" Parker clapped her hands, delighted, so Geraint had another sip as he tried to build an even better Guinness moustache for Parker's amusement.

Frances shook her head. *He's like a child trapped in a yeti's body.* But in spite of his size, she simply could not imagine him harming a fly. Parker even less so. "Why are you two in anger management?"

Parker's face turned pink. "Oh, I'd rather not say, thank you very much."

"Geraint, how about you?"

"Ditto."

"What? Why not?"

"Because. It's embarrassing."

"More embarrassing than my video?"

"Well, no, but—no offence, Frances, you set the embarrass-ment bar very high."

"I won't judge you," said Frances. A white lie.

Geraint took a long pull from his Guinness. He set the glass down and closed his eyes. "All right. If you must know, I urinated in my ex-boss's fountain."

Parker wrinkled her freckly nose. "That's it?"

"A neighbour saw me do it. I need to be very clear that *I did not see the neighbour*. But it means I was charged with"—he closed his eyes again and said in a strangled whisper—"committing an in-decent act."

"But why would that land you in anger management?" asked Frances.

"Oh. Well, I also got charged with mischief over five thousand dollars."

"For peeing in a fountain?" asked Parker.

"No. For spray-painting something on his Lamborghini Hur-acan." Geraint downed the rest of his pint and raised three fingers when the server walked past.

"What did you spray-paint?" asked Frances.

"Just one word." He cocked his head, thinking. "Or is it two? I wrote it as one but grammatically it may be two. Frances, you're the writer. Is *man whore* two words, or one?"

Frances, mid-sip, snorted Guinness up her nose, which gave her a coughing fit. Geraint slapped her on the back. "Two," she sputtered.

"Why did you do it?" asked Parker.

He rested his massive hands on the table. "That's a longer story."

"So tell us," said Frances. "We've got time."

GERAINT'S STORY, PART 1

Geraint had always been big for his age. The kids at school teased him mercilessly about his accent, his clothes (lots of hand-knit sweaters from both his nice great-aunt and his mean one), his size, and his name. They called him Gargantuan or Gorgon. They also called him the R-word because his grades were in the toilet. His vocabulary was well above average—his father had drunkenly recited the poetry of the Thomases, both Dylan and R.S., after dinner every night—but he was well behind in reading and writing. It wasn't until he was eleven that one of his teachers suggested he get tested, and lo and behold they discovered he had dyslexia.

In middle school, the teasing took the form of bestiality jokes. *Hey Geraint, what do you call a Welshman with lots of girlfriends? A shepherd!* Or: *Really, officer, I was only helping the sheep over the fence!* How the Welsh had been cursed with this particular reputation, he did not know.

But in high school, his size became an asset. He wasn't athletic, but he was *big* and, as the rugby coach said, he was *Welsh*, which meant the game was in his blood. They made him a tight-head prop on the team, because he didn't need to be particularly fast; he just needed to be strong and throw his weight around in a scrum. It gave him some status at school, and he even dated a few girls, which he found to be equal parts nerve-wracking and delightful.

Yet none of these girls came close to Darlene.

Darlene had it all going on: confidence, an effortless charm, a good sense of humour (even if it was occasionally mean-spirited). She was hardly a brainiac, but then, neither was Geraint.

And she was gorgeous. A thick mane of long auburn hair, a curvy figure . . . She could literally take Geraint's breath away just by passing him in the halls. To top it off she was semi-famous: in eleventh grade she'd been cast in a North America–wide bubble gum commercial, and for months he couldn't watch TV without seeing her, blowing a huge bubble that eventually popped all over her adorable face. "It's bubble-yummy bubble gummy!" she'd declare. Geraint thought she was perfection itself. But she was light years out of his league.

Then, near the end of twelfth grade, Geraint scored the winning try at the provincial rugby championships. As a prop, he was hardly the top scorer on the team, and generally managed to get in one or two tries per season if he was lucky. On that particular day, it was a muddy slog along the try line; the forward pack kept smashing into the defence but couldn't break through. Then suddenly the ball came loose in a ruck, and Geraint managed to snatch it and dive over the line. Darlene was on the sidelines, watching. He caught her eye and she cheered like mad.

That night there was a party at the house of one of the forwards. Darlene sought him out and they chatted, and when they stepped onto the patio for some fresh air, he asked if he could kiss her. She laughed and said, "You don't need to ask permission, just do it" (which, Geraint took pains to tell Frances and Parker, sounded *very wrong* in a twenty-first-century context, but back then it didn't seem so strange, and also he *did* ask permission), so he kissed her, and her mouth *actually tasted like bubble gum*. It was everything he'd dreamed of and more. He swore he could hear the angels singing. (This was the second time Geraint saw Frances's eyes glaze over, the first time being during the rugby talk; but he was fairly certain it was the beer, not his heartfelt story.) Then a pile of his teammates spilled out the patio doors and she pulled away and the angels abruptly stopped singing.

A week later, he gathered up the courage to ask her to prom.

She told him she was already going with someone else. "Perhaps I could take you out some evening after that?" Geraint ventured.

"Ooh, love to, can't. I'm leaving, like, right after grad."

"Where to?"

Her eyes lit up. "Los Angeles. I have a third cousin who lives in Orange County. I'm going to get an agent, audition for pilot season. I want to be the next Lindsay Lohan."

"Well, if anyone can do it, you can. You've got loads of talent."

"You really think so?"

"I know so."

Perhaps she could see he was crestfallen. Or perhaps she just appreciated his vote of confidence. Because she took his hand in hers and said, "Tell you what. If we're both still single when we turn thirty, let's look each other up and go on that date."

Fast forward twelve years ("Thank Christ," he thought he heard Frances mutter). Geraint, having trained as an automotive technician after high school, had started a new job working for Ron Neumann at Ron's first-ever Quicky Muffler shop. Geraint loved his job and he worshipped Ron; Ron was a shrewd business-man and such a bon vivant! Sure, his humour could sometimes be off-colour, verging on racist or sexist or some other kind of "ist." Sometimes he poked fun at Geraint for his size, like the day Geraint wore a new pair of skinny jeans and a form-fitting shirt to work and Ron said, "Christ, Geraint, you look like ten pounds of shit stuffed into a five-pound bag!" But he always made a point, afterwards, of slapping Geraint on the back. "Ah, you know I'm just having a laugh, Ger. You're my right-hand man!"

The jokes bothered Geraint's fellow mechanic Jorge more than they bothered Geraint. "You shouldn't let him say stuff like that to you," Jorge would say on the occasions they grabbed a beer after work.

But Geraint brushed it off. "It's his way of bonding." Still, it

must have bothered him more than he realized, because one day after work—probably after Ron had delivered a few more fat jokes—
Geraint decided to pop into a new gym that had opened in his
neighbourhood. "Hello," he'd said to the auburn-haired woman
behind the desk. "I just want to ask how much it is to join, or if
you offer a free trial period—" He stopped mid-sentence, worried
he was hallucinating. "Darlene?"

It was indeed Darlene. And she was just as beautiful as ever.
"Hi, Geraint." She sounded subdued.

"When did you get back?"

"About a year ago."

"I kept looking for you on the big screen."

"Yes, well . . . turns out there are a lot of young women
down there with the same dream as mine." She gave him a rueful
smile.

"Perhaps. But no one quite like you."

"There were hundreds of girls like me. And some of them also
happened to be a lot more talented." And then Geraint understood: she was embarrassed. Embarrassed that she'd ever thought
she could have made it in such a competitive industry.

"I highly doubt they were more talented. Perhaps they were
just luckier. Right time, right place."

She smiled. "That's sweet of you to say."

"Well, I mean it."

She pulled out a flyer and handed it to him. "You were asking
about memberships."

Then he remembered. "I just turned thirty," he blurted. "By
my calculations, you must be thirty, too."

She looked at him askance. "You don't need to rub it in."

"Are you married? Seeing anyone?"

"Not at the moment, no."

"Well, then," he smiled. "I believe we owe each other a date."

GERAINT'S STORY, PART 2

Geraint continued: "We dated for a couple of years. We weren't exclusive, because she wanted to see other people; I mean, I guess *I* was exclusive because I only dated her. But when she turned thirty-three her biological clock started ticking, and who was the guy who was always there for her, through thick and thin? Who answered her calls at any time of the day or night? Who fixed her toilet every time it went on the fritz? Who paid her rent a few times when she was short of cash? Who drove all the way out to Surrey to pick her up when her date with a gang member went sideways?" Geraint pointed proudly at himself. "Me."

"A love story for the ages," Frances murmured, then gave herself a metaphorical kick; she was getting judgy-drunk.

The server walked past, and Geraint held up three fingers again. "We got married in a simple ceremony. Just a few of our family and friends, including Jorge and Ron. We bought a wee fixer-upper in East Van, close to Burnaby. Darlene didn't love it, she wanted something fancier on the west side, but it was what we could afford. I spent evenings and weekends doing renovations. Once a year we took a trip to Cabo. Then, five years ago, Keanu was born."

Frances had to force herself not to make a face. "*Keanu?*"

"Such a great name," said Parker with genuine enthusiasm. "I love Keanu Reeves."

"Darlene met him once when she was living in LA," said Geraint proudly.

"She was in one of his movies?" asked Parker.

"No, but she was a server at an after-party for one of his movies, and she always remembered his kind smile when he took two mini-quiches from her tray—Frances, are you all right? You look like you're in pain."

"I'm good. Really."

Geraint returned to his happy land of nostalgia. "I didn't think I could love anyone more than Darlene, but Keanu . . . oh, he's perfection." He broke into a goofy, jumble-toothed grin. "Almost five, with his mom's hair and my face. As you can imagine, he is quite the handsome lad—Frances, are you sure you're okay?"

Frances nodded, thinking, *I have got to stop drinking.* Which was exactly the moment three new pints landed on the table.

"I was so happy. We had a simple life; I was saving my pennies to open up my own Quicky Muffler franchise, so we could improve our financial situation. I wanted to give Darlene at least a fraction of the life she deserved. I thought she was happy, too. She'd quit her job at the gym, but she'd signed up with an extras agency—sorry, she prefers the term *background*—and she got work here and there on shows that were shooting in town. You know the movie *Deadpool*?"

"Starring Ryan Reynolds," said Parker. "Darlene was in that?"

Geraint nodded. "The sequel. You can see her in a street scene with Mr. Reynolds. Well, half of her. It's a crowd scene; she's partially in frame. At any rate, I think she was still secretly hoping she might get discovered."

"And really, why wouldn't she," said Frances before she could stop herself.

"My sentiments exactly! I told her I had a good feeling about it." Geraint grew suddenly somber. He downed the last of his second pint and picked up the third. "Then last month I did one of my weekly trips to a few of the other Quicky Muffler franchises. Ron trusted me to go on his behalf, do a general check-in. The visits took less time than usual, so I came back to the flagship shop early and walked into Ron's office.

"He was sitting at his desk with his pants around his ankles. Darlene was on his lap, skirt hiked, top off . . . They were . . ."

Parker's mouth dropped open. Frances's did not. "Saw that coming," she muttered under her beer-breath.

"Do you know what Ron said? *Oops.* That's it. *Oops.*" Tears welled up in Geraint's eyes. "I walked out. Wandered the streets for hours. Then parked my car a few blocks from Ron's house, hid in the bushes, and did what I did."

"He deserved it one hundred percent," said Parker fiercely.

"It had been going on for at least two years, apparently. I had no idea. I mean—they were a bit overly friendly with each other the odd time we had Ron for a barbecue. And he did French kiss her right in front of me last New Year's Eve, but I chalked it up to the eggnog and mistletoe. And once he went to a sales conference in Vegas, and Darlene went to Vegas at the same time with her girlfriend Christine, and when I saw a photo of her and Ron on Facebook outside Cirque du Soleil she told me it was just a crazy coincidence that they'd run into each other." Frances did nothing to hide her expression this time. Even Parker was giving him the same incredulous look. "Okay, okay, I see how it sounds in retrospect. But you have to understand, I'm a very trusting person."

Frances picked up her new pint. "If it makes you feel any better, I trusted my husband implicitly, and he'd been lying to me for decades." The beer was having a truth serum effect. She had the feeling she was slurring her words. "He walked out on me over seven months ago. The day I flipped out on that kid was our twenty-fifth wedding anniversary."

"That's brutal," said Parker.

"I'm so sorry, Frances," Geraint added. Then, hesitantly: "Was there someone else?"

"Yes." She burped softly. "Kelly."

"Let me guess. She's younger than you," said Geraint.

"I bet she spells Kelly with an *i*," said Parker.

"Bet people mistake her for his daughter all the time."

"Bet she's just looking for a sugar daddy—"

"Wrong on all fronts. Kelly is age appropriate. And he definitely doesn't spell Kelly with an *i*."

Parker understood immediately. "Oh. I can't believe I was being so hetero-normative."

It took Geraint a few more seconds. "Hetero-*what*?" Then: "O-oh."

"And he's a dentist, so. Definitely not looking for a sugar daddy."

"Did you know that your husband was . . . ?" asked Geraint, tilting his head, which Frances took to mean *not straight*. It was the question she saw in every single person's eyes when they found out Jeremy had left her for a man, but most of them never dared to ask.

"No. I didn't."

"But in hindsight?" asked Parker.

This was the question she tortured herself with. Were there signs? She'd never found a secret stash of magazines or caught him watching porn, of any type. Once she'd come home to find him watching a *Magic Mike* movie by himself. Was that a clue? Was he less physically affectionate than some husbands? Did they have sex less often than other couples? She suspected the answer to that one was *yes*, since for the last decade at least she could count the number of times they'd had sex in any given year on two hands and still have fingers to spare. Even early on in their marriage, sex had sometimes been an afterthought. But she'd had nothing, or no one, to compare it to. With the exception of Jeanette, she and her circle of girlfriends didn't share intimate details about their sex lives. Frances had just assumed they were all in the same boat, that sexual desires and appetites waned as people got older. "That's harder to say," she answered. "He started spending more late nights 'at the office' in our last year together. And he was definitely more distant." She had a sip of her Guinness.

"At least you know it wasn't your fault," said Geraint.

"What do you mean?"

"Well, if he'd left you for another woman, you might make yourself crazy trying to figure out if you were to blame. I wonder that all the time with Darlene. Should I have tried to take her on more holidays even though we couldn't afford it? Should I have made a bigger effort to dress better, or lose ten pounds, or not chew with my mouth open, or not cry during Tim Hortons ads like she was always pressing me to do?" He sighed. "*Of course* Darlene fell for Ron. He's richer, smarter, better looking, more ambitious. But your husband left you for a man."

"Geraint's right," said Parker. "There's literally nothing you could have done differently because it had nothing to do with you."

Frances looked at the two of them, their expressions earnest and heartfelt. How could she explain to them that it had *everything* to do with her? That if Jeremy had left her for another woman, she'd still be devastated; she'd still wake up at three in the morning with dark, spiralling thoughts of dying alone and unloved. But at least she could have held on to the idea that their twenty-five-year marriage hadn't been a sham. She could have continued to believe that he'd genuinely loved her for at least some of those years. She wouldn't have to endure people's prurient curiosity when they found out. She wouldn't have to wonder if every single time she and Jeremy had had sex he was quietly revolted. The questions were relentless, never-ending. Had he chosen her all those years ago because she seemed just gullible enough that she'd never detect his secret? And/or because to this day she still had a boyish figure, meaning tiny boobs?

And most important of all: Had he ever really loved her? The answer, to her, seemed clear: Of course not. He'd liked her well enough. But love? She'd wasted the best years of her life with a man who'd used her as his beard. She'd been living in her very own *Truman Show.*

She looked at Geraint and Parker, trying to think of how to articulate some of this, but when she saw the looks on their faces, she realized she didn't need to because she'd just said all of her darkest thoughts out loud.

Geraint stood up. He pulled Frances to her feet and enveloped her in a monstrous hug. It was, she imagined, like being hugged by Hagrid. Or by an anthropomorphically safe and cuddly silverback gorilla (his arms were almost as hairy). Frances hated herself for starting to weep, but the hug felt too good to wriggle free, so she just stayed there. She felt Parker's hand, gently rubbing her back.

These people will never be my friends, she thought. *But I suppose they aren't the worst people in the world.*

13

Parker wandered up and down outside the Safeway at Broadway and Macdonald, trying her best to walk in a straight line. Alexei had called her on his way home from his parents' place and offered to pick her up. Normally she would have gone with him to his mom and dad's; she loved going for Sunday dinner with him, because Alexei's mom doted on her and stuffed her full of homemade *avgolemono*, *keftedes*, and all sorts of other Greek delicacies. Alexei's older sister and her husband and two little kids were usually there, and it was loud and argumentative, but in a nice way. And they always made her feel so welcome! Aside from the odd time she'd been invited to a friend's house in Penticton, she'd seldom experienced big family dinners like this; she and her mom had kept separate schedules, partly due to Sharon's work as an esthetician and partly due to her active dating life. If they ever did sit down for dinner together, it was usually a frozen pizza or Chinese takeout, and more often than not Sharon's latest boyfriend would be there, too, and aside from maybe Fred—who knew an awful lot about snakes and other cold-blooded reptiles and was trying to get his hands on a pet boa constrictor—none of them were what you'd call a good conversationalist.

But, thanks to their stupid community service shift, Parker had had to beg off this week. "Tell them I'm under the weather," she'd said to Alexei.

"I'll bring you leftovers," he replied.

She'd been disappointed, but also a touch relieved. The thought of pretending that things were okay, that she was okay, had been giving her increasing anxiety. She was a terrible actress; Sharon had told her as much after her one and only role as one of the Pink Ladies in her high school's production of *Grease*.

Speaking of Sharon.

Parker had told her nothing.

Well, not nothing. They still had their bimonthly talks, and Parker just pretended nothing had changed. As far as Sharon knew, her daughter was still working on *Knights of the Castle*. "Sebastian Trevor's kind of a creepy lech, though." That was as close as she'd gotten to anything resembling the truth. "And not nearly as good-looking in person as he is onscreen."

"Well, I still wouldn't kick him out of bed for eating crackers," Sharon had said; then she'd proceeded to tell Parker all about her latest sculpting class. "I'm making a clay replica of my vagina!"

Parker waited at a red light to cross the street. She still couldn't believe she'd gone for drinks with her fellow garbage pickers, but the thought of the empty apartment had been too much to bear. She'd downed almost three pints! Almost, because she couldn't finish the last one. They'd finally ordered food to absorb some of the alcohol, so a shepherd's pie sloshed around in her belly along with the Guinness. She'd never been much of a drinker, and she was pretty sure she was loaded.

But boy, had she learned a lot about those two! A lot of very private things! Parker had listened, riveted, as Geraint and Frances shared their stories. She'd also felt hugely relieved, because the spotlight had never turned on her. She supposed there were parts of her story she could tell them (not that she wanted to talk about any of it, ever), but she couldn't tell them the most important part—the Origin Story, as she thought of it—because of the NDA. And The Thing that happened at the mall filled her with a crushing shame. *It's so much worse than what either of them did*, she thought.

Parker was almost at the corner. She saw the Blood Money Mazda parked on the side of the road, and Alexei sitting in the driver's seat. When he spotted her, his face lit up. He waved. Parker stumbled to the car and climbed in. "I've got massive amounts of leftovers for you," he started. "Whoa. You're drunk."

Parker nodded. "I am." Then she rolled down her window and puked, splattering the side of the Blood Money Mazda and the pavement below.

14

Geraint walked home, even though it was a few miles. Three pints of Guinness had barely made a dent in his sobriety, but he didn't want to risk blowing over the limit if he was pulled over. At least the skies had cleared.

He ambled across the Burrard Bridge, gazing out at the inlet and the lights twinkling on the North Shore, and headed into the West End, past the shops displaying Pride flags and the cozy little restaurants, until he arrived at the generic 1970s-era apart-hotel that had been his home for the past two months. He let himself into his unit on the sixth floor.

When he'd come home from his night of vandalism, Darlene had been waiting up for him, sitting on the overstuffed floral couch that barely fit in their tiny living room. Geraint was the fixer-upper, but Darlene was the decorator; she was always telling him he had the worst taste, in art, in haircuts, in clothes—"I swear you must be colour-blind," she often said. He'd been happy to let her take that on, especially if it made her appreciate their little love nest more, but if he had one teeny complaint (which he kept to himself), it was that she seemed to have no sense of proportion. The house, and the rooms, were small. The furniture she chose was large.

"Hello, Darlene," he'd said, lowering himself into the matching enormous armchair. He'd waited for her to apologize, to beg forgiveness, to tell him it would never happen again, that it was just the classic seven-year itch, that Ron meant nothing to her.

He already knew he would forgive her, although he'd make her suffer somewhat, perhaps milk her regret for more back tickles, maybe even the odd foot rub, although she hated rubbing his feet. ("They're like Neanderthal feet," she said.) He'd find a new job, demand his franchise deposit back, perhaps open his own auto repair shop . . .

"I want a divorce."

Geraint blinked. This did not follow the script in his head. "Is Keanu—"

"Sound asleep. I just checked on him."

Geraint tried to collect his thoughts. "Are you . . . in love with Ron?"

"Maybe? I think so. I don't know."

He was finding it hard to breathe. "*How can you not know? You've just said you want a divorce!* You want to blow up our lives and you don't even know if you love him—"

"I know I don't love you."

Geraint had worried he would faint, fall right off the over-stuffed armchair and hit his head on the big oak coffee table.

Darlene had wrapped her arms around herself. "This was all a terrible mistake. I never should have dated you, I certainly never should have married you, but you were *there*, and I so wanted a baby, and I . . . I somehow thought I *could* love you, that the love would come, but—"

As she'd talked, the cuckoo clock—the sole possession of Geraint's that he'd insisted on having in their living room despite Darlene's protests, because it had belonged to his nice great-aunt—ticked loudly in the background.

"You've never loved me?"

"I'm sorry, Geraint. You're a nice guy, and I tried. I really did."

"Will you move in with Ron?"

"No, no, we're not at that stage, not yet."

"Then where will you go?"

Darlene looked puzzled. "I'm not going anywhere."

"But . . . but this house is just as much mine as it is yours. And you're the one who—"

"Our boy needs his mother, Geraint. Especially at a time like this. Surely you can see that."

He did, sort of. But didn't he also need his father? "He's my son, too."

"You'll still see him. Why don't we talk about a schedule once we've both had a good night's sleep?" She stood. Adjusted her skirt. The same skirt that had been hiked up to her waist just hours earlier in Ron's office. Geraint tried to force the image from his brain.

"Okay," he'd said, his mind like mush. He'd stood, too, and started to head towards the stairs, but Darlene had blocked his path and thrust a slip of paper into his hands. He'd looked at it blankly. "What's this?"

"The address for an apart-hotel downtown. I've booked you a room. Good monthly rate."

"You want me to go there . . . now?"

"It's for the best, Ger. I've packed you a bag."

And so he'd left. Looking back, he knew it was a tactical error, but in the moment he'd been in total shock.

Over the next few days he'd lived in a bubble of denial, waiting for Darlene to show up and beg him to come home. But the police were the only ones to show up, and he realized later that it must have been Darlene who'd given them his new address.

Luckily for him, he had a sympathetic lawyer who, in a moment of oversharing, ranted about her ex-husband's serial infidelity for at least an hour, then charged him for said hour—but it was worth it because she pushed hard for the Crown to agree to alternative measures.

So here he was, two months later, still living in a beige box that contained the ghosts of countless sad humans before him. They were evident in the stains on the mattress, the cigarette burns on the carpet, and the hole punched into the wall (now covered by a suspiciously low-hanging picture of a sunset). Darlene had dropped off some of his woodworking supplies, but the space was claustrophobically small; there was no room to make his birdhouses, and even if there was, where on earth would he put them?

Keanu came to stay with him every Wednesday night and every other weekend, which was paltry and unfair. When Darlene had presented him with the schedule, he'd said he'd need to run it by a lawyer. "Get a lawyer involved if you want," she'd said. "But Ron says that under the circumstances, things might not go in your favour. He says you're lucky I'm giving you any time with our son at all, given that criminal charges have been laid against you." She was quoting Ron a lot, he'd noticed.

Even on the days he and Keanu were together Geraint felt his absence, because all he could think about when his boy was with him was that he would soon be gone again. He loved Keanu so much, and Keanu loved him, but how could an almost-five-year-old hold on to those feelings if he only saw his daddy three nights out of fourteen?

Geraint glanced at his cuckoo clock—the one thing Darlene had happily agreed to let him take from their house. It was twenty to eight, and almost time to call Keanu. Geraint FaceTimed every night before his son went to bed, so that his image would be imprinted on Keanu's mind as he fell asleep. He ran the tap and poured himself a large glass of water. He guzzled it down and poured himself another. Then he sat down on the black leather (leatherette?) couch, which made a farting sound—it was Keanu's favourite thing about his daddy's apartment—and called his son.

Keanu's little face lit up the screen. "Daddy, hi!"

"Hello, my sweet boy."

"My birfday is in less than ten sleeps!"

"Are you excited?"

"Yes! But Daddy—Mommy won't let me bring Franklin to bed."

"Who's Franklin?"

"My turtle."

"A new stuffy?"

Keanu giggled. "No, Daddy, a real, live turtle! Mommy's friend gave it to me. He said it was an early birfday present."

"Mommy's friend?"

"The man you work for. Ron."

So Ron was still very much around. Ron was still—*effing* his wife. Ron, who still owed him money. Ron, who'd had a restraining order taken out against him, and who was now, apparently, giving Geraint's son the gift of a reptile.

"Well, your mommy's probably right, Kee. You *and* Franklin will get a better night's sleep. And imagine how excited you'll both be to see each other in the morning."

Keanu considered this. "I think he'll be most excited," he said.

"Who wouldn't be excited to see you?"

"Are *you* excited when you see me, Daddy?"

"Oh, Kee, you have no idea. Over-the-moon excited." Geraint blinked back tears. He refused to let his son see him cry.

"Make the couch fart."

Geraint wiggled his bum around and the couch farted, and Keanu laughed. He heard Darlene's voice in the background.

"Mommy says I have to go now."

Mommy can go eff herself. "Well, Mommy knows best."

"I love you, Daddy."

"I love you, too, Keanu."

"To the moon and back?"

"To the moon and back."

Then his little face was gone.

Geraint sat back on the couch and stared into the middle distance. The clock chimed eight o'clock.

Cuckoo. Cuckold. Cuckoo. Cuckold. Cuckoo. Cuckold. Cuckoo. Cuckold.

15

obo-calls. Leaf blowers. Manspreaders. Man*splainers*. People who go thirty in a fifty zone. People who warble when they whistle. People who whistle tunelessly. People who whistle, period. People who play their music loudly in public parks—surprise, we don't all share your lousy taste in music! People who talk in movie theatres. Dog owners who don't pick up after their pets. Loud talkers. Close talkers. Mumblers. People who take a crazy amount of time to order their coffee—just make up your mind before you hit the front of the line already, how hard can it be?" Geraint paused for a breath. "Golly, Frances. You have a very, very long list of triggers. I'm only on page one of . . ." he shuffled through the papers ". . . three."

It was week two of anger management. Dennis had asked them to break into two groups to share their homework. Because there were only five of them this week, Frances, Geraint, and Parker had formed one group, pushing their desks into a triangle. Byron and Wayson formed the other. Frances wondered what had happened to Jimmy and Roy. Had they violated their conditions somehow? Taken another swing at their girlfriend or wife?

"I don't think I'm unusual," she said to Geraint, who was wearing his green track suit again; he looked like a giant Kermit the Frog. "Just thorough. Let me see your list of triggers." Geraint handed her his list, which Frances read aloud: "One: Finding out my wife is having an affair with my boss. Two: Animal cruelty. Three: People who don't treat the elderly with the respect they deserve." She flipped the paper over, but it was blank. "Seriously, Geraint? That's it? Human beings don't annoy you on a daily basis?"

"I'm not generally an angry person."

"Oh, for the love of—Parker, what did you write?" Frances reached for Parker's sparkly purple notebook.

Parker's hands shot out and clamped down over the notebook. "*Nope.*" Her expression was fierce.

Frances drew her hands back, startled. "Okay, sorry."

Parker's face crumpled. "I'm sorry. I didn't mean . . . I just—I didn't do the homework." She took the book back and held it close to her chest. *The way a woman might hold onto her purse while walking down a dark alley*, thought Frances, unsettled.

"Okay, class," Dennis said. "Any observations you've made, any discoveries?" Frances raised her hand. "Frances?"

"My observation is that none of us"—she indicated the three of them—"should even be here." She turned towards Byron and Wayson. "Sorry, I can't speak for you two. Based on the stories you told last week, maybe you *do* deserve to be here? No offence intended."

"None taken," said Wayson.

"We totally deserve to be here," added Byron.

"My . . . 'anger episode'"—she used air quotes—"was circumstantial. And this man"—she pointed to Geraint—"belongs in this class the same way Winnie-the-Pooh belongs in this class, which is *not at all*. And you can't tell me *she* belongs here." Frances pointed at Parker. "What did she do, step on an ant colony by mistake?"

"Ha ha!" Geraint laughed. "Exactly! Parker couldn't harm a fly!"

Dennis's Adam's apple started bobbing up and down like it had a life of its own, and it occurred to Frances that he knew exactly why each of them was here. She glanced at Parker, who had drawn her red hair over her face like a shield. "Well, Frances," Dennis tittered nervously. "Whether or not you belong here is beyond my purview. You're welcome to take this up with your diversion officer, but I don't recommend it. It could do more harm than good." He turned to the chalkboard. "Now we are going to begin to try to understand the feelings behind your anger, because when you understand *where* the anger comes from, you can better address your triggers." He wrote FEELINGS in capital letters and underlined it, not once but twice. "I want you to identify a problem, a situation, or a person that has triggered your anger in the past." He wrote PROBLEM on the board. "Then identify your goal"—he wrote GOAL—"in solving this problem and spend some time making a list of various ways you might achieve your goal *without anger*. Try to get some words down on paper without thinking about it too much. You have fifteen minutes. Begin."

Still holding onto her notebook for dear life, Parker pushed her desk back to its original spot. Only when she was away from potentially prying eyes did she open it. *Like she's hiding state secrets*, thought Frances as she rooted in her bag for her notepad and pen. She started to write:

> *Problem: lying douchebag husband left me and entire life exploded because of it.*
> *Goal: To not feel like shit all the time. To get some semblance of my life back.*
> *How to achieve this goal:*

Frances stared at the page for a long time.

With seven seconds remaining, she wrote:

> *Fucked if I know.*

"All right," said Dennis when time was up, "who's willing to share?" No one volunteered. Dennis sighed. "Come on, people. Work with me here." Geraint raised his hand. "Thank you, Geraint."

Geraint extricated himself from the desk and stood. "Problems. One: Wife cheating on me with my boss. Two: Wife doesn't love me, possibly never has. Three: Wife kicked me out of the house. Four: Because I wrote *man whore* on my boss's car, I was fired, so, five: I have no money coming in, and six: my savings are wiped out, and therefore seven: I'm worried I'll wind up living in a pup tent in Stanley Park."

Dennis blinked. "Um, okay, for this exercise I was thinking we'd stick to *one* problem—"

"And eight: I only get to see my child on Wednesday nights and every other weekend."

"*What?*" said Frances.

"That's bullshit," said Parker.

"Dads always get the short end of the stick," said Byron. "You should come with me to my Fathers' Rights Group—"

"Okay, okay," said Dennis, "let's allow Geraint to finish."

"Goal. To find a job, and a place to live that doesn't smell like cheese, old farts, and despair." He looked down at his piece of paper. "And most important, to see more of my child, because it's like a dark chasm opens up in my heart when we are apart." Geraint's face had gone an alarming shade of red. "How to achieve these goals. Well, Dennis, it's not very easy, is it? I want to apply for jobs but what do I write on the applications when I'm asked if I have a criminal record? *Jury's still out?* And my wife says I'm lucky to see my son at all because of this." He swept his hand around the room. "So, I don't see myself achieving *that* goal any time soon."

Dennis scratched the back of his neck. "Um. Okay. I guess I wasn't as clear as I could have been. I wanted you all to pick one *smaller* problem that has triggered anger in the past, like . . .

waiting in line forever at the bank, or . . . putting together a piece of IKEA furniture." He put down his chalk, his forehead glistening with sweat. "Let's take a fifteen-minute break."

Geraint lumbered from the room, emitting a series of small bleats as he went.

Frances and Parker found him at the vending machine, buying a bag of ketchup-flavoured chips. "I'm sorry you don't get to be with your son more often, Geraint," said Frances.

"That sucks," said Parker. "Especially since you obviously *want* to spend more time with him. My dad never even wanted to meet me, and then he died, so."

"That's terrible, Parker," said Frances.

"And also, who wouldn't want to meet you?" added Geraint.

She shrugged. "He was the lead singer in a cover band. Him and my mom hooked up when they played a gig in Penticton. She says he looked like Chester Bennington's doppelgänger." They looked at her blankly. "From the band Linkin Park?" She chose a bag of Twizzlers from the vending machine. "She tracked him down through their website and told him, and he said he wanted nothing to do with it. Meaning, us. She was gonna do the whole DNA thing, sue him for child support and all? But he got electro-cuted on stage at an outdoor concert and—" She ran a hand across her throat, adding a sound effect. Frances and Geraint stared.

"Well, that . . . is tragic," said Frances.

Again, Parker shrugged. "You know what they say: You don't miss what you never had. But you"—she pointed at Geraint—"know exactly what you're missing." Parker shoved her Twizzlers into the large pocket of her hand-sewn shirt, which looked more like a painting smock, and headed to the washroom.

"She's a smart young thing," said Geraint, as he shoved an abnormally red chip into his mouth. He extended the bag towards Frances. She shook her head, not because she didn't love chips but because ketchup flavour was a singularly Canadian abomination. "Do you have children, Frances?"

"Two. My son lives in Sydney, Australia. I miss him every day. And my daughter lives in our basement suite, and sometimes I wish she lived in Sydney, Australia."

"You don't mean that," said Geraint.

"No. I don't."

Geraint's phone pinged. He dug into his track suit pocket and his face lit up when he saw the message. "It's Keanu. He's sent me a selfie from his mom's phone." All Frances could see was a ring of orange surrounding a dark hole. "I think it's his nostril." Geraint scrolled through his phone, looking for a better photo. "Here's my wee fellow." He showed her a picture of a chubby little boy with a mass of black hair and the eyes and nose of his father. "See? Didn't I tell you? Isn't he handsome?"

"He's the spitting image of you, Geraint," Frances said politely.

"It's his birthday this Saturday. Turning five."

"Sweet age."

"I won't get to see him on the official day."

"Why not?"

"Darlene called dibs."

"Ask her if you can split the day."

He shook his head. "Don't want to push my luck. I have him on Sunday."

"What do you have planned?"

"Well, that's the problem. I can't afford to take him and his pals anywhere special, what with being unemployed."

"Trust me, Geraint, children are happy with the basics. My kids' favourite parties were the ones we had right in our own backyard. We'd turn on the sprinkler and put out a few hula hoops and you'd think they were at Disneyland."

"Yes, but I live in a cramped apart-hotel." He looked straight at her. "*You* live in a house. You have plenty of space to entertain."

The words hung in the air between them. "How do you know I live in a house?"

"You said so the very first time we did our community service. You said, *My house isn't far from here.* Also, you just said you have a backyard."

Frances cleared her throat. "Kids don't take up a lot of space. I'm sure your place will be fine—"

"It smells like stale smoke and cabbage."

"I thought you said it smelled like old farts and cheese."

"All of the above."

"Kids don't notice things like that."

"But their parents do. And some of them are very judgmental."

"You just have to ignore them."

"And there's no room for games like pin the tail on the donkey. Certainly not enough room for a piñata. Keanu would *love* a piñata. But a piñata requires outdoor space." He gazed at her, unblinking.

Nope. Not falling for it. "Why not have the party in a park?"

"What if it rains?" He tipped his head back and shook the remaining chips into his mouth. A ring of red ketchup flavouring encircled his mouth.

"Well," said Frances, just as Parker returned, "I'm sure you'll think of something."

"Think of something for what?" asked Parker.

"Keanu's birthday party this weekend," said Geraint. "I need a larger space."

"I'd offer up our place," said Parker, "but it's the size of a postage stamp. My boyfriend's an amazing baker, though. I'm sure he'd be happy to make Keanu a birthday cake."

"Really? That is such a generous offer, Parker," said Geraint, all while gazing at Frances. "So thoughtful. Such a kind and selfless gesture."

It was a stare-off. And Frances blinked first. Without an ounce of sincerity in her voice she said, "I have an idea. Why don't you have the party at my place?"

". . . And would your backyard accommodate a bouncy castle, because I think I could just about cover a bouncy castle." Geraint peppered Frances with questions as he drove her home; he'd insisted on doing so when he'd found out her car was in the shop. Even though it was cold and dark and pouring with rain, Frances regretted taking him up on his offer; she longed for the relative peace and quiet of the bus.

"A bouncy castle would be fine," she said. "As long as you keep it away from my garden beds."

"And because I don't want to pick favourites, I'd like to invite his entire pre-kindergarten class. That would be upwards of twenty children, I take it that's okay?"

"That is a lot of children, Geraint."

"They're good kids, trust me. Well, except for Santino. And Corey. Do you have pets?"

"A cat. Mr. Pickles."

"I'd advise locking the cat in the basement. Along with anything fragile." He let out a gentle burp, and Frances swore she could smell ketchup chips. "And of course we have to invite Parker and her fellow, and any of the parents who'd like to stay, so . . . it might bring the number closer to forty."

"Jesus, Geraint."

"Shoes: on or off?"

"Off."

"Silly String: for or against?"

"Against."

"What if we only used it outside"—

"No Silly String, Geraint. None. Nada."

"What about the piñata?"

"Fine. Turn left here. I'm in the next block." She couldn't wait to bolt from the car.

"Thank you, Frances. I appreciate this so very, very, very, very, very—"

"You're welcome. This is me." Geraint parked his Subaru in front of her house. "Wowee zowee, Frances. Nice digs. Guess I went into the wrong profession, eh? Should've been a writer."

"Never too late, Geraint. All you need is a notebook and a good idea."

"Really?" Then he caught her look. "Oh. You're being sarcastic again."

She reached for the door handle, ready to make her escape.

"Can I ask you something?"

"I've already said no to a pony."

"Do you ever wish your ex had died, instead?"

Her fingers fell away from the door handle. The question threw her, not because it was inappropriate, but because it was like he'd crawled into her brain and read her worst thoughts. "All the time."

"Do you have . . . scenarios?"

She nodded. "I swing between exceedingly unimaginative—he steps off a curb and gets hit by a bus—to unique, like, we're hiking on the North Shore and a cougar drops from a tree and claws out his throat."

"Jeepers." Geraint clutched his own throat.

"Or we're kayaking in Maui, and a grey whale breaches right in front of Jeremy's kayak. It tips, and he's unconscious and can't escape. Or we're on a weekend getaway in New York City, which we did every year for our anniversary, and he steps onto the elevator at our hotel, but the elevator isn't there, it's just a shaft, and he plunges twenty floors and goes *splat*."

"Wowee zowee."

"Or he walks past a construction site and a concrete slab just"—she smacked her hands together and Geraint jumped—"pancakes him." She looked at him. "How about you?"

"Mine involve a horrible diagnosis. Incurable cancer. ALS. Early onset Alzheimer's. It's a rapid decline and Darlene has to rely on me one hundred percent. She can't do without me."

Frances looked at him askance. "And you think my scenarios are fucked up."

"How is that more effed-up than a cougar tearing out your husband's throat?"

"Because you want your wife to *need* you. To be completely at your mercy, even if she doesn't love you."

"Yes, but in my version I wouldn't know she doesn't love me, would I? I'd live in blissful ignorance while spoon-feeding her and changing her diaper."

Frances pondered this for a while. "I will concede that your version isn't half-bad." They were both quiet for a moment. Then, to Frances's alarm, Geraint lurched towards her. *Oh, shit on a stick, is he going to try to kiss me?*

No. He just reached past her and opened her door. "I'm glad to know you, Frances," he said.

"I'm . . . glad to know you, too, Geraint," she said.

And she realized she almost meant it.

16

He doesn't look dangerous. But then again, neither did Ted Bundy." Daisy was helping Frances hang a colourful Happy Birthday banner in the kitchen, her eyes constantly straying to Geraint, who was setting up a rented bouncy castle in the back-yard. For once he wasn't wearing one of his signature track suits; instead he wore a pair of jeans and a bulky dark green sweater. The sweater rode up his belly and the sleeves stopped midway between elbow and wrist. Frances suspected he'd accidentally put it in the dryer.

"He's not a serial killer, Daisy." Frances had put a bit more effort into her appearance for the party and wore a pink cashmere sweater with a simple black skirt. Lipstick had even been applied.

"No, but he might be some other kind of predator," her daughter continued. "Didn't you tell me he got charged with an indecent act?" Daisy made a judgy face. It was, Frances had to concede, even judgier than her own judgy face, and that was saying something.

"That was a misunderstanding. He had no idea one of the neighbours was out walking her Shiba Inu. He's as much a criminal as I am."

"Well, Mother. Technically speaking, you *are* a criminal." Said with the arrogant assuredness of youth.

"Thank you, Daughter, for the reminder. As I've told you already, you don't have to stay."

"What, and leave you and Grandma alone with a flasher?"

"Daisy, he is *not* a flasher—"

"Are you sure about that?" Daisy indicated Geraint, who was currently showing at least two inches of bum crack.

"Who's a flasher?" Cordelia returned from the bathroom. Frances had picked her up and driven her here, which she tried to do once or twice a month.

"No one, Grandma," said Daisy. "It's just a story I read about a man who was charged with an indecent act. Everyone thought he wasn't so bad until he committed multiple murders at a children's birthday party." Daisy tore open a jumbo-sized bag of potato chips and poured them into a bowl, thoroughly enjoying herself. Frances just rolled her eyes.

Cordelia perched on a stool by the island. "Where is Jeremy?"

Daisy shot her mother a look. "He's out of town on business," she said, and Frances mouthed a thank you.

"Also, you should know, there's a grizzly bear in your garden."

"Actually Mom, he's a—" *A what?* she wondered. "An acquaintance of mine. He's human, just . . . very bear-*like*." The doorbell rang. She wiped her hands on her apron and hurried to the door.

Parker stood on the porch, a young man beside her. He was not much more than Parker's height and unassumingly handsome. They'd both dressed up for the occasion, Parker in a red-and-white polka-dot dress with colourful striped tights, the young man in a conservative button-up shirt and grey trousers. Between them, they carried a large cake covered in tinfoil. "Frances, this is Alexei," said Parker. She beamed with pride as she added, "My beau."

"Hello, Alexei. Welcome. Come in."

Geraint joined them in the kitchen and introductions were made. Parker and Alexei put down the cake and carefully unveiled it. It was cut and iced to look like a fire truck. "Fire trucks are

Keanu's favourite thing in the world!" Geraint exclaimed. "How did you know?"

"He's a five-year-old boy, so we figured we had a fifty-fifty chance of nailing it," said Alexei proudly. "Plus they were my favourite thing when I was five."

"It's absolutely incredible," said Geraint.

"*You're* incredible," Cordelia replied, approaching Geraint. She put her hands on his chest. "You are very, very big."

"I suppose I am, Cordelia."

"Please, call me Cordy. I bet you give great hugs." Cordelia held out her arms. Geraint gamely embraced her, and Cordelia giggled like a schoolgirl while Frances and Daisy looked at each other, wide-eyed.

Geraint released Cordelia and glanced at his watch. "Time to pick up Keanu. Back in a jiffy. I do hope you don't get overrun with guests before I get back."

The doorbell rang just moments after he'd left. As Frances headed to the door, she shouted over her shoulder, "Daisy, make sure Mr. Pickles is locked up downstairs."

But it wasn't a party guest.

It was Jules.

"Hello, Frances. May I come in?"

Frances stared at her coldly. "Now is not a good time. I'm hosting a party. To which you were not invited."

"Jules! Come in, come in!" Cordelia had appeared behind them. Frances shook her head. Last weekend her mother hadn't remembered Jules. Clearly she was having a lucid day.

Good for Cordelia; bad for Frances.

Daisy threw her arms around Jules when she entered the kitchen. "Auntie Jules!" She introduced her to Parker and Alexei.

"Nice to meet you," said Jules. "I'm Frances's—"

"Lawyer," said Frances.

Daisy gave her mom a quizzical look. "She's also your best—"

"Lawyer. Best criminal defence lawyer in town."

Jules smiled at Frances. It was the smile she used when she was about to tear someone a new asshole in court. "And as your lawyer, I have something I need to discuss with you. Privately." She grabbed Frances's arm in an iron grip and marched her up the stairs, into Frances's book-lined office. "Really?" she said when they were alone. "I'm your lawyer now? Not your friend of, what, twenty-four years? Surely I'm allowed one fuck-up in *twenty-four* years?"

"It was more than a fuck-up, Jules, it was a betrayal. You lied to me."

"That is untrue. I never lied. I merely withheld information."

"Do *not* try your lawyer tactics with me."

"Look. It was stupid and shitty. If it had been up to me, I'd never have laid eyes on Jeremy again. But you know Carmen. She's a psychologist and notoriously bipartisan. I said I didn't think we should invite him, but she insisted."

"Insisted on inviting him over me."

"Frances. We have you over three times a week on average."

"But never with other people. Your other guests were my friends, too, Jules. Is it because I'm single and he's not? Do I ruin your seating plan?"

Jules exhaled. "Do you want the truth?"

She wasn't sure she did. "Of course."

"You're not a lot of fun to be around." Frances opened her mouth to retort. "Let me finish. You're in pain. And you *should* be in pain. Everything you're feeling makes sense. And Carmen and I are here for you, you know that. But let me cast your mind back to the last time we had you over with our mutual couple friends. Charles mentioned he and George were going to Paris for their anniversary and you stood up so quickly your chair fell over. You locked yourself in the toilet for half an hour, then sniffled your way through dessert. Then later, when Mahshid said Reza was going on another business trip, you snorted and said, *Better hope it's really a business trip.* You were miserable the entire evening. *And* you explicitly told me afterwards, *Please don't put me through that again.*"

Frances sighed. "Okay. Point taken. But I didn't say *Have my shitty ex over instead.*"

"You did not."

"How often have you seen him since we split?"

"Twice. The first time Carmen made us go for coffee with him. Last Saturday was the first time we had him over, and the first time I met Kelly."

"Did you like him?"

Jules shrugged. "He's fine. I mean, he's a dentist, so . . ." Jules faked a yawn. "And he's balding." Frances suspected this was all for her benefit, but she'd take it.

"Did you talk about me?"

"Jeremy asked after you, before you showed up."

"What did you tell him?"

"I told him you were doing great."

"Thank you for lying."

"Then suddenly there you were on the doorstep. After you left he was in a terrible funk. And not because you'd damaged his car, because he didn't know that yet."

She did her best to sound puzzled. "His car? I don't know what you're talking about."

"You are the worst liar." She placed a hand on Frances's arm. "You will always be my best friend. I am your ally in this. But we've known Jeremy for almost as long as we've known you. You didn't really think we'd just completely ostracize him, did you?"

"I one hundred percent did."

"Look, I know you don't want to hear this, but I have some sympathy for his situation, too. I was deep in the closet until I was in my late twenties, so I know what it must have felt like for him."

"No."

"What do you mean, *no*?"

"I don't want to hear about *poor Jeremy*. He is a liar and a philanderer, and if I can no longer shit-talk him to you, then I think we are done."

Jules gazed at her, unblinking. "You know, Francy-Pants, I rather thought that as a writer, you'd be able to see the shades of grey."

"Oh, you'd be surprised. We're good at it on the page, but less so in real life."

"Well, I cannot imagine my life without you, so . . . shit-talk away. But let me state for the record that I think you're being rather petulant and immature." Jules pulled Frances into a hug. Frances kept her arms stiffly by her side, but Jules lifted Frances's left arm, then her right, and forced her to hug her back.

"Can I ask you something?" Frances asked.

"Of course."

"Did you or Carmen suspect that he was gay?"

"You've asked me this before."

"I know."

"What's the definition of stupidity, Frances?"

"Doing the same thing over and over and expecting different results?"

"You can ask the question over and over and I will give you the exact same answer: No. We did not. Contrary to popular belief, our community does not have built-in gaydar. But I did notice that he seemed increasingly unhappy. And I think you did, too."

Frances said nothing. Yes, she had noticed. But she hadn't wanted to examine his unhappiness too closely.

"And now I would like a large glass of white wine," said Jules.

As they left Frances's office, she added: "Oh, and by the way, unless you don't want your charges diverted, you'll need to write a new apology letter. And only when you're sober. That first one was a piece of shit."

"It must be interesting, working in a bunch of different places," Parker was saying to Daisy when Frances and Jules returned to the kitchen.

"Yes and no," said Daisy. "Most of the work is super boring. Like, last week I did secretarial work at an accounting firm. *Yawn.*"

"I dated an accountant once," said Cordelia cheerfully as she popped a mini sausage roll into her mouth. "Dull as dishwater."

Alexei started to cough, and Parker cleared her throat. "Alexei's an accountant, almost. He's just getting his last few credits."

Daisy flushed with embarrassment. "I didn't mean—I mean, that sounds fascinating . . ."

"It's okay," smiled Alexei. "No one believes me, but I love what I do. It's like solving new mathematical puzzles every day, but with a human element."

Frances poured a glass of wine for Jules and one for herself. "Forgive my mother, Alexei. She has dementia. I have no excuse for my daughter, however."

Daisy glared at her mom before changing the subject. "What about you, Parker?" asked Daisy. "Are you working? Or, um, are you allowed to, under your . . . current situation?"

Parker squirmed on her kitchen stool. "I'm between jobs right now."

"Parker's an incredible designer and seamstress," Alexei said with pride. "She made her dress."

"Seriously?" said Daisy. "I love that dress. I'm in love with your style."

Parker's ears turned pink with pleasure and embarrassment. "Thanks. I do a lot of upcycling, making my own creations with used clothes and fabric remnants."

"Her portfolio got her a job on a TV show," said Alexei, and Frances could have sworn she saw Parker give him a warning look.

"I was a wardrobe assistant," she said. "For a nanosecond."

"On what show?" asked Daisy.

Parker was saved by the doorbell. Frances put down her glass. "Prepare for the onslaught."

But when she got to the door, it was Geraint. Keanu was hoisted over his shoulder, sound asleep. Frances led them to the living room, where Geraint laid Keanu on the couch. Frances saw that the boy was indeed adorable, with his abundance of black hair and his little mouth hanging open, dead to the world.

She and Geraint tiptoed out, and she closed the sliding door that separated kitchen from living room. "Keanu's friends haven't shown up yet . . . Are you sure you gave them the right address?"

Geraint's smile wobbled. "Darlene told me she didn't give out the invitations. She said she could hardly ask his classmates to go to two parties two days in a row."

"Oh, Geraint," said Frances. "That wasn't her decision to make."

Cordelia gave him another hug and held onto him longer than was comfortable or polite.

"Darlene and Ron took Keanu and his entire pre-kindergarten class to Flyover Canada yesterday. Then they had a big party at the Spaghetti Factory. With a magician. Then the three of them stayed overnight at a fancy hotel and Keanu spent the better part of today in the hotel pool. Oh, and they got him a Lego set. Of Hogwarts. As in, the entire bloody castle. Worth hundreds of dollars. I also got him a Harry Potter Lego set." He held up a small, gift-wrapped box. "The potions class."

"This Darlene person sounds like a bitch," said Cordelia.

Jules cleared her throat. "Geraint, I'm Jules. Could I pour you a glass of wine? Because it seems to me you could use one."

"Thank you, Jules, yes." Jules poured him a large glass and he gulped half of it down in one go.

"Daddy?" Keanu had opened the sliding door. He gazed up at them, a pint-sized version of his father, rubbing his eyes, a little disoriented. When he spotted Geraint, his face lit up. "Daddy, Daddy, Daddy." He launched himself at Geraint, who hoisted him into the air. The boy wrapped his arms and legs around him. Geraint blew razzberries into his arm and Keanu giggled. "I'm so happy to see you, Daddy."

"Me too, my dear boy, me too."

Keanu had the same incredible stores of optimism and cheer as his father. He was delighted with everything. "Daddy, my cake is a fire engine! I love fire engines!" Then, "You got a bouncy castle! I love bouncy castles!" The two of them—full-size and pint-size—headed to the patio doors. "C'mon," said Keanu, waving his chubby arms. "Come and play!" Cordelia took no convincing. She shot outside and climbed into the bouncy castle with Keanu. When the two of them had had enough, Frances and Jules looked at each other and shrugged. "Fuck it," said Jules. They headed into the yard, kicked off their shoes, and climbed in.

The party expanded. The Sihotas came over with their kids. Jules called Carmen, who showed up fresh from her soccer game and took a turn in the bouncy castle. When she emerged, she found Frances. "Did my wife throw me under the bus?"

"She did."

"Good. Inviting Jeremy really was my idea, not hers."

Cheryl Underwood came outside to tell them to pipe down, and Frances tried to appease her with a piece of cake. "I've been wanting to talk to you for weeks," Cheryl said in an accusing tone, and Frances steeled herself, waiting for her to say she'd seen the video. "I've been retired for years. As you probably know, I'm home a lot. So I notice things. And I know Jeremy hasn't been here in a long time."

Frances tried to conceal her impatience. "What's your point, Cheryl?"

"My point is that I know what it's like to suddenly be on your own. So if you ever want company or a cup of tea—I'm around."

This was not at all what Frances had expected. "Thank you, Cheryl, I really appreciate that—"

"This cake is awfully dry."

Frances smiled. She knew she would never, ever take Cheryl up on her offer. "Would you like another piece?"

Cheryl shrugged. "Well, if it helps you get rid of it."

Later, when the neighbours had gone home, they took the party back inside. Keanu opened his presents: a set of signed *Phoebe Unknown* books from Frances, a fire truck puzzle from Parker and Alexei, and the Lego set from Geraint. Carmen handed him her muddied soccer ball. Keanu was giddy with excitement. He told Parker and Alexei the cake was the most delicious thing he'd eaten in his entire life.

By seven o'clock Keanu was falling asleep on his feet. Geraint wanted to help tidy up, but Frances insisted he take Keanu home. Parker and Alexei left shortly afterwards. Jules and Carmen offered to drive Cordelia back to Shady Pines, and Frances gratefully accepted.

Once they were gone, Daisy actually helped her mom clean up. They moved back and forth, carrying dirty plates and cups into the kitchen. "I can't believe I'm saying this, but I kind of like your criminal friends."

"I'm not sure I'd call them either of those things."

"Well, it's the first time you've hosted people here since Dad left."

"That's not true."

"It is." Frances cast her mind back over the past eight or nine months and realized her daughter was right. Daisy started the dishwasher. "How did someone like Parker wind up in anger management?"

"I still don't know. I asked her once, but she didn't want to go there." Frances picked up a cloth and started wiping down the counters. "It can't have been that bad, though. She's such a nice young girl. A bit awkward, perhaps, hums to herself, scribbles in her notebook . . . when we collect garbage, she puts her headphones on and barely says a word to us."

Daisy picked up her phone and started thumb-typing. "No offence, but maybe you two oldsters aren't the most scintillating company."

"You know, for someone who considers herself a social justice warrior, you are remarkably ageist."

"I found her on IMDb."

"What's IMDb?"

"Internet Movie Database. Wardrobe assistant. Just one show listed, and only for a couple of episodes. *Knights of the Castle.*"

"I've heard of that show. With that British actor, what's-his-name."

"Sebastian Trevor. Hot for an old guy."

"When did she work on it?"

"A few months ago."

"I wonder why it didn't work out." But before Frances could give it any more thought, Mr. Pickles wandered in and barfed up a massive hairball, and Parker was quickly forgotten.

17

It was an afternoon like any other. The triplet bachelor brothers, along with their spinster sister, were standing in the village square, vociferously debating what to have for their afternoon tea. "I fancy scones with sultanas," said Bartholomew.

"I'd prefer crumpets," said Buford.

Suddenly there was a rumbling, followed by a roar. They tilted their heads upwards, towards the noise, just in time to see a wall of snow cascading down the mountainside.

Avalanches were not unusual in their part of the world, situated as they were in a valley ringed by mountains, so they simply resumed their conversation. "What about cucumber sandwiches?" asked Basil. "I do love a cucumber sandwich."

"Baby," said Cressida.

"Now, Cressida, I'm not being a baby, I just happen to like cucumbers—"

"Baby." She pointed down, where, lying between their feet, wrapped like a mummy in blankets, was a sleeping, apple-cheeked baby girl.

They searched high and low for the girl's parents. But it wasn't until spring, when the snow melted and the first wildflowers started to unfurl, that they found them, halfway up the mountain, perfectly preserved in ice. The baby had her father's green

138

eyes and her mother's fiery red hair. Buford observed that they weren't dressed for the weather. Bartholomew observed that it was foolhardy for anyone to attempt a mountain crossing in the winter. Basil observed the empty baby carrier on the father's back and posited that the force of the avalanche had shot the baby out of the carrier like a cannon, landing, miraculously unharmed thanks to her swaddling, at their feet.

At first they'd had no idea what to do with the baby or how to care for her. Not one of them had ever wanted children; they preferred a life of the mind. A baby meant focusing on things other than their passions: physics (Bartholomew), entomology (Buford), history (Basil), languages and music (Cressida). But after only a few short weeks they found themselves arguing over who would give the baby her bottle, because there was nothing like being on the receiving end of one of her heart-stopping, life-affirming, feel-good-right-down-to-your-toes smiles.

Cressida found herself wondering sometimes about the baby girl's parents. Why would they risk their daughter's life to traverse a mountain pass in the dead of winter?

Unless staying hadn't been an option.

Unless staying was much more dangerous than attempting to leave.

O ne more page!" begged Keanu. He was tucked into Geraint's bed. On the nights his son stayed over, Geraint gave him the bedroom and he slept on the leather (leatherette?) couch.

Geraint wanted to read more, too. *That Frances can really spin a yarn*, he thought. "Darling boy, it's already far past your bedtime. We'll read more over breakfast, okay?" Geraint carefully placed *Phoebe Unknown* on the bedside table. "Did you have a nice time today?"

"The best time, Daddy. But all my times with you are the best." Keanu gave him a big hug.

"I love you, Kee."

"I love you, too, Daddy."

Geraint stood. "Nighty-night, dear boy."

"Nighty-night, Daddy. Leave the door open."

"I will. And the hall light will be on all night. Remember, I'm just on the other side of this wall if you need anything. You can do our secret knock."

"Daddy?"

"Yes?"

"Mommy's friend Ron told me I should start calling him Daddy."

Geraint froze. "Oh yes? And what did you say?"

"I told him I already have a daddy. He told me he could be my daddy, too."

"He did, did he?"

"I don't want Ron to be my daddy, Daddy."

"Well, don't you worry about that, my boy. I will always—*always*—be your daddy, okay? Ron can choose a different name." *Like Turd Muffin. Or Butt Face. Or Poo Head*, thought Geraint, his lack of imagination catching up with him.

Keanu yawned and rolled onto his side, which meant he was close to sleep. "Okay, Daddy."

Geraint stood in the doorway until he heard Keanu's breathing deepen. When he was sure he was asleep, he walked back into the living room and grabbed a cushion from the couch. He stepped onto the tiny balcony and closed the door behind him.

And even though he knew that countless other lonely men and women had sat on that cushion, farted on it, slept on it, drooled on it, and god only knows what else on it, he shoved it into his face and screamed into it with all his might.

18

Ron sounds like he's either truly stupid or truly despicable," Frances declared. The three of them were walking along a wooded path in Stanley Park in their garbage-picking clothes, all of them dwarfed by the looming coniferous trees. It was drizzling lightly, and Frances breathed in the air, which was alive with the fragrant scents of humus and pine needles. She felt a moment of something close to bliss, which lasted until she picked up a pair of sodden extra-large men's underwear in her claw.

"He's definitely not stupid," said Geraint.

"My mom had this one boyfriend who lived with us for a couple of years?" said Parker, inflecting the statement into a question. Her pink headphones dangled around her neck. "Abelard? He told me one night I could call him Dad."

"And did you?" asked Geraint.

"Heck no. He was a colossal jerk." She didn't tell them about the times he'd smacked Sharon or screamed at a nine-year-old Parker till she'd hidden under her bed. He'd finally crossed the line one day when he smacked Parker, too. Sharon went ballistic. When he'd come home from the pub later that night, Sharon's biker gang friend Gary (who had a strict skin care regime and got regular facials, gratis, from Sharon) was guarding her front door with a baseball bat. Abelard's belongings were strewn on the ground outside the trailer home. Gary had given him forty-five minutes to clear out of town. Abelard only needed thirty.

"The worst part is," Geraint continued, "I used to think Ron was my friend. But he's stolen my wife, my money—now he's trying to steal my child."

"He stole your money?" asked Frances.

"Not *stole*, exactly. I'd been saving for years to put a deposit down on a Quicky Muffler franchise. Just a few weeks before I found Ron and Darlene"—he shuddered, still traumatized by the memory—"I handed him a cheque."

"For how much?" asked Parker.

"Fifty grand."

"Whoa."

"Now, of course, I don't *want* to run one of his franchises. And he has made it very clear that he would never *let* me run one of his franchises after what I did to his car. But when I sent him an email asking for the deposit back, he refused. He said it was non-refundable and I would know that if I'd read the fine print."

"And did you?" asked Frances. "Read the fine print."

"Yes." Then, sheepishly: "But only after he told me I should have read the fine print."

"And does it say . . . ?"

He nodded glumly. "The deposit is non-refundable."

"Geraint, that is insane. And maybe not even legal. I'm sure, if you checked with a contract lawyer—"

"More lawyer's fees, no thank you."

"Okay," said Frances, "I know it wouldn't be easy under the circumstances, but have you thought about trying to talk to him in person?"

"I can't."

"Well, you *can*, you're just choosing not to."

"No. I can't. I'm not allowed within one hundred metres of him. He got a restraining order against me, even though I never laid a hand on him."

Frances and Parker looked at each other, both having the same thought. "What if someone *else* talked to him?" asked Parker.

"I suppose that would be okay," he said glumly. "But who in their right mind would want to do that?"

"This certainly proves the adage that money can't buy taste," Frances said a while later. They were outside Ron's villa. The rain had stopped, but the clouds were still thick, low hanging. The Lamborghini was parked in the driveway, with a brand-new paint job, lime-green this time. Their own cars—all three of them because they'd gone home to shower and change after their garbage-picking shift—were parked in a neat, environmentally unfriendly row down the block.

"Is that the fountain you . . ." Parker began.

"It is."

"Before we do this," said Frances. "Does he have a dog?"

"No."

"Is there any chance Darlene might be with him?"

He shook his head. "Ron prefers that they keep separate residences. Plus she'll be picking Keanu up from pre-kindergarten right about now."

Frances turned to Parker, suddenly uneasy. They hadn't exactly thought this through. "Ready?"

Parker nodded. "Ready." The two of them took a few steps towards the house.

Geraint stepped in front of them, blocking their path. "No. I'm sorry, ladies, I know you mean well, but I can't in good conscience put you in the line of fire."

"We're only going to ask him politely to give you your money back," said Frances.

"It's just that he's not a nice person. He wouldn't physically harm you, but he might yell. He's scary when he yells."

"We can handle yelling. Can't we, Parker?"

Parker nodded. "When I was a barista, customers used to yell at me all the time."

"Geraint, stay in your car. We won't be long."

Geraint chewed his lip. "You're sure about this?"

Frances looked towards the house. The truth was, she was not at all sure. But all she said to Geraint was, "Look at it this way. It won't make things any worse."

19

I t made things worse.

20

Frances rang the bell. The theme music from *Jaws* echoed through the house. Parker rang it again, just to hear the *DA-da. DA-da. Da-da-da-da-da-da-da-da* again.

It took a good minute for Ron to come to the door. He was dressed in obscenely tiny gym shorts and an undershirt, and he was sweating; Frances guessed they'd interrupted a home workout. He had bland, manufactured good looks: a chiselled jaw, teeth so white they were almost blue, and a full head of hair that looked suspiciously like hair plugs. He also looked like someone who enjoyed his booze; he was drifting towards jowly, and broken red capillaries criss-crossed his cheeks and nose.

"Hello," Frances began, but she was immediately cut off.

"If you're Jehovah's Witnesses, you can fuck off."

"We're not Jehovah's Witnesses."

"And if you're from a political party, you can doubly fuck off."

"Nope, no political affiliation."

He studied Frances, his eyes narrowing. Frances swallowed, uneasy under his gaze. "You look awfully familiar. Did we hook up back in the day?"

"We most definitely did not."

"We're here on behalf of Geraint Blevins?" said Parker, and Frances felt annoyed that Parker again inflected a statement like a question; to her ears, it sounded weak.

"Really." Ron's interest was piqued. "And how do you two know Geraint?"

Frances froze. They hadn't talked about what they would say.

"We're in the same night school course?" said Parker, and even if she'd made it sound like she was asking a question again, Frances was grateful for her effortless half-truth.

"We understand you have a restraining order against him," said Frances.

"Damn right I do, man's a nut case. Be careful around him."

"Come now," said Frances, "he's perfectly harmless."

Ron lowered his voice. "Look, I shouldn't be telling you this, but—he vandalized my car. Cost me an arm and a leg to get it repainted."

"Well," said Frances, "technically it cost your *insurance company* a lot of money."

"Worse, he's been charged with indecent exposure. Ladies, the guy's a perv."

"He is not," said Parker, no question mark in sight.

"Hey, it's your funeral. But if he turns on you, don't say I didn't warn you. A real Jekyll and Hyde, that one."

"Duly noted," said Frances. "Now, back to the reason for our visit. We'd like you to give him his deposit back." Beside her, Parker nodded.

Ron stared at them for a moment. Then he started to laugh. "Geraint sent two of his lady friends to do his dirty business. What a pussy."

Frances bristled at the word. "He didn't send us. We offered."

"He would have come himself if it weren't for your restraining order," Parker added, "which, I don't know, makes it seem like maybe you're more afraid of him than he is of you." Parker shot a look at Frances, pink-cheeked and pleased with herself.

Ron crossed his arms over his chest. "As if I'd ever be afraid of that buffoon. And the deposit's non-refundable. Idiot didn't bother to read the contract, that's on him." He started to close the door.

"You're right," said Frances, aiming to sound conciliatory, "he should have read it. But he trusted you. And now that he isn't going to be opening a Quicky Muffler—"

"Of course he isn't. I wouldn't let a convicted felon run one of my franchises."

"He's not a convicted felon," said Parker. "At least, not yet anyway."

"And he needs that money," Frances added. "You fired him."

"Of *course* I fired him, he vandalized my car and pissed in my fountain!"

"Because you were sleeping with his wife," said Frances.

"Not to quibble, but I *am* sleeping with his wife. Present tense." He bestowed another lecherous grin upon them.

"Look," said Frances. "You have the chance to do the right thing here, the kind thing."

Ron's eyes suddenly lit up with recognition. He wagged a triumphant finger in Frances's face. "I know where I've seen you."

"I don't think you do."

"You're the crazy bitch from that video! *That's* how you know Geraint. You're in that airy-fairy alternative program with him, aren't you?"

Beside her, Parker stiffened. "I need to ask you to apologize for calling my friend a bitch?"

"It's okay, Parker," Frances began, but Parker cut her off.

"Apologize."

Ron smiled indulgently at Parker. "Aren't you just a ball of fire."

Then he reached out and patted Parker on the head.

* * *

From the driver's seat of his Subaru, Geraint strained forward for a better view. It looked as if Ron had possibly touched Parker's head. And now it looked as if Parker had grabbed his hand and—no, it couldn't be, Parker wouldn't bite someone!

HONK!! He leapt back in alarm. He'd leaned so far forward he'd hit the horn.

He saw Ron, cradling his hand, staring down the block.

He and Ron locked eyes.

Oh dear.

He watched as Ron pushed past Frances and Parker and strode down the long driveway towards him in his workout shorts. "Hey! Hey, Geraint."

Geraint stepped out of his car. "Ron. I don't want any trouble." They were still well over a hundred metres apart.

"I don't either," Ron replied, his tone surprisingly conciliatory. "We should just talk things through. Man to man. Bit cowardly, wouldn't you say, sending two ladies in your place?"

"I'd have come myself if you hadn't got the restraining order."

"About that. I was angry in the moment. You know what my car means to me."

"Yes, well. You know what my wife means to me."

Ron bowed his head. "Touché." Then he held out his arms. "Come on, old pal. Let's hug it out." Geraint hesitated, but only for a moment. He started to walk towards Ron.

"Geraint, stop!" Frances shouted as she and Parker ran in their direction.

But it was too late.

When Geraint was about twenty metres away from him, Ron whipped out his phone and started recording. "Don't come any closer, Geraint! I'm warning you!"

Geraint looked around, confused. "But you just said—"

"Please don't hurt me!"

"I'm not going to—"

Ron started to shake his phone, then he pointed it at the sky. "No, Geraint! Please, stop hurting me."

"You evil prick!" someone roared, and it took Frances a moment to realize that the someone was Parker, who took a running leap and latched herself onto Ron's back like a succubus and started to punch him in the back of the head with her fists.

Ron flailed, trying to get hold of her. "Aagh, get off me!"

Parker grabbed his hand and bent it back until he yelped in pain and his phone fell to the ground. "Grab it, Frances!" Frances was motionless, in shock, but only for a split second; she did as she was told and scooped up the phone. Parker hopped off Ron's back and took it from her.

Geraint and Frances both stared, slack-jawed, as Parker made a beeline for her car. Ron tried to follow her, but Geraint's rugby training came back to him and he handily blocked Ron's path. They all watched, agog, as Parker laid Ron's phone down under her left front tire. She started her car and drove over the phone. She reversed over the phone. Back and forth, a few times. The phone made a satisfying crunchy sound.

Then she sped off.

The three of them stood in a neat little row, gaping, stunned. "What. The. Fuck," said Ron. He looked near tears. Then he started jogging back towards his house.

Frances and Geraint stood rooted to the spot, trying to make sense of what had just unfolded. Finally Frances found her voice. "I suspect Ron's going to use his landline to call the police."

"I suspect you're right."

The two of them made a dash for their cars and drove away as fast as the thirty-kilometre speed limit would allow.

21

P arker screeched around another corner in the tony Shaughnessy neighbourhood, past the Tudor and Classical man-
sions on their expansive manicured grounds, going double
the speed limit. It was only when she took a speed bump at sixty
kilometres an hour and felt the *thwump* in her bones that she came
back to herself. Adrenaline coursed through her body. She slowed
the car down. The last thing she needed was to be pulled over by
the cops. Once she was far enough away from Ron's house, she
pulled over and rested her head on the steering wheel.

Holy-triple-moly.

She had never been an angry or outspoken person, ever. Sharon
had had a lot of boyfriends (her grandpa liked to say, "Your mother
goes through boyfriends like a dysentery patient goes through toilet paper"), and while some of them had been nice, some of them
had not. Karl had been the worst; he'd snuck into her bedroom a
few times when she'd been sleeping and . . .

Luckily Sharon's relationship with Karl had been short-lived.
From that point on, Parker had made a point of drawing as little
attention to herself as possible. One boyfriend, she couldn't remember his name, had called her "quieter than a mouse," in a tone that
was halfway between a criticism and a compliment. On her report
cards teachers would say, "Parker is so well behaved," which Parker
took as praise until her mother had said, "It's what they write when
you haven't stood out for them in any way."

Even during her encounter with Sebastian Trevor, she'd acted more out of fear than anger.

But the guy at the mall—that was more than anger. That was rage. And today—definitely rage, only this time she'd incorporated a few of the tricks she'd learned in self-defence classes. Alexei had signed her up for them a couple of months ago. She hadn't wanted to go. But from the very first session, she'd felt empowered. Her instructor—a towering, muscular Swede named Björn—had told her, "You can be on the short side and still be fierce. In fact sometimes it's an advantage because people take you for granted."

Well, that misogynistic poop of a man had taken her for granted. She'd felt the fury start to build when he'd dared to call Frances a bitch. And in such a casual way, like he was so much better than she was just by virtue of his sex. Then he had refused to apologize; and then he had *patted her on the head*. Like she was a child or a puppy. Like he thought it was totally within his rights to touch her, to treat her like a plaything, the way Sebastian thought it was totally within his rights to force her onto her knees . . .

Her self-defence classes had kicked in and she'd bitten down hard on the meaty part of Ron's hand.

Then that creep had tried to entrap Geraint! Geraint, who was just about the sweetest man Parker had ever met. Something had to be done to stop him.

But now, as Parker sat in the car, reality started to set in. Ron would call the cops. She'd destroyed his phone, and while they'd probably been out of range of his security cameras, his neighbourhood was peppered with the things—she knew from watching tons of *Real Housewives* franchises with Sharon that rich people loved their surveillance equipment. If she was charged with assault again, there wasn't a judge out there who'd go easy on her. She'd wind up with a criminal record, and then what?

She started the car and pulled out carefully into traffic. But as she drove away, quietly humming "My Favourite Things" from *The Sound of Music* to try to calm herself down, mindful of staying just below the speed limit, an even worse thought entered her head.

If she got caught, she would almost certainly bring Frances and Geraint down with her.

22

Geraint stood outside the front doors of the high school the following night, waiting for Frances. He wore a bright yellow rain slicker with the hood up, but even that didn't protect him from the sideways-slanting rain, which was coming down hard.

He saw her car pull in, and a few moments later she hurried up the steps, holding a large *Merde Il Pleut* umbrella. "Anything?" he asked anxiously.

She shook her head, lowering her umbrella. "Nothing. You?"

"Nothing." He held the door open for her. "The silence feels ominous."

"Yes." They headed up the stairs, feet squelching. "I'm so sorry, Geraint. That did not go as I'd hoped."

"Please don't apologize. I know you were only trying to help."

"You tried to warn us. He really is an awful human being." They reached the top of the stairs—and stopped dead in their tracks.

Parker was at the far end of the hall, getting a snack from the vending machine.

They ducked back into the stairwell.

"I feel that I've misread her," said Geraint.

"Very much so. She's less Rory in *Gilmore Girls*, more . . ."

"Regan in *The Exorcist*."

"Maybe she has a personality disorder?"

"I had a great-aunt like that. One minute she was serving you cookies and warm milk, the next minute she was chasing you around the kitchen with a meat mallet."

They were both quiet for a moment. "I think you need to ask her why she's in anger management," said Geraint.

"Me? Why me?"

"Because she terrifies me, ha ha, oh goodness, she's coming straight towards us!"

Parker joined them, clutching a Mars bar and wearing a loose-fitting grey sweatshirt and jeans. Geraint attempted to sound cheerful and upbeat. "Parker, hello! You're looking well," he lied, because she looked awful, tired and drawn.

"Have you guys heard from the police?" she whispered. They shook their heads. "Me neither." Parker wrapped her arms around herself. "I'm so sorry. I mean, I know *I'll* be in trouble if he called them, but I never meant to get you guys in trouble, too." She looked like she might cry. Frances felt a flood of sympathy for her, this poor girl who was no older than her daughter. Geraint felt a flood of sympathy, too, and wanted to give her a hug. Then he remembered her reaction when Ron had patted her on the head and took a step back instead.

"This isn't your fault," said Frances. "Besides, if none of us have heard a peep, then chances are he didn't call."

"Maybe he was too embarrassed," said Geraint. "He was Goliath, smote by David." Parker looked at him blankly. "You're David," he clarified.

"I think we're probably off the hook," said Frances. All three of them felt a little bit lighter as they headed into the classroom, where Dennis stood at his desk.

Chatting with Carol Jansen.

When Dennis saw them, he gave them a pitying look. "You three," Carol said. "Come with me."

She pulled them into an empty classroom. "Sit." They sat. Carol, who wore a shirt that read *The More People I Meet, The More I Love My Cat*, leaned against the teacher's desk, arms crossed over her broad chest. "I have a friend on the police force. He took a complaint from a citizen named Ron Neumann yesterday about three individuals. Two he knew by name, Geraint Blevins and Frances Partridge. The third he said was *a crazy young ginger.*" She paused. "My friend looked up the two names in the database and saw they were clients of mine. So he gave me a call." She looked at them sternly. "Did you, or did you not, pay Ron Neumann a visit yesterday?"

Frances leapt in, praying Geraint and Parker would follow her lead. "We did."

"He's saying the three of you attacked him in broad daylight."

"*What?*" said Frances, dredging up her eighth-grade acting skills. "That is ridiculous! The three of us did not attack him." This was true; only one of them had attacked him. "We only tried to talk with him."

"He's saying Geraint violated his restraining order."

"Also not true. Geraint stayed at least one hundred metres away from him at all times, even when Ron tried to approach *him*." Beside her, Geraint nodded nervously.

"He's saying Ms. Poplawski bit him, jumped him, beat him on the side of the head, almost broke his fingers, and ran over his phone."

Frances glanced at Parker, who had pulled the strings on her hoodie so tight, only her mouth and nose stuck out. She swore she could hear the girl humming to herself.

"Carol—may I call you Carol?" asked Geraint.

"No."

"Ms. Jansen. My ex-boss is over six feet tall and well over two hundred pounds. You could fit three Parkers into one of him. Can you imagine this wispy young girl attacking a man Ron's size?" Geraint started to laugh. Frances joined in. "Ha ha ha ha ha ha ha ha ha ha." They let it go on for a bit too long. Carol just gazed at them stonily until they stopped.

Frances thought she heard Parker sing something like "Whiskers on kittens."

"These are wild accusations," said Frances, "especially if he doesn't have any proof." She let this hang for a moment.

"He says things took place just out of range of his security cameras," Carol said, glancing sharply at the three of them when they collectively exhaled. "And there were no witnesses. Which is odd, because a number of his neighbours were home. The police got the feeling none of them like him very much."

"He's not a very likeable person," said Frances, and again she could have sworn she heard Parker sing something about cream-coloured ponies.

"Why did you go to his house in the first place?"

"He owes Geraint fifty thousand dollars."

"That's a big chunk of change. What for?"

"I'd put a down payment on one of his Quicky Muffler franchises," said Geraint.

Carol made a face. "Ron owns Quicky Muffler? I had some engine work done at the flagship store last year. They did a crappy job."

"I'm very sorry to hear that," said Geraint. "You have my word, the franchises are run almost entirely by good people. But Ron likes to cut corners on occasion." He leaned forward in his desk. "If you'd allow it, I would be more than happy to have a look at your engine."

Carol considered this. "Been a long time since anyone's been near my engine."

"That's not good. Your engine should definitely have regular maintenance."

"I've tried fiddling with it myself a few times, but . . ."

"I could make your engine purr in no time."

Frances shot Parker a look—*Are you hearing this?* But Parker was still buried in her nondescript hoodie and singing quietly to herself.

Carol picked up her Bic pen and clicked it repeatedly, open-shut, open-shut. "You realize that if any of what Ron said is true, you'd get pulled out of the alternative measures program, and from what I know about each of your cases, you'd be found guilty of the charges against you and wind up with permanent records." She trained her penetrating gaze on each of them. "But it's his word against yours. I'll let the police officer know that, after a thorough investigation, I've found there is no basis for Ron Neumann's complaint."

"Thank you so much, Carol," Geraint said.

"Now get back to class."

The three of them marched single file out of the room. When they were safely out of earshot, Parker emerged from her hoodie and blurted, "Oh my god, you guys were amazing. I was so scared, I completely clammed up. If there's any way I can pay you back—"

"There is, actually," said Frances as they reached the classroom door. "You can tell us what landed you in anger management."

Parker took a deep breath. "Okay. I can do that." She tore open her Mars bar. "I broke a guy's leg?" Then, almost as an afterthought: "Oh, and his collarbone?" She bit into her chocolate bar. "Oh, and I gave him a concussion?" Then she walked into the classroom, leaving Frances and Geraint to pick their jaws up off the floor.

They got the full story after class, in a brightly lit doughnut shop not too far from the school. The three of them sat at the very back with large cups of tea. Geraint had also got a jelly doughnut for himself and a cruller for Parker. "A couple of months ago I went to the Pacific Centre mall to try to find a briefcase for Alexei," Parker began. "I went into Hugo Boss. And I noticed this guy was watching me." Parker grimaced. "He had on a tight white T-shirt even though it was January, and big bulgy muscles, and his head was shaved. And he came up to me as I was leaving the store and said, *If being sexy was a crime, you'd be guilty as charged.*" She shuddered. Frances noticed that she never once looked up at them, but instead stared down at her tea.

"I was super polite. I said something like, *Oh, ha ha, how nice of you to say but I have a boyfriend, so—have a nice day!*" Parker shook her head. "But he kept following me, in and out of stores. I was starting to get freaked out."

"Of course you were," Frances said.

"So I hopped on an escalator to get away from him. But he got on, like, right behind me. And now he was leaning into me and making these annoying, quiet smooching sounds. Then he started saying really gross stuff, like, *I wanna take you home and—*" She stopped, ashamed.

"Then he touched my hair. And I don't know, I just lost it." She closed her eyes, remembering. "I whipped around and smacked him in the chest as hard as I could with both hands. He wasn't holding onto anything and he lost his balance. The look on his face when he started to fall—" She opened her eyes and saw that Frances's and Geraint's eyes were wide as pancakes. "Thank god there was no one riding behind him. He tumbled all the way down and landed in a heap on the floor. At first I thought I'd killed him. Then he moved, and I felt so relieved, but then he started to yell, *That bitch pushed me!* So I took off. But there were, like, security cameras everywhere, and a handful of witnesses, and also I felt super guilty? So the next day I went with Alexei to the police station and I turned myself in."

"Surely they understood it was self-defence," Frances said.

"I don't know. It was his word against mine. My legal aid lawyer told me he was able to get me alternative measures because I turned myself in, and also because one of the shop owners had noticed the guy was following me. But he also warned me I couldn't mess it up. And I don't want to mess it up." Tears welled up in her eyes. "I didn't mean to hurt him. I just wanted him to *leave me alone*." The tears spilled over, landing on her cruller, one after another.

Frances grabbed her hand and squeezed it. "Of course you did."

"I'm so sorry that happened to you, Parker," Geraint added, his own eyes looking rather moist.

Parker's tears flowed freely now. "I just don't understand why this keeps happening to me lately. The second time in three months! It's like I'm wearing a perfume called Eau de Creepy Guys, like I'm doing something to attract them."

"Sorry," said Frances. "Did you say the second time in three months?"

Parker's eyes grew wide. She clamped a hand over her mouth.

Frances and Geraint shared a concerned look. "Parker," said Frances gently, "you can tell us anything."

Parker shook her head vigorously. "No. I can't."

"What if Geraint left, and you and I—"

"It wouldn't make a difference. I seriously can't."

"Why not?" asked Geraint.

Parker glanced around the coffee shop, deserted except for the bored-looking teenaged boy behind the counter. She lowered her voice to a whisper. "Because I signed an NDA."

Frances and Geraint took this in. "Well, but you could still tell *us*," said Geraint. "We all have so much on each other at this point, we're pretty much forced to keep each other's secrets. Mutually assured destruction and all that."

Parker considered this. Part of her wanted to tell them, even though it was humiliating. The weight of her secret was getting unbearable. But the lawyer had told her that if she broke the NDA, they would come after her for breach of contract. They'd force her to pay the money back. Worse, he'd implied that they could sue her for defamation and she would never work again.

"I can't. I'm sorry, but I just can't." She pushed her chair back and walked out, leaving most of her cruller behind.

Geraint shook his head. "That poor girl."

Frances nodded, pensive. "Two incidents in three months. You know what Parker was doing three months ago?"

"What?"

"Working in the wardrobe department on *Knights of the Castle*."

"Ooh, what? I love that show so much! When Queen Maribelle serves a roast to her duplicitous uncle Algernon and after he's done she reveals he's just eaten his own son—"

"My point is—what if something happened to her on that show?"

Geraint looked confused. "You're not suggesting—"

"Yes. I am. Someone she worked for? A producer?"

"Like, a Harvey what's-his-ding situation?" His mouth was ringed with icing sugar.

Frances nodded. "It would explain why her career in television seems to have begun and ended so abruptly." Geraint's face clouded. He ate the last crumbs of his jelly-filled doughnut, then picked up Parker's leftover cruller and took a bite. "She cried all over that, Geraint. And her nose was running."

He put the cruller down. "What can we do?"

Frances sighed. "Not much of anything right now, I don't think. Except be there for her."

"I can do that," he said. "I'm good at that." Then he picked the cruller back up and ate the rest of it—tears, snot, and all.

23

S he was being toured around a dark, dank one-bedroom apartment. "The ad didn't mention it was in a basement."

"It's not a basement. It's a garden suite." The landlady sounded a lot like Margaret Atwood. Oh. It *was* Margaret Atwood. "Ms. Atwood, I'm a huge fan. I've read everything you've written. Well, almost everything, I might have missed one or two of the dystopias."

"There's a hot plate on the counter," said Margaret Atwood. "And a bar fridge. Doesn't have a lot of space, but since you're sad and alone it will probably fit what you need. Which I'm guessing is mostly wine."

"Ha ha ha ha. Your trademark caustic wit. I'm a writer, too, you know. Maybe I could cook you dinner on the hot plate sometime and we could talk craft—"

"Sorry, place is already rented."

"No, it's not. You just said—"

"Bye-bye now."

Frances's alarm went off just as Margaret Atwood was shoving her out the door. She felt surprisingly clear-headed because, for the first time in a long while, she'd had nothing to drink the night before.

Mr. Pickles trotted ahead of her into the kitchen. Daisy was already there, making a smoothie in her plaid pajamas. "You're up early," said Frances.

"The temp agency called. I have a month-long gig at a new PR firm." She shoved a banana into the blender.

"That's good." Frances put on the kettle. "How was your evening last night?"

"Fine."

"What did you do?"

"Nothing much." She turned on the blender, letting it run for a very long time.

Frances waited till the noise stopped. "You had dinner with your father."

Daisy poured her smoothie into a glass, giving the leftovers—all of a few mouthfuls—to her mom in a teacup. "He's still my dad."

"Of course he is." In theory, Frances knew it was good and right and healthy for Daisy to still see Jeremy. But in reality it killed her. She preferred Max's way of dealing with his dad, which was to break off all contact. "How did he look?"

"I don't know. Like Dad."

"Heavier? Thinner?"

"The same."

Then, unable to stop herself: "Was Kelly there?"

A pause. "Yes."

"How many times have you met him now?"

"Not a lot. Like, maybe three."

"Do you like him?"

"Mom, you can't do this."

"Can you blame me for being curious?"

"Do you really want to know? Because I'll tell you if you do."

Frances knew she should say no, for her own psychological well-being. "Yes."

"He's fine. Nice. Not super handsome but well put together. He tries way too hard with me, like, laughs too hard at my jokes, asks a million questions about my life but doesn't really listen to the answers."

"Rude."

"Because he's so nervous. I think he's worried I hate him because he's seen as the homewrecker—"

"Not 'seen as,' *is*—"

"And I think he feels really guilty about that—"

"As he should."

"There. Now I've told you. No more questions." Daisy had bright pink patches on her cheeks, a sure sign that she was feeling stressed.

Frances knew she should quit her badgering. But knowing and doing were two different things. "So, you like him."

"Mom, I just said—"

"That wasn't a question. It was a statement."

"I didn't say I liked him."

"Are they touchy-feely?"

"That *is* a question, and no, they're not, and I am done."

"Do they make googly eyes at one another?"

"Mother! Stop putting me in the middle!" Daisy picked up her smoothie and walked out.

Once she'd eaten breakfast, Frances drove to the Vancouver Aquatic Centre, a good half-hour earlier than usual in hopes she might avoid The Turtle.

No such luck. There he was, in the medium lane, taking up more than his fair share of space. She placed her fins and a pull buoy down by the edge of the pool and hopped in, just as a man she'd never seen before sauntered up. He was about her age, average height, with a face that was somewhere between handsome and ugly. *He looks like Daniel Craig's brother*, she thought. He gave her the briefest of smiles before he hopped in and pushed off just ahead of her. *Jerk.*

Frances's competitive nature kicked in. She was determined to show him up. She pushed off and swam as fast as she could, managing to pass him at about the thirty-five-metre mark. But it took everything she had, and she was exhausted and breathless when she reached the end. So she had to let him go ahead again, which was humiliating, especially when he smirked at her before pushing off. This time she hung back, letting him get at least a twenty-five-metre lead.

She'd swum for over half an hour, passing The Turtle at least four times, when she stopped at the end of the pool to grab her pull buoy. It wasn't there. As she scanned the pool deck, Daniel Craig's brother swam towards her, and she saw it: *her* pull buoy, wedged between his muscular thighs. Wedged right up against his nuggets! When he reached the end she said, "Excuse me, that's my pull buoy."

"What's that?" He had an accent.

"The pull buoy. It's mine."

"Oh. Sorry." He pulled it out from between his legs and handed it to her. "You might want to put your name on it."

"You mean, like this?" She indicated the large *FRANCES* written in black Sharpie on the side.

He grinned again. "Yeah, like that." Then he hoisted himself out of the pool, workout done.

"British dickhead," Frances muttered.

He stopped. Gave her a hard stare. "That word is extremely offensive."

Frances felt the heat rise in her face. "I'm sorry, I didn't mean—"

"I'm *Scottish*," he replied. Then he started to laugh at his own joke as he sauntered away.

* * *

"I read a very interesting and not entirely depressing article on climate change this morning," Norah said a while later. She and Maryam sat across from Frances.

"Tell us more about it," said Maryam, and Norah did, in minute detail.

"I'm repainting my kitchen," said Maryam when Norah was finished. "I'm trying to decide between eggshell and cream."

"Please don't do this," said Frances. "It's a sweet gesture. But I'm fine. Talk about your projects. I want to hear everything."

Norah exhaled with relief. "Oh, thank goodness, because I really need to vent." She told them about the cover art she'd just received for her fall novel. "I hated it. So I wrote a very measured email to my publisher, and you know what she said? *Our marketing team feels this is the best approach.* My opinion means nothing!"

"Norah, Maryam, hello." Sabrina Faizal, executive director of Bookapalooza, stood over their table, wearing a beautiful camel-coloured wool coat and a jaunty black beret, a to-go coffee in her leather-gloved hands.

Maryam almost spit out her coffee. "Sabrina!"

"What a lovely surprise!" Norah almost shrieked.

"I trust you've both received your invitations to the festival."

"Yes and we can't wait!" said Maryam with overwrought enthusiasm.

"*So* excited!" added Norah. They both had manically large smiles plastered on their faces.

Frances had also received an invitation to the festival, as it had lined up with what was supposed to be her fall book release. Then the video had gone viral and the invitation had been rescinded. A clipped, cold email from an underling. Sabrina had never reached out personally, even though Frances had participated in

Bookapalooza for years. She'd considered Sabrina a friend. "Hi, Sabrina," she said. Sabrina swivelled her head and locked eyes with Frances.

The change in Sabrina's expression would have been comical if it weren't so hurtful. Her voice lost all its warmth. "Hello, Frances. Well, I should get going." With a curt nod to Norah and Maryam, she walked away.

An awkward silence descended on the table. Then Norah pushed back her seat. "Goodness, I forgot, I have a thing."

"Me too," said Maryam. "We have the same . . . thing." They pulled on their coats and scuttled out. *Like cockroaches*, Frances thought unkindly. She knew what was going through their heads. They were afraid of being found guilty by association. Afraid that they might get uninvited now, too. Afraid that by being seen with her, their careers might also suffer. And she couldn't totally blame them because they'd all heard the rumours that these things, while hard to prove, really did happen in their insular industry.

Frances slowly gathered her things. She suspected that next week Norah and Maryam would cancel their coffee date with excuses about deadlines. And if they didn't, she would.

She left the coffee shop and walked the few blocks home. Anxiety bubbled through her. The *coldness* in Sabrina's voice. The look on her face. There was a finality to it: *You are dead to me*. She'd been able to tell herself that her reputation would eventually bounce back, along with her ability to write. But it struck her now that even if she found the will to write again, she might never find anyone with the will to publish her. Her reputation might never be resuscitated.

When she got home it was only eleven o'clock. The house was quiet. Mr. Pickles was sound asleep in the bay window in a puddle of weak sunlight. She had nothing to do until another community service shift at three.

It was abundantly clear that she could not be home alone with her spiralling thoughts. So she filled Mr. Pickles's bowl with kibble, headed back out to her car, and drove to Shady Pines.

"Frances. What are you doing here?" Cordelia was in her room, applying liberal layers of eyeshadow.

"Just thought I'd pop by for a visit." She watched as Cordelia slipped one of her nicest dresses over her head, black, knee-length, with a zipper up the back. "Wow, you're awfully dolled up." Her mom could no longer navigate zippers, so Frances zipped her up.

"I'm going on a date."

"With Harvey?" Her mom would sometimes tell her she was waiting for Harvey to pick her up to take her to dinner or to the drive-in.

"Who's Harvey?" Cordelia said now, and Frances's heart sank. "I'm going on a date with Alfred."

Alfred. Frances tried to think; had her mom ever mentioned an old beau named Alfred? Was this someone else from her past? She was about to ask when there was a knock at the door. Frances answered. A man who bore an uncanny resemblance to Dobby the house-elf stood in the hall. He smiled warmly. "You must be the daughter. I'm Alfred." Frances's eyebrows shot up.

"He's my new beau," Cordelia said to Frances in a stage whisper.

"We're going to play bingo in the lounge," said Alfred.

Frances tried to shake off her surprise. "I'll come with you," she said, "help you play—"

"That won't be necessary," Cordelia said, her voice firm. She linked arms with Alfred. Then, with a slight hint of reproach as they left her room: "Surely you have something better to do with your day than spend it here with me."

* * *

Frances found Jamal by the nurse's station. "What's up with my mom and this Alfred fellow?"

Jamal smiled. "It's a recent development. They seem pretty sweet on each other. He's a nice guy. In the very early stages of the disease."

"Okay but . . . I don't think my mother should be dating."

He gave her an inquisitive look. "Why not?"

"Because . . ." *Because she needs to honour the memory of my wonderful stepfather. Because she'll need me less. Because it doesn't seem fair that my mom has a more active dating life than I do.*

Jamal smiled. "Would it help if I told you Jeremy seems okay with it?" Frances didn't understand the question at first. She'd never told Jamal about their break-up, because—well, why would she? "We talked about it briefly yesterday, when he was here."

"He was here?"

Jamal looked puzzled. "He's here every Wednesday. But you know that. Frances, are you all right?"

She was already making a beeline for her car.

"Siri, call Asshole," she said as she pulled out of the parking lot.

"Calling: Asshole. Mobile."

The phone rang. Once, twice. "Frances. I'm so glad you finally called—"

"You've been visiting my mother behind my back."

A pause. "Okay, we can talk about that."

"I explicitly told you not to."

"She was my mother-in-law for twenty-five years."

"And now she isn't, so do me a favour and stay the hell away from her."

"Do you think that's what's best for Cordelia?"

"She has Alzheimer's, Jeremy. Give it a few weeks and she'll forget you ever existed. God, what I wouldn't give for a case of dementia so I could forget about you, too!"

There was a long pause on the other end of the phone. "That is a truly awful thing to say."

She knew that it was. She regretted her words on so many levels as soon as they were out of her mouth. But—as Jeremy himself used to say—you can't put the shit back in the donkey.

So before he could say another recriminating word, she hung up.

Frances was still roiling with a noxious mixture of anger, guilt, and despair when she pulled up on the banks of the Fraser River half an hour later. She could see Parker sitting by herself at a picnic table. Frances grabbed her reflective vest from the trunk and walked towards her.

As she got closer, she saw that Parker was drawing in her purple notebook. Frances noted with some satisfaction that the pink headphones were nowhere to be seen.

Her misery dissipated somewhat. Parker was Daisy's age, give or take a year, a sweet girl with a generally sunny disposition. And something terrible had happened to her.

"Hey, Parker," she said as she slid in across from her.

Parker slammed her notebook shut. "Hi! Sorry. I didn't hear you coming."

"How are you doing?"

"Fine?"

"Are you?"

Parker didn't respond.

"I hope you don't mind me asking, but—is your mother in the picture?"

"Oh yes. She's down in Mexico with her latest boyfriend."

"Are you close? What I mean is, can you talk to her?"

Parker felt the heat rise in her face. "I don't know how to answer that."

Frances nodded. "I know there are things you can't say. But if you ever need an ear—I'm a phone call away."

"Thanks. That means a lot, especially coming from one of my all-time favourite authors."

Frances raised her eyebrows, surprised.

"Your books rocked my world when I was growing up. I must've read the *Phoebe Unknown* series at least five times."

"Wow."

"They got me through some rough patches. Like, if my mom was dating someone who didn't like kids, I'd just go to my room and escape into the world of that little mountain village and pretend Basil, Buford, Bartholomew, and Cressida were raising me, too. And the fact that Phoebe had red hair, well . . ."

Frances smiled. "I must have known I was going to meet you one day."

They heard tires crunching on gravel. Carol's white pickup truck pulled into the lot. She lowered herself from the cab. Frances noticed she was wearing makeup. "I come bearing a fresh supply of gloves and garbage bags." She grabbed a large plastic bin from the flatbed. "Where's Geraint?"

"I'm sure he'll be here any minute," said Frances. "He's usually the first to arrive."

But when Geraint finally showed up he was on foot and a full twenty minutes late. "So sorry. Couldn't find car keys. Had to take bus. Very discombobulated." He was sweaty, out of breath, and out of sorts.

"Is something wrong?" asked Parker.

"Got some news before I left." He smiled, but it looked more like a grimace. "Seems Ron asked Keanu a lot of questions about his birthday party. Such as, what was the name of the woman who hosted the party? He thought it was an interesting coincidence that your name matched the name of the woman who showed up at his house recently. The same woman who has charges against her. For assault. Of a minor." His voice rose an octave as he continued. "So Ron and Darlene's lawyer—because they have a lawyer now, *ha ha ha*—has filed an emergency notice of application asking for them to get sole parenting of Keanu. Because they feel he isn't safe with me. Because I consort with *child abusers* and even took Keanu to said child abuser's house." Geraint's voice was now just a squeak.

"Oh my god, Geraint," murmured Parker.

"That's awful," said Frances. "He's awful."

Geraint dropped to his knees, not quite avoiding a large pile of dog shit. "I can't lose my son!" He started to weep.

Frances realized, not without shame, that it gave her an odd bit of comfort to know that in a bad-day contest, hers would now come a distant second.

24

arol happened to have her gym bag in the truck, so she loaned Geraint a pair of neon green workout tights. They fit in the waist but stopped just below his knees, like knickerbockers. *He looks like the Friendly Giant,* Frances thought, then realized she was probably the only one who was old enough to get the reference.

He put his soiled trousers into a garbage bag. "Can I leave these in your trunk?" he asked Frances.

She made a face. "Geraint, just throw them out."

"But they're perfectly good trousers."

"They're for garbage picking, and they're covered in dog poo."

"Which washes out." Normally Frances would have refused, but Geraint was suffering enough already. So she made sure he sealed the bag tightly and let him put it in the trunk.

Carol accompanied them on the first half-hour of their route, walking side by side with Geraint. She had a lot of advice to impart because she'd had an acrimonious divorce, too, and her ex had tried to get sole custody of their kids. "He lost," she said. "And he had to pay part of my legal bills because the judge declared him a vexatious litigant. So my number one advice is, lawyer up. And get a good one."

"But lawyers are expensive. And I'm in a bit of a financial bind at the moment."

"Is your son important to you?"

"He's everything to me."

"Then get. A good. Lawyer. I'd recommend mine but he's dead. Brain aneurism." On that cheery note she gave Geraint a comforting pat on the arm and headed back to her truck.

Geraint barely said a word during the rest of their shift. Frances and Parker tried to pick up the slack. "Geraint, what would you rather: Have the ability to see ten minutes into the future or ten years?" asked Frances.

He just let out a long sigh.

"What would you rather," Parker asked, "have telekinesis or telepathy?"

He simply sighed again, only this time, it sounded more like a moan.

Frances and Parker shared a look that said, *This is serious.*

When they were done their shift he asked, "Don't suppose you want to go for a drink?" He looked utterly woebegone.

"Sorry," Frances said, apologetic. "Jules and I have a standing date at a burger joint. Carmen's a strict vegan, so when she plays pickleball on Thursday nights Jules gets her meat fix."

"I like Jules," said Geraint. "And I love burgers."

Jesus, the hangdog look.

"Also, she's a lawyer," he said.

"A criminal defence lawyer."

"Still. She knows law stuff."

Frances tried to harden her heart. But he'd had such a lousy day, lousier than hers. "Would you like to join us, Geraint?"

"Well, all right. If you insist."

"Alexei's got night school," Parker said. "And I like burgers, too."

So Frances texted Jules to give her the heads-up, then drove Geraint to Bells and Whistles on Dunbar, Parker following behind in her Mazda. Even though Geraint's pants were safely stored in her trunk, a faint whiff of dog shit filled the car. Frances cracked her window open. With the exception of a periodic, juicy sniffle, Geraint was still unusually quiet.

But the moment he saw Jules, the words spilled out of him. "Jules, they want to take my child away from me," he said as he slid into the booth. He told her the entire story, stopping only so they could place their order. Jules looked inquisitively at his neon green tights but kept her questions to herself.

"Do you think your ex-wife . . ." Jules began.

"Wife. Technically she is still my wife."

"Is she driving this or is Ron?"

"I'm quite certain it's Ron. He doesn't even like children. He's told me that a million times. I think he's just doing it because he can."

The server put a pitcher of beer on the table, and Jules filled their glasses. "First and foremost, you need a good lawyer."

"That's exactly what our diversion officer said. I was hoping you might know someone who is good but also, how do I put this . . . *cheap*. I'm rather broke at the moment."

Frances tried to catch Jules's eye. But their burgers had arrived, and Jules got busy putting ketchup on hers. "I don't know people from that world, I'm afraid. But Frances—"

"Also knows no one from that world," Frances said.

Jules glanced up from her burger and saw the pleading look on Frances's face. Her eyes narrowed. "Are you sure about that?"

"Mmm-hmm. But I do know that everyone is entitled to legal representation, so I'd suggest you contact the legal aid society, Geraint. They may be able to help you out."

"That's a great idea," said Geraint. "Thank you, Frances. You are such a good friend."

Jules gave her a hard, steely look. "Isn't she, though? So selfless. Always putting others' needs ahead of her own."

Parker nodded as she popped a fry into her mouth. "You're a good person, Frances."

Frances knew she needed to change the subject. "Guess what I learned today. My mother has a boyfriend."

"Cordy?" said Geraint.

"Yup. Alfred. He looks like the Dalai Lama, only older."

"That's so sweet," said Parker.

"Is it? I find it all a bit unsettling."

"Of course you find it unsettling," said Jules. "Your mother's love life is more active than yours."

"That has nothing to do with it."

"Then again, *anyone's* love life is more active than yours," Jules continued. "You haven't had sex in, what, eight months?"

"Eight *months?*" Parker sounded horrified.

"Gosh, Frances. That's two-thirds of a year," said Geraint. Frances wasn't about to tell them that it had actually been three-quarters of a year, because she and Jeremy hadn't had sex at all during their last month together.

"Poor Frances." Parker made a sad face, which was all kinds of irritating.

"Sex isn't everything," Frances stated.

"No, but it isn't nothing," said Jules.

"Have you thought about starting to date again?" asked Geraint.

"Nope, not going there."

"I've tried repeatedly to get her to sign up for a dating site," said Jules.

"Oh, Frances, you should," said Geraint. "You'd be a hot commodity!"

"Thank you, but that's entirely false, and may I point out I don't see you dating."

"No, but it's only been a few months for me. And I still cling to the hope that Darlene will realize the error of her ways and come back to me."

"You do realize that's highly unlikely."

"Well, it's more likely than your Jeremy coming back to you," Geraint replied, not unkindly. But the words stung because the truth was she did harbour the smallest shred of hope that Jeremy might realize, sexuality aside, that he was simply happier with her than he was with Kelly. She'd imagined them coming to some sort of arrangement, à la Leonard Bernstein and his wife, Felicia. She thought she could manage the rest of her life without sex if it meant having him back, because everything else in their marriage had worked so well. She had never admitted these thoughts to anyone, not even to Jules, because she knew it didn't look good on her that she'd be so quick to take such an unsatisfactory deal.

She extricated herself from the booth. "I am done with this conversation. And more importantly, I need to pee."

When she returned a few minutes later, the three of them were in the midst of an animated discussion, which ended abruptly when they saw her. "What?"

"What, what?" asked Jules.

"What were you talking about?"

"Nothing important."

Frances knew they'd been gossiping about her barren sex life. So when the server came by she asked for the bill; it was time to bring the night to a close.

Parker offered to drive Geraint home. Frances made him collect his trousers from her trunk first. Jules waited with her until they were gone. "Why did you do that?"

"Why did I do what?" Feigning innocence.

"Jeremy is a family lawyer. A very good one."

"So? There are thousands of good family lawyers out there."

"Who will charge him an arm and a leg."

"No more than Jeremy would."

"Except you could get him to do it for nothing by tapping into his enormous stores of guilt."

Frances took a deep breath. "I know you think I'm being selfish, and that I should be the better person—"

"Yes and yes."

"But he's been visiting my mother behind my back."

Jules fixed her with an incredulous look. "So? She was his mother-in-law. They had a great relationship."

"She's not his mother-in-law anymore."

Jules took a deep breath. "Francy-Pants, I do not like the person you are right now. You are not thinking of your mother's best interests, nor Geraint's, and you know it." Frances opened her mouth, but Jules held up a hand. "I think you're enjoying wallowing in your misery. And it's frankly very unattractive." On that note, Jules abruptly crossed the street and climbed into her car.

Frances mulled her friend's words on the short drive home. She knew Jules wasn't wrong. By the time she let herself into the house, she'd made up her mind to text Jeremy. She would keep it brief; acknowledge she'd overreacted and that she knew it was in Cordelia's best interests for him to keep up his visits. All she would ask in return is that he continue to stick to a schedule, so their paths would never have to cross.

She wandered into the kitchen to make herself a mug of tea. A registered letter was propped up on the counter; Daisy must have signed for it.

She tore it open and skimmed it.

It was a notice of family claim.

Jeremy had finally, officially, filed for divorce.

25

At 8:05 on Saturday morning, Geraint left his apart-hotel in his favourite track suit (the green one, obviously), Mötley Crüe's "Smokin' in the Boys Room" ringing in his ears. Geraint liked his next-door neighbour's taste in music; he just didn't like that it blared at all hours, day or night.

He was determined not to go back to the apartment until his secret scheduled Zoom call with Jules and Parker and Frances's daughter, Daisy, that afternoon. He needed to occupy himself. Doing what, he didn't know. Normally he would be picking up Keanu right about now; it was his weekend. But Darlene (and Ron, he was certain this was all Ron) had quashed that, too.

When he'd arrived home from Bells and Whistles on Thursday night, he'd FaceTimed Keanu like he always did, using Darlene's number like he always did. Keanu had answered, his face so close to the screen he was just a fleshy blur. "Daddy, they're taking me away, but I told them I'm supposed to be with you."

Geraint tried not to show his alarm. "I'm sorry, dear boy, who is taking you away?"

Darlene's face appeared on the screen. "Kee, time for bed, we're getting up bright and early."

"But Daddy's reading me *Phoebe Unknown*."

"I know, darling, and I'm sorry. But I'll read you a different story tonight."

"I want Daddy."

"I know you do, love, but tonight it's going to be me."

"But Daddy reads better. He does the voices."

"Tell you what, if you're a good boy and go upstairs, I'll make you waffles for breakfast, how's that sound?"

"With chocolate chips?"

"With chocolate chips."

That seemed to appease Keanu, because Geraint heard his little feet clomping up the stairs. He waited until he was sure Keanu couldn't hear. "What does he mean, you're taking him away?"

"Ron's taking us to the Chateau Whistler," she said, unable to keep the delight out of her voice. "He's booked us a suite."

"But it's my weekend," he said. "You and Ron can go any time. Or go this weekend, just the two of you. He doesn't want Keanu there anyway."

"Well, he doesn't want Keanu with *you*, Geraint. You brought our child into the home of a known child abuser."

"She is *not* a child abuser. She's a child *assaulter*." Geraint realized as he said it that he wasn't helping his cause. "Darlene, it was one child. And she didn't hit him, she just . . . yelled at him. And shook him a little."

"Listen to yourself."

"She's a children's author, for heaven's sake! She simply had a bad day."

"What if she has another bad day when our child is in her home?"

"Darlene. I know there are all sorts of ways you think I'm lacking. But you *know* I'm a good father. I would never put him in harm's way."

She softened a bit. "I know you wouldn't. But Ron says—"

"Pardon my French, but *eff* Ron. This is all him, isn't it? Applying for sole custody—it's all his idea. Surely you don't think Keanu would be better off without having me in his life?"

She hesitated. "He's just trying to keep us safe."

"Do you really believe that? He's only doing this to make my life hell."

"Geraint, that's ridiculous. You're hurt, I get that. But he's only trying to do what's best for Keanu and me."

"He's a snake, Darlene, a venomous snake."

"Okay, I'm hanging up now."

"It's *my* weekend and he's just as much my child as yours!"

"We're going to Whistler, Geraint. And if I were you, I'd be more focused on your court appearance because you're going to need all the help you can get." The screen went black.

He'd slept poorly that night and the next, and not just because of his heavy-metal-loving neighbour. He'd thought about making plans with a friend to help pass the time, but the only names he could come up with were Frances and Parker, and he was quite certain neither of them needed more Geraint time than they already got. He wasn't as foolish as Frances believed him to be. He'd seen her pained look when he'd asked to tag along to the burger joint on Thursday.

Before he'd gotten married, he'd had a decent circle of friends. But Darlene had made it clear that she didn't like his crowd, so he'd started spending less time with them. Then they'd bought the house and had Keanu, and between raising a small child and doing the renovations, he'd stopped seeing his friends entirely— something he deeply regretted now. The only other person he could think of was Jorge, his former colleague at Quicky Muffler, but he was sure Jorge wouldn't want to come anywhere near him after all that had gone down.

He walked the entirety of the Stanley Park seawall, listening to Joni Mitchell and Jann Arden, which weren't the wisest choices because some of their vocals brought him to tears. He wandered past the towering totem poles, the majestic Lions Gate Bridge, the massive tankers anchored offshore, and the imposing Siwash Rock.

Normally these sights would fill his heart with wonder and awe. But today they barely registered. Even his favourite statue, of Olympic runner Harry Jerome, elicited nothing more than a passing glance.

The circuit took close to three hours. Afterwards he stopped for a late breakfast at De Dutch Pannekoek House, because pancakes always boosted his spirits. Then he popped into the Home Hardware on Davie Street, because who didn't love browsing the crowded shelves of a Home Hardware? He could spend at least half an hour in there. He turned the corner to check out the garden supply aisle, even though he had nothing resembling a garden right now, and there, as if his earlier thoughts had conjured him, was Jorge.

Geraint ducked out of sight. When Jorge had opened his own franchise, well over a year ago, Geraint had missed him terribly. But he didn't want Jorge to see him now. It would be awkward for both of them. Jorge would have heard all the sordid details about Geraint's situation, and he didn't think he could bear seeing the pity in his face, or worse, the disappointment. So he scuttled in the opposite direction, to the paint supplies aisle, and stood there for a few minutes, waiting.

"Geraint?" It was Jorge, standing at the far end of the aisle.

"Oh. Hello, Jorge."

"It's so good to see you, man." Jorge strode up to Geraint and gave him a big hug. Geraint burst into tears.

Jorge insisted on taking him for coffee at Blenz down the street. "I kept meaning to reach out after I heard," he said, "but I dunno, life is so busy with the shop, the kids . . ." He shrugged his broad shoulders. "Lousy excuses, I know."

"Not lousy at all. Completely understandable."

Jorge shook his head. "Fucking Ron. I remember him flirting with your ex at a few work parties. Guy's a pig." He lowered his voice. "Also, so you know, me and the other guys think what you did to his Lamborghini was freaking perfect."

"Would have been more perfect if I hadn't got caught."

Jorge laughed. "Dude, of course you were going to get caught."

"How are Luisa and the boys? Matteo and Diego?"

"They're all good. Truth be told I feel like I barely get to lay eyes on them with the hours I work. I'm telling you, man, you dodged a bullet, not opening a franchise."

"Well, except he owes me my depo—"

But Jorge was on a roll. "I thought it was gonna make my life better, you know? Having to deal with Ron less, being my own boss. But he still manages to get up in your grill. I've been busting my balls for the past year and a half and I'm barely making ends meet."

"Not enough customers?"

"Plenty of customers. I just hadn't factored in how much money goes back to corporate. The monthly invoice is nuts. Feels kinda hinky, but hey. I'm no accountant."

Geraint thought about this. "I'm not either. But I know an almost-accountant. I could ask if he'd have a look."

"Suppose it wouldn't hurt. I have to go in to work later today, I can scan a bunch of stuff and send it your way." Jorge polished off his coffee. "But enough of my shit. How are you? You working?"

Geraint shook his head. "I'm pretty much unemployable at the moment."

"Come work for me," Jorge said. "Soon as you're done your alternative whatchamacallit. I could sure use someone with your commitment and skills."

"You just said you're barely breaking even."

"Yeah, but you're an amazing mechanic. Maybe you'd bring in more business."

Geraint felt a flutter of hope, but only for a moment. "I don't think Ron would like your hiring choice."

Jorge's face fell. "Yeah, I guess you're right." He looked at his phone. "I'm sorry, man, I've gotta run. I'm late to pick up the kids from soccer."

The two men said their goodbyes on the sidewalk. Geraint looked at his Seiko: one o'clock. Two more hours to kill before his Zoom call, then an entire evening to kill after that. He walked the length of Denman Street, arriving eventually at *A-maze-ing Laughter*, the sculptures by Yue Minjun. A group of larger-than-life identical men, all in bronze, all in different poses, laughed with genuine joy, some of them doubled over, others with arms in the air. Geraint loved these sculptures. But today, among them, Geraint broke down. He wept openly and loudly.

A group of tourists gave him a wide berth, except for one elderly woman. She tucked a five-dollar bill into his hand, thinking it was a performance piece.

26

Parker fell asleep just before midnight on Saturday, only to wake with a start at 2 a.m. She lay awake for a couple of hours before finally being pulled under again. It had been her pattern for the past few months. At 9 a.m. she was in a deep sleep when she became aware of Alexei's hands, stroking her back, her bum, her thighs. He wrapped his arms around her and she could feel his heat, his soft skin.

"I need to pee." She hopped out of bed and spent just long enough in the bathroom that by the time she emerged, Alexei was up and making them coffee in the kitchen.

She used to love lazy Sunday morning sex with Alexei. Correction: she used to love sex with Alexei, period. Until the incident with Sebastian, they'd had sex like bonobos. They couldn't get enough of each other. They'd be in the middle of making dinner, or halfway through a Netflix documentary, or brushing their teeth, and have to stop to do the deed. A few times they'd had to make use of a Starbucks washroom. Once they'd even done it in Alexei's parents' garden shed. But now, even though she was still overwhelmingly attracted to Alexei, she felt more like a female panda than a bonobo—seldom in the mood. *Lethargic* was the word that came to mind.

When she entered the tiny kitchen in her unicorn pajamas, Alexei was standing at the counter, making her a latte in just his boxers and undershirt. He wasn't tall but he was ripped, and as

Parker watched him she was overwhelmed yet again with the feeling that she didn't deserve this amazing guy. He had been relentlessly supportive, even though she knew he thought signing the NDA was a huge mistake. As more time passed, she felt that way, too. But he never said a word and she loved him for it, because it was done. There was nothing she could do.

He worked so hard to buoy her spirits. She knew it couldn't be fun, coming home to an unemployed Eeyore day after day. In fact she could see it was taking a toll on him.

Sometimes she wondered how much longer he'd put up with her.

Her phone buzzed. "It's a text from Geraint," she said. "He's hoping to talk to you about looking at some paperwork for a friend of his."

"Sure. Give him my number."

A moment later, Alexei's phone rang; it was Geraint. Parker left them to it and went to the bathroom to brush her teeth; they needed to leave for Frances's house in half an hour. While she was spitting toothpaste into the sink, her phone rang. "Call from: Sharon," said the AI voice.

Reluctantly, Parker picked up. "Hi, Mom."

"*Hola, mi hija. Cómo estás?*"

"I'm fine. How are you?"

"Great." Her mom's voice was rippling with excitement. "I have some interest in my vagina."

That took Parker a moment.

"A gallery owner down here. Another ex-pat. He says he might use my sculptures in an upcoming exhibit."

"Mom, that's amazing."

"You're not the only creative one in this family."

"I never thought I was."

"So listen, I have a small favour . . . The gallery owner—Chuck's his name—he's a huge fan of Sebastian Trevor. Says *Storm Shadows* is one of his all-time favourite movies." Parker felt a pain in her stomach. "I told him you were working with him, and, well, I was thinking, if you could get a signed photo or two and courier them down—it might just grease the wheels, if you know what I mean."

Parker took a deep breath. "I don't work on the show anymore."

". . . Sorry, what?"

"I don't work on the show anymore."

"You're kidding. Why not?" Before Parker could respond, Sharon continued: "Parker, baby girl, what did you do? Was it your verbal diarrhea? Because we've talked about that a million times."

Parker lay back on the pillows and closed her eyes. She was dying to tell her mom the truth, to shout it to her. But even if she could, she had the awful feeling that Sharon would still find a way to blame her, and Parker was doing a pretty good job of that herself. "It wasn't that. They just had to make some cuts. And you know what they say. Last one in, first one out."

"Yes, but if you'd made yourself indispensable . . ."

"Good luck with your vaginas, Sharon. I have to run."

Parker hung up. It was the first time she'd ever hung up on her mom.

When it was time to leave, Alexei had to drag her off the bed.

27

'm so sorry, Frances," said Jules as they jogged through the Endowment Lands. They were now up to two minutes of running, one minute of walking. "I mean, we knew it was coming, but it still stings." Her watch beeped and they started to walk.

"I don't know why it's upset me so much. I suppose it's the finality of it."

"What are you going to do?"

"For now? Nothing. I have thirty days to respond."

"So, you'll respond on day thirty?"

"Perhaps day twenty-nine, if I'm feeling generous."

"You're naughty."

"And Jules?"

"Yes?"

"I'm going to try, okay?"

"Try what?"

"To stop wallowing."

Jules's watch beeped, and they started running again. "Well, thank Christ for that," she said.

When they got back to Frances's house, Jules invited herself in for coffee. "I can whip up some breakfast," said Frances as they kicked off their running shoes and headed for the kitchen.

Frances stopped at the entrance. Daisy was seated at the kitchen table, along with Geraint, Parker, and Alexei. They were eating from a big spread that, judging from the bags, someone had picked up from Siegel's Bagels. Daisy's laptop was open in front of her. "Um, hello. Why are you all in my kitchen?"

"We need to talk to you," said Jules, suddenly all business. She pulled a chair out and motioned to Frances. "Sit."

Frances did not sit. "Guys"—Daisy cleared her throat loudly— "*folx*, this has a strange intervention-type vibe." No one corrected her. "Okay, have I been drinking rather excessively the past number of months? Yes. But I've cut back a lot lately."

"That's not why we're here," said Daisy.

"And actually, I'm just here because Parker and I don't get to see each other much during the week," said Alexei sheepishly.

"We're concerned about your inability to move forward," said Jules. "You're stuck."

"And morose. And bitter and depressed. Oh, and sometimes maudlin," added Daisy.

"So, this is an intervention to criticize my personality?"

"I like your personality, Frances," said Parker.

"So do I," said Geraint cheerfully. Bagel crumbs and poppy seeds littered his red track suit. "Most of the time."

"This isn't about changing your personality," said Jules. "It's about getting you unstuck."

"Didn't I just tell you, I'm going to try to stop wallowing?" said Frances.

"You did. And that's terrific. Because what we've done is our way of helping you begin that journey."

Frances looked at them, suddenly uneasy. "What have you done?"

"We've set up a dating profile for you on Silver Solos," said Daisy.

"You did not."

"We did. It went live last night."

Frances stared at them, incredulous. "You did—without my—when??"

"We had a Zoom call yesterday," said Daisy.

"A *Zoom* call? My dating life is none of your business!"

"No, it isn't," said Jules, "but your happiness is, and it breaks our collective heart to see you so miserable most of the time."

"I am not miserable most of the time." Five sets of eyes stared skeptically back at her, six if you counted Mr. Pickles, who sat purring on Alexei's lap. "And it's rather offensive that you think a new man might be the answer to my misery, especially while I'm still grieving the loss of a twenty-five-year marriage."

"This isn't about finding a replacement," said Jules. "It's about getting you back out there again. Regaining some self-confidence."

"Maybe making a new friend or two," added Geraint.

"Getting laid," said Daisy bluntly.

"You don't have to be looking for Mr. Right," said Jules. "Just . . . Mr. Right Now."

Frances crossed her arms. "No. Hard no. You need to take it down immediately."

"You've had five matches already," said Daisy.

Five matches. For a moment Frances felt an old, familiar flutter that took her back to seventh grade, when a friend of hers had told her that Cameron Fowler thought she was cute. Frances, who'd felt hideous and undesirable with her flat chest and braces, had felt the flutter then. Till she'd found out a few days later from Cameron himself that he thought she was cute "the way a snaggle-toothed chihuahua is cute. So fugly it's adorable."

Flutter-feelings could be dangerous.

"We haven't looked at the matches," Jules said. "We thought we should wait for you."

"That's when your ethics kicked in?"

"Aren't you curious?" asked Geraint. "I know I am!"

Of course she was curious.

She pulled up a chair.

Jules had chosen her profile photo: a head shot of Frances down at the beach after one of their runs, laughing. "Ugh, I'm perspiring! And I'm not wearing any makeup."

"You want matches to be attracted to the real you," said Jules.

"Exactly. You look gorgeous and authentic," said Parker.

"And look at those biceps," added Daisy.

Frances felt secretly delighted. She read her bio aloud. "*I'm a self-employed woman in my mid-fifties. I love swimming and hate running, but I force myself to do it anyway. I enjoy dinner parties, travel, and word games (my day gets off to a terrible start if I don't get to 'genius' in Spelling Bee). I'm a voracious reader. I've been told I have a sharp tongue, but a kind heart.*"

"I suggested that sentence," said Geraint, pleased with himself.

"*I'm looking for someone who leans towards optimism, has a good sense of humour, likes to stay physically and mentally active, and enjoys socializing and having new experiences.* Bit generic, if you ask me."

"We're not all writers," said Jules.

"Okay," said Daisy, "are we ready for the fun part?" She clicked on the first match.

First up was Marcus. He had a generic profile photo—dark hair (possibly thanks to Grecian Formula), a bland face, and perhaps the beginnings of a double chin, although it was hard to tell from the angle. They scrolled through the rest of his shots, most of which featured him holding fish.

"Oh my god, who does that anymore?" groaned Daisy.

"Also, I can't help but notice he has the bulbous nose of an alcoholic," added Geraint. "My father, may he rest in peace, had a very similar schnozz."

"Next," Jules pronounced.

Piotr looked more promising. He had a head of salt-and-pepper grey hair, piercing blue eyes, and a slender build. In a few photos he appeared to be wearing some sort of military uniform. "He's kind of cute," said Parker.

"He's a follower of Odinism." Alexei pointed at a caption under one of his photos.

"What's Odinism?" asked Geraint.

"A form of neo-paganism that attracts white supremacists," said Alexei.

"Next," said Jules.

Next was Arthur.

"Oh, that's unfortunate," said Geraint with a wince as they studied his profile photo.

"He looks like a potato with legs," said Parker.

"A very old, wrinkly potato," said Daisy.

"It says in his bio he's looking for someone to help him around the house," said Jules. "Code for nurse with a purse. Next."

Lionel was decent-looking. They scrolled through his photos and read his bio, which was generic and uninspired. "A possibility?" asked Jules.

"I don't know," said Daisy. "He mentions his *love language*." She and Parker both made a face.

"I think that sounds sweet," said Geraint.

"It's a seriously overused buzzword," said Daisy.

"And see what's in the background of his profile photo," said Alexei. Daisy zoomed in on the image and they all leaned in for a closer look.

"The old Benny's Bagels on Broadway," said Frances.

"That building got torn down almost ten years ago," said Alexei. "Meaning these photos are super old."

Geraint high-fived Alexei. "Good detective work, my friend." Alexei beamed.

"Okay," said Jules. "Fifth and final. Remember, Frances—these are early days."

"Exactly," said Daisy. "Don't lose heart if the first batch isn't to your liking—"

"Just click on it," said Frances. "Let's get it over with."

When Keith's profile photo appeared onscreen, everyone said a collective "Ooooh."

"Hello, Keith," said Jules. "You have a beautiful smile."

"Silver fox," murmured Daisy.

"He's good-looking without being *too* good-looking," said Parker, and Geraint and Alexei nodded in agreement.

Frances was annoyed that yet again she felt a flutter of excitement. "Anyone can choose one good photo. Let's see the rest."

In one shot he was skiing. In another he stood in front of the Eiffel Tower. In a third, he was in a kayak, and in a fourth, he was wearing a business suit. There were no selfies, no fish photos, no shirtless photos, no photos taken in bed. "*I'm a fifty-eight-year-old financial planner,*" Alexei read aloud. "*I love the great outdoors, but I also love going to the ballet, or enjoying a quiet night at home watching Netflix. I'm looking for a woman who likes to seize the day, and who, like me, wants companionship and hopefully more.*"

"You should send him a message," said Parker.

"Based on what? His bio is awfully generic. Besides, I wouldn't know what to say."

Daisy rolled her eyes. "How about, *Hello?*"

Frances shook her head. "I need some time to think about it—" Beside her, Daisy started typing. "What are you doing?" She saw Daisy hit the return key. "Daisy. You wouldn't—"

"I would. And I did."

"You are awful!" Then: "What did you say?"

"I said, *Hi Keith, it's Frances. I see we're a match.*"

Frances's stomach clenched. "Okay, this is certifiably horrible. It's worse than being back in high school."

"Mom, relax. Sometimes they respond, sometimes they don't. You can't take it personally."

"Easy for you to say."

"If he doesn't respond, there will be more matches," said Jules. "This is only your first day on the site—"

Ping.

The room went quiet. Frances peered over her daughter's shoulder. Daisy read his response out loud: "*Frances, I was hoping you'd message me.*" Parker and Geraint actually clapped. "*How has your day been so far?*" Daisy pushed her laptop towards Frances. "Now it's your turn."

Frances thought for a moment. Eventually she typed:

Day not bad. Went for a run with my best friend. More plod than run.

He responded quickly:

I used to run a lot. Until my knees rebelled and said no.

The trick is to start in your fifties, like I did. ☺

Ha-ha, smart. Tell me more about yourself.

I'm divorced. Two grown kids.

Frances smiled.

Ditto.

And so it began.

28

Do your children make you feel like a fossil all the time?

God, yes, Frances typed. My daughter thinks people over fifty should have their tongues surgically remov—

"Frances, are you listening?" asked Dennis. He stood over her desk. Tonight's cheap suit was a shimmery mucous green.

"Yes, Dennis, of course."

"What was I saying?"

"You were saying . . . anger, bad?"

Dennis sighed. "No, Frances, that's *not* what I was saying. And also, anger isn't a *bad* emotion, it's a very useful emotion. It's how we *deal* with anger that we're here to work on. Now, kindly put away your phone. Participation counts for everything in this class."

Frances defiantly typed *ed* and pressed send before she slipped her phone into her purse.

She and Keith had been texting off and on like this for a few days. And she had to admit, she hadn't felt this giddy and alive in a long time.

"On that note," Dennis said as he returned to the front of the class, "some of you may think that in trying to manage your anger, you can't stand up for yourselves or express a strong emotion. Nothing could be further from the truth. What we want to do is learn to stand up for ourselves without"—he wrote AGGRESSION in large letters on the board and underlined it three times—"but instead with"—he wrote ASSERTIVENESS on the board and underlined it three times.

"He really loves doing that," Geraint whispered from his seat behind Frances.

"Let's break into your smaller groups. I want you to ask each other these questions." Dennis passed around a sheet of paper. "And try to answer them honestly."

Byron and Wayson pushed their desks together at the back. Frances, Geraint, and Parker formed their triangle near the front. "Were you texting Keith?" Parker asked.

Frances nodded.

"It's so exciting!"

"You must be dying to meet him," said Geraint.

"No, not really."

"Why not?" asked Parker.

"Because there's a strong chance that reality will be a disappointment. This way it can stay fun. And no one gets hurt."

"That is a very pessimistic attitude," said Geraint.

Frances cut him off. "Yes, it is," she said cheerily. "More important, have you found a lawyer?"

Geraint smiled. "As a matter of fact, I have."

Relief washed over Frances. "That's great news."

"Best of all, he isn't going to cost me a penny."

"Even better! Who did you get?"

He pointed two thumbs at himself. "This guy!"

"Geraint, you're not . . ."

"Representing myself? I am!"

Good god, thought Frances.

Parker pursed her lips. "Are you sure that's a good idea?"

"Well, legal aid is backed up, so this is what I can afford if I want to get this dealt with quickly; therefore it will have to do. And I've been doing my research. It seems pretty straightforward. I simply file a response. Then as far as I can tell from my Google search, we'll get a hearing date—"

Parker cleared her throat. "Dennis, my ten o'clock."

Frances picked up the sheet of paper. "Geraint, let's start with you. *Do you struggle with decision making?*"

"Do I struggle with decision making . . . No." Then: "At least, I don't think I do. Or maybe I do . . . I guess I do . . . or do I? Aaaagh, that's a tough one!"

Frances and Parker shared a look. "*Do you struggle to speak up if someone interrupts you?*"

"No, I don't think I—"

"I had an omelette for dinner last night," Frances interrupted.

"Sounds yummy," said Geraint. "I had—"

"Alexei made us spaghetti with meatballs," said Parker.

"Mmm, meatballs," he said with a grin.

Frances stared hard at Geraint. "Do you see what just happened?"

"Yes," he said. Then: "No."

"You let us both interrupt you," said Parker.

"Ohhhhh. Clever!"

"*Do you say 'sorry' a lot, even when you have nothing to be sorry for?*" Frances read.

"I don't think I do," said Geraint, just as Frances pushed over his water bottle, spilling some of the liquid onto his lap. "Oops, sorry! So sorry!" He grabbed the bottle and set it upright. Frances pushed it over again. "Sorry—ah, okay. I see what you did there."

"*Do you let others push their work onto you?*"

"Well, yes. Ron was always giving me more work because he knew I'd never say no."

"*Do you let people make fun of you?*"

"Sometimes. But is that always a bad thing? Isn't it good to be able to laugh at yourself?"

"I think it depends on whether or not you find it funny or hurtful," said Parker.

"Ron did make a lot of jokes about my appearance. And my intelligence, or lack thereof."

"Why do you think you let him?" asked Frances.

Geraint shrugged. "It was just easier that way. I'm a very non-confrontational person. And Ron's an Alpha. He likes to win, even if he doesn't want the prize."

Dennis approached. "How are things going here?"

"We've discovered that Geraint's a pushover who needs to learn to stand up for himself," said Frances.

"Without . . ." Dennis said leadingly.

"Aggression," said Parker.

"And with . . ."

"Assertiveness," the three of them said in unison.

Dennis clapped his hands, delighted. "Excellent! We'll be working on ways to help you with that next week. In the meantime, let's all take a fifteen-minute break."

Frances immediately checked her phone. Keith had texted her back.

My son once told me I was redundant.

Frances texted back: Sorry for the slow response. I take a . . . *Don't lie,* she told herself . . . night school course on Wednesdays.

Ah. I thought you'd decided I was redundant.

LOL no.

My son also tells me no one uses LOL anymore. LOL.

Frances was trying to think of a response when Keith texted again.

Can we meet in person?

Oh god.

Tomorrow night if you're free? I know a good wine bar.

She stared at her phone.

All this texting is giving me a repetitive strain injury. ☺

She kept staring at her phone.

Frances, you still there?

When Parker and Geraint returned with their vending machine snacks a moment later, Frances still sat clutching her phone, frozen with indecision. She didn't even take a Hawkins Cheezie when Geraint offered her one, which was Geraint's first sign that something was very wrong. "What is it? Are you okay?"

"Keith wants to meet in person."

"That's great," said Parker.

"No. It's not great. I think I should—what's the word—ghost him."

"Why on earth would you do that?" asked Geraint.

Because it's easy to be witty when you have time to craft a response. Because I'm terrified I'll see the disappointment in his eyes. Because I don't think I can bear being rejected, not after everything I've been through. I would have to kill myself and make it look like an accident so my children wouldn't bear the psychological scars of a mother who'd committed suicide—

Parker interrupted her reverie. "I totally get it if you're nervous."

"Of course I'm nervous. I haven't been on a date in *thirty years*."

"Wow. That's longer than I've been alive!" said Parker, earning herself the stink-eye from Frances. "Look, don't think of it as a date. Think of it as a meet-'n'-greet. Limit it to one drink. That's what I did when I was on Tinder. If we weren't connecting, I was out of there in half an hour. You can talk to anyone for half an hour."

Frances thought about this. On the whole, it was probably true. But then another thought occurred to her. "What if he's seen the video?"

"Have you shared your last names?" asked Parker.

"Yes."

"Did you immediately google him?"

"Yes—oh god."

"Exactly. High probability he's seen it. But, Frances, this is good news, because he still wants to meet you."

"But that automatically makes me think there's something wrong with him. *I* wouldn't want to meet me if I saw that video."

"You're overthinking it," said Geraint, who now had a ring of orange Cheezie dust around his mouth. "Most people who watch it see a woman who was having a bad day. That's what I thought."

Geraint's words made her feel better. "Do I have to tell him about . . . ?" She waved her hand around the room.

"If he brings it up, be honest," said Parker. "But if he doesn't, you don't need to tell him. Not yet."

Frances felt reassured. "Thank you, Parker," she said, meaning it.

"Ask yourself this: What's the worst thing that could happen?"

"He turns out to be a scammer who drugs me, kills me, and drains my bank accounts," Frances said with no hesitation.

Geraint looked alarmed. "Oh goodness, I *have* read about cases like that."

"Class is back in session." Dennis walked into the room with a Diet Coke. "Phones away." He stared at Frances, who still clutched hers in both hands.

Before she tossed her phone back into her purse, she quickly fired off one last text.

Okay. One drink.

She comforted herself with the thought that if he did drug her, kill her, and drain her bank accounts, at least her obituary would no longer lead with the infamous video.

29

Frances had been standing under the awning of the False Creek wine bar for at least five minutes. The rain was coming down in sheets. Her hair, never her strong point, was a frizzy mess.

She'd agonized over her outfit like a teenager, trying on multiple combinations before circling back to her old standby: a beloved off-white cashmere V-neck sweater and a pair of black jeans, coupled with her pair of short black boots (one of only two pairs of footwear she owned that Daisy hadn't denounced as "old lady shoes").

Speaking of Daisy, she hadn't dared ask her for fashion advice, for two reasons: one, she didn't think she could bear Daisy's overly critical eye, and two . . . she hadn't told Daisy she was going on a date. She hadn't told Jules, either. The only people who knew were Geraint and Parker. Keeping it quiet had been a conscious decision on her part; if things went sideways, she would only have to tell the story once. No one else would ever need to know.

Her phone started to buzz. She pulled it out of her purse, convinced that it was Keith, cancelling their date at the last minute. But it was Jeremy again. He'd been calling once a day since he'd filed for divorce. And she'd been ignoring those calls. She told herself she wasn't wallowing; her energies were simply focused elsewhere.

She looked at her watch: six minutes past their designated meeting time. Parker had told her, "You don't want to get there first. Five to seven minutes late is perfect, because it hasn't crossed over into inconsiderate yet, but it also gives you a chance to see if *he* is considerate: Did he make an effort to show up on time? And for the record, if he *still* isn't there at quarter past, get up and leave. If he's that late without texting or phoning you with a really good excuse, he's a jerk." Parker had been full of pearls of wisdom like this. "Keep talk of your ex to a minimum. This is about the present, not the past. And if all he can talk about is *his* ex, cut the evening short and leave because he is *not* ready to date. Oh, and don't show him photos of Mr. Pickles, not on the first date." Frances was exhausted by the time Parker was done, but also deeply impressed. She also realized that Parker had spoken with self-assuredness and hadn't made any of her statements sound like questions.

Seven minutes past the designated meeting time, Frances took a deep breath in and let a deep breath out. Then she opened the door and walked in.

The wine bar was dimly lit, the tables and chairs in blond wood. She spotted him immediately. He was at a table halfway back, in a button-up shirt and casual navy blazer. She was pleased to see that he looked mostly like his pictures. Better still, he smiled warmly when he saw her—there wasn't a flicker of disappointment on his face.

He stood, and she had a moment to register that he was softer around the middle than she'd imagined. Then again, he was probably noticing inconsistencies in her, too. Overall, he came as advertised. "Frances, hello." They gave each other an awkward, quick hug and she caught a noseful of strong aftershave. *Small thing,*

Frances. Let it go. She sat down across from him, and they started to talk.

And talk.

". . . My story is as old as time, I suppose. Once both our kids had left the house my wife and I looked at each other and realized we had nothing in common."

"Was it amicable?"

"Yes and no. I think people who say their divorces were amicable are either lying or seeing the past through rose-coloured glasses. But overall it wasn't too bad. We can be in the same room if we absolutely have to." He had a sip of his Merlot. "How about you and your ex?"

"Not so amicable, I'm afraid. It ended rather spectacularly." He looked at her inquisitively. "He told me he'd been having an affair for a few months. With a man. So it was a lot to process."

"Wow. No kidding."

"To be honest, it's possibly too early for me to be doing this"— she indicated the two of them—"but my friends . . ."

"Ah, yes. The well-meaning friends." He looked her in the eye. "I'm glad they pushed."

Frances felt a jolt in her nethers.

"Oh my god, are you Frances Partridge?" The voice at Frances's elbow was very familiar. "Because you're my favourite author of all time." A dog-eared copy of *Phoebe Unknown* landed on the table, along with a pen. "Would you mind signing this?" Frances looked up to see Parker, her hair in two Pippi Longstocking–like pigtails, her orange faux fur coat draped over her arm.

Frances didn't play along. "Keith, this is Parker, one of my well-meaning friends, and I made the mistake of telling her where we'd be tonight."

Parker gave Keith an unabashedly cheerful wave.

"Hi, Parker," said Keith.

Frances pivoted in her seat and scanned the bar. Sure enough, Geraint sat a few tables back, trying to hide behind a menu. "Excuse me a moment." She slid off her chair, grabbed Parker's arm, and marched her over to Geraint, grabbing the menu out of his hands. "What do you two think you're doing?"

"Don't be angry," said Geraint. "When I got home the other night I punched 'drugging, killing, dates' into Google and, goodness gracious, there were a *lot* of articles. I just wanted to see the man with my own eyes. And possibly follow you both if you decided to go home with him, just so I'd know exactly where to tell the police to start their search if you disappeared."

"And I just wanted to pump you up," said Parker.

"Are you very mad?" asked Geraint.

She sighed. "Mad? No. Exasperated, yes." She motioned to them both. "Come on." They followed her back to Keith's table. "Keith, you've met Parker. This is Geraint, another of my well-meaning friends. He just wanted to make sure you weren't a con artist or a murderer."

"I guess you'll never know for sure," joked Keith, but his grin died under Geraint's glower. "How can I put your mind at ease?"

"I'd like to see a valid piece of photo ID."

"Geraint, for heaven's sake," said Frances.

"Not a problem." Keith pulled out his wallet and handed Geraint his driver's licence. Geraint borrowed Parker's pen and made a show of writing Keith's information down on a cocktail napkin.

"And now it's time for you both to leave," said Frances.

"But I was about to order the deep-fried pickles," Geraint started.

"Go," said Frances.

They went.

When they were gone, Frances exhaled loudly. "I'm so sorry about that."

"Are you kidding? You have amazing friends who clearly think the world of you."

I do, she thought with surprise.

"How do you know them?"

Frances hesitated. She could obfuscate. She could say, "Oh, just around," or, "They're in my night school class."

Instead she told him the whole truth and nothing but.

"So, if you want to just settle the bill and never see me again, I completely understand," she said when she was done.

Keith smiled. "I don't scare that easily. And since we're being honest . . . I'd already seen the video."

"Parker figured as much."

He reached across the table and put his hand over hers. "It's fine, Frances. You had one really bad day, and you clearly regret what you did. I wouldn't be here if it bothered me."

They stayed for a second glass of wine. He suggested a third but, not wanting to get ahead of herself, and wanting to stay in some form of control, she declined. They left the bar together. He waited with her in the rain until her Uber showed up.

"I'd like to see you again," he said.

"I'd like to see you again, too."

"How about this weekend? I could cook you dinner at my place."

It only took her a moment to respond. "I'd like that." Her Uber pulled up. "Goodnight, Keith."

"Goodnight, Frances." He gave her a soft kiss on the lips. Her inner voice said, *Ugh, that aftershave.*

But also, *God, his lips feel so good.*

30

ow could you not tell us? I'm your best friend!" Jules sat across from Frances on the patio at The Ellis, in what Daisy referred to as "the cool part of Kitsilano." Because it was a beautiful April day, they'd decided to go for brunch after their Saturday run, and Daisy, fresh from a yoga class, had joined them. She sat beside her auntie Jules, looking indignant.

"And I'm your daughter!"

"Sorry! I didn't want to have to tell you if it went sideways."

"But we're here for you under any and all circumstances—*especially* if it goes sideways," said Jules. "We are your pillars of support."

"*And* you told Geraint and Parker," pouted Daisy.

"Only because they were there when he asked me out." Frances had a sip of her water. "Now, do you want to keep chastising me, or do you want to know everything?"

"I believe the answer to that question is obvious," said Jules.

So Frances told them about her evening. She told them about his warm smile, their easy banter. She also told them about his cloying aftershave ("Poor soul, he probably had no idea," said Jules) and his trend towards doughiness ("Well, it gets harder to stay trim as you age," said Daisy, adding, "Look at you"). "And now he's invited me to dinner. At his place. Tonight."

Daisy actually squealed. "Oh my god, Mom's gonna get laid."

"Please don't say that," she said, even though it was all she'd thought about for the past two days—the possibility of where the evening might lead.

"You'll be fine. It isn't something you unlearn," said Jules.

"It's like riding a bike," said Daisy.

Then Jules added, just as the server arrived with their California bennies: "And if you're lucky, the bike will give you a fabulous orgasm." Jules and Daisy cackled with laughter as the server beat a hasty retreat.

Frances wanted to die. "I'm glad you both find this so amusing. But I have ridden only one bike for over twenty-five years. I got very used to that bike. The position, the way it rode." She dug into her food. "Truth be told, I've only ridden a few bikes in my entire life."

Daisy made a sad face. "That is so tragic, Mom." She popped a hash brown into her mouth and grinned devilishly. "I've ridden loads of bikes. Most with crossbars, but a few step-throughs."

"Even I rode a few crossbars back in the day," Jules said through a mouthful of eggs.

"What are you going to wear?" asked Daisy.

"I don't know. I was thinking maybe casual, like jeans and a blouse?"

"Just not your mom jeans."

"No, I was thinking of the dark blue ones."

"Those *are* your mom jeans."

"I think you should consider a dress," said Jules. "Nothing too fancy or overly sexy—"

"But just sexy enough," said Daisy.

". . . I have that Eileen Fisher sheath."

"No!" they said in unison. "No Eileen Fisher!"

"Tell you what, when we're done here, we'll stop by Twist Fashions," said Jules.

"I can't. I am literally earning zero dollars aside from the odd royalty cheque."

"It will be my treat," said Jules. "An early birthday gift." She could see Frances was about to protest. "I'm doing this. End of discussion. Now, what's your underwear situation?"

Frances shovelled some avocado and egg into her mouth and pretended to take a great interest in all the gorgeous young things in Lululemon who jogged, cycled, rollerbladed, and scootered by. "Fine."

"Liar," said Daisy. She turned to Jules. "Her bras are beige and threadbare. And she has granny underwear. I think she buys all her stuff in bulk at Walmart."

"I do not," said Frances stiffly. "I buy them in bulk at Costco."

Jules groaned. "When is the last time you bought new ones?"

"I don't know. Five years? Seven?"

Jules shook her head in bewilderment and pity. "Oh, Frances. What is *wrong* with you?"

"What is wrong with *you*? You'd think I'd just told you I like to torture small animals."

Jules put down her knife and fork. "Okay, I'm also taking you to Diane's Lingerie this afternoon. You will buy yourself a new bra and a few new pairs of panties." Frances was about to protest. "Think of it as an investment in your future. Oh, and you also need to book a wax."

"Hundred percent," said Daisy.

"How would either of you know if I need to book a wax?"

"We've been to the beach with you. We've been on holiday with you," said Jules. "It's like you have a woolly mammoth grazing on your vagina."

"I was going to say it's like Grizzly Adams is camped out on her vagina," said Daisy, "but your analogy is better."

The server returned to collect their plates, just in time to hear Jules say: "Seriously, it's amazing you can contain it in your swimsuit. Your bush is like a giant stationary tumbleweed."

Frances thought she might spontaneously combust from embarrassment. "I can't believe you two. Daisy, you've told me countless times the entire beauty industry is a misogynistic sham, created by male-run corporations to make women feel ashamed of their bodies so they spend millions on useless products."

"All true. But Mother, there are exceptions. Like, kids born with harelips, or other facial deformities, should have access to cosmetic surgery."

"You're comparing my pubic hair to a deformity?"

Daisy shrugged.

"You two are being downright cruel."

"Sometimes, Frances, you have to be cruel to be kind," said Jules.

"So you think I should be like a prepubescent teenage girl down there? That goes against everything I, and I would have thought you, stand for!"

"That isn't at all what we're saying," said Daisy. "Just—bring it down a notch."

"Less woolly mammoth," said Jules. "More . . . marmot." That set them both off into fits of hysterical laughter again. Frances did not join in.

But although their teasing stung, she was grateful for their guidance. She felt completely overwhelmed, anxious, and unprepared. It made everything less nerve-wracking to give herself over to their advice; at least now she had a clear agenda, with practical steps to take.

Daisy headed off to meet friends after brunch, and Jules took Frances to Twist on West 4th. They found a perfect teal blue wool dress that was just the right amount of sexy and looked great with Frances's hair. Next they stopped at Diane's Lingerie on South Granville, where Frances, with the help of a wonderful saleswoman, purchased the prettiest—and definitely most expensive—bra and panty set she'd ever owned in her entire life.

Jules drove her back to Broadway and Macdonald. "You're on

your own now, grasshopper. There are loads of waxing places along here. Just look for one that's busy."

Frances hopped out of the car with her shopping bags. "Thank you, dear Jules."

"I'll be sending you all the good vibes." Jules blew her a kiss and drove away.

In her fifty-five years on this planet, Frances had never waxed any part of her body, which she supposed might make her eligible for inclusion in the *Guinness Book of World Records*. But when she was younger it just wasn't a thing, at least not that she was aware of. She remembered the first time she'd shaved her legs, she'd included her thighs because she didn't know any better. And she remembered trying a depilatory once that stank to high heaven of deadly chemicals and felt like it was burning off her skin. By the time waxing was a thing, or at least a thing that she knew about, she and Jeremy had been married for a number of years and it had never even occurred to her to put herself through that kind of torment.

She wandered for a while, finally settling on an unassuming, tiny shop. It wasn't busy, far from it, but the prices were cheaper than the other ones she'd passed. Frances reasoned that, especially after her bra and undie purchase, she needed to be budget-conscious, and surely one wax was as good as the next.

A woman whose nametag read Vera was behind the counter when she entered. "What do you want?"

Frances stared at her blankly.

"Bikini, French Bikini, Brazilian, Between the Cheeks . . ."

"Bikini," said Frances, because it sounded the least invasive.

Vera hustled her into a small, nondescript room at the back and gave her a paper sheet. "Take off your clothes from the waist down." Then she left.

Frances did as she was told and lay under the paper sheet in the closet-sized sterile room, gazing at the water-stained gypsum ceiling. A few minutes later Vera returned and unceremoniously pulled back the sheet. Then she replaced the sheet and left the room.

Frances was confused. Was this normal? A moment later Vera returned with another woman, possibly her boss. Vera pulled back the sheet again and together they examined Frances's pubic region while speaking rapidly in Vietnamese. The second woman eventually left. "My manager," said Vera. "I showed her because this is a big job. Costs extra, okay?"

"Um . . . okay," said Frances, because she felt incredibly vulnerable lying on a table with her muff on full display and she just wanted to get it over with.

A few minutes later, Vera poured warm wax on Frances's thighs and parts of her pubic area. It felt wonderful. They waited while the wax hardened.

"This is gonna sting a little." Vera tore the now-hardened wax from her thigh.

It wasn't child-birth-level pain. But it was a lot more than "a little sting." Vera ripped the next piece of wax off, then the next. It was sharp, searing. By the time she finished, Frances was whimpering, tears of pain leaking down her face.

Finally it was over. Frances felt like she'd just run ten kilometres at top speed with wasps stinging her thighs along the way. She was breathless, exhausted.

"Okay," said Vera. "We're gonna take a short break. Then we'll do another round to get the rest of it."

At 7:05, Frances rode up to the nineteenth floor of a Yaletown condo that overlooked False Creek. Her thighs were still rather tender, but she felt good in her new lingerie and dress. It was thinking about possibly removing them later that made her feel sick.

When she stepped off the elevator, Keith poked his head out of a unit down the hall. "Frances, hello." With a familiar fluttering in her chest, she headed towards him. He looked handsome in a black sweater and jeans. He gave her a kiss on the cheek, and she smelled the cloying aftershave again. *If we continue to see each other, I can gently broach the subject.*

He beckoned her inside, taking her coat and the bottle of wine she proffered. "Beautiful dress," he said. "Let me get you a drink."

She wandered over to the floor-to-ceiling windows, trying to calm her nerves. The view was spectacular; lights from the sailboats moored in the creek reflected off the water's surface. The living room itself was generic, and the decor screamed of someone who'd had to start from scratch with little design sense. Two pictures hung on the walls: one was a large photo of English Bay, the other, a silhouette of a moose.

Keith joined her at the windows and handed her a glass of red wine. "It's a Cab Sauv from California," he told her. "One of my favourites. And I've made us a lasagna. My son would say that's a little retro, but it's one thing I know how to do well." He clinked her glass with his own.

Frances had a large mouthful.

When it was time to eat dinner, she had to force down the food. It wasn't the taste, which was fine if a bit bland; it was her nerves, and the worry that *if* they got naked later she didn't want to be bloated and gassy. Their conversation was a bit more stilted this time, perhaps because they were both thinking about where the evening might lead. He told her about his work as a financial planner, and Frances had to force her eyes not to glaze over. When there was a lull in the conversation she said, "Tell me about your favourite places in Paris." She'd been to Paris many times, both on holiday with Jeremy and also to promote her novels when they were translated into French. Oh, how she'd loved those trips, allowing herself to get lost on the side streets, buying herself one indulgent *pâtisserie* per day; she especially loved the late-night dinners with her chain-smoking publisher, eating too much rich French food and drinking too much wonderful French wine, and conversing until the wee hours. *Maybe the French won't cancel me*, she suddenly thought; they had a much higher tolerance for some forms of bad behaviour.

Keith looked at her, puzzled. "I've never been to Paris."

"Yes, you have. The photo on Silver Solos."

"Oh," he laughed. "That's not Paris, that's Vegas. I was down there for a conference."

"Oh. Ha ha."

"I did go to Europe once, with my ex. Bus tour. Six countries in ten days. Exhausting!"

Frances told herself she was being ridiculous for feeling disappointed. So he didn't travel as much as she did, or in the way she did. Was she that much of a snob that she'd let that bother her? *Small potatoes!*

But when he excused himself to go to the washroom, she poured herself another glass of wine and gulped it down before he returned.

She helped him clear the dishes. It was while they were rinsing plates that Keith leaned in and properly kissed her. His tongue probed her mouth, a little too greedily perhaps, but it still sent jolts of electricity to her groin. He pulled her close, ran his hands up her back and squeezed her bum. She could feel his erection through his jeans. "Let's leave the dishes for later, shall we?" he said.

He took her hand and pulled her towards the bedroom.

Well, she thought as she lay naked on Keith's bed exactly seven minutes later, she'd done it. She'd had sex with someone other than Jeremy.

There hadn't been a lot of foreplay, which meant it had hurt quite a bit when he entered her because she was still dry. And it was far from inventive: missionary style from start to finish (approximately three of those seven minutes), *pump-a, pump-a, pump-a.* And the sounds he made were disconcerting, best described as *bleats.* The moment he was done he'd collapsed on top of her with his full weight. Then he'd gotten up and headed to the bathroom. So he clearly wasn't going to reciprocate. Even Jeremy had always been good about making sure she had an orgasm, too. It was true he hadn't gone down on her for years and years, but he'd known how to use his fingers and that had sufficed.

But, hey, it was their first time. Surely the next time would be better. And regardless of the quality, *she'd done it.* Sex with a new man, after thirty years! She lifted her arms in the air and gave herself a high-five, just as Keith farted loudly in the bathroom.

A moment later he stepped out, wearing a robe, a grin on his face. He sauntered—no, it was more of a strut, he was *strutting like a peacock*—up to the bed and kissed her forehead. "I want to show you something. I think you're really going to like it." He left the room, and Frances got up to pee and clean herself. Sitting on the bathroom counter was a prescription bottle of Viagra. She guessed he'd taken one when he'd gone to the washroom during dinner.

When she came out of the bathroom he still wasn't back. She wasn't sure what to do. Should she put her clothes back on? Should she get back into bed? Was she staying the night? Did she *want* to stay the night? She didn't think she did. She'd just pulled on her sexy new underwear when he returned and dropped a heavy plastic bag onto the bed with a *thwunk.*

He grinned. "Go on. Check it out."

Frances peered inside. It was a towering stack of paper. She saw, printed on the first page, the words: *Mutiny of Fire*.

No. He wouldn't.

"My manuscript."

Oh god. He would.

"I've been working on it in my spare time for the past couple of years. Eight hundred and sixty-two pages. After I found out you were an author—it just felt like serendipity."

Frances felt light-headed and extremely vulnerable in her almost-naked state. "Did it, now."

"I've given it to a couple of friends to read, but they're not professionals, so it's hard to know how seriously to take their feedback. But you're an actual published author, so I thought you could read it and give me your comments. Not that I think you'd have a lot, it's pretty polished. Then, if you like it, maybe you could introduce me to your agent or your publisher. Or both."

Frances heard a ringing in her ears. "Is this why you wanted to go out with me? So I'd read your manuscript?"

"No, of course not. Finding out you were an author was just an added bonus." He flopped down on the bed beside her, his now-limp penis dangling out of his robe like a banana slug. Frances stood and began searching for the rest of her clothes. "What are you doing? You can stay the night. You could even read the first few chapters. Or wait, I could read them *to* you—"

"I'm not reading your manuscript," she managed to say, even though her lips felt numb.

". . . What?"

"I'm not. Reading. Your manuscript."

"But you don't even know what it's about."

"Let me guess. It's post-apocalyptic. And/or it involves zombies. Or swashbuckling. Or Hitler has been cryogenically frozen and has just been brought back to life. And there's a love interest, a buxom blonde who can't help but fall for the hero and have lots of sex with him, in spite of his flaws."

"You're wrong." Keith gazed at her stonily. "The woman is *raven-haired*." Frances pulled her dress over her head. "Why are you being like this? I'm just asking a small favour—"

"How much do you charge an hour?"

"I don't see how that's relevant."

"Humour me. How much?"

"Two hundred."

"Okay. Well, if I were to take on this 'small favour'—actually read your manuscript, which I guarantee is not as good as you think it is, and give you thoughtful, considered notes—I'm guessing it would take about a week. So, forty hours, times two hundred—sure, I'll read and note your manuscript. If you pay me eight thousand dollars."

"That's insane."

"No, what's insane is the fact that we are both professionals, yet you believe your time is worth two hundred an hour and my time is worth nothing."

"Oh, come on—is this some form of drawbridge mentality? Like, once I'm published I'm going to do my best not to let anyone else in?"

She balled up her nylons and shoved them into her purse. "Yes, Keith. That's it. I am threatened by the possibility you're an immense talent." She walked to the bedroom door. "Thanks for the underwhelming sex."

On her way out she passed by an alcove off the kitchen. She just happened to see his recycling bin.

Sitting on top was an empty Safeway lasagna box.

31

Frances sliced through the water, head down, heart pounding, not just because she was swimming hard, but because she could not get her disastrous date out of her head. *I am such a colossal idiot.* The date, which was supposed to help lift her self-esteem, had only jammed it further into the toilet. Had he only slept with her because he wanted her to read his manuscript? Worse: Had he thought that would be a *fair exchange?* Mediocre sex for what was guaranteed to be over eight hundred pages of excrement? *No living author is allowed to write a book that is over eight hundred pages,* she thought. *Unless you're Donna Tartt or Ann-Marie Mac-Donald. In which case you can write double that and I will read every delicious damn word.*

Daisy had been home when Frances got in, so she'd had to tell her everything. Not about the sex—no child needed to hear about that—but about the rest of it. Daisy had been furious on her mother's behalf. They'd stayed up late drinking wine and watching reruns of *Family Law* so Frances could have a laugh and be soothed by the presence of Victor Garber.

She got to the end of the pool and grabbed her pull buoy. "Unh-unh-unh. That's mine." The British—*no, Scottish*—guy had swum up beside her. "Look, I even put my name on it." He turned it around; he'd written *Dickhead* in large black lettering on the side.

He burst out laughing.

She did not even crack a smile. "Wow. You really like laughing at your own jokes."

"You say that like it's a bad thing."

She grabbed her own pull buoy and pushed off. To hell with Daniel Craig's brother. To hell with men, period. She would be celibate for the rest of her days, try to do better with her female friendships, and invest in a really good vibrator, maybe two. Perhaps she could move to Sydney, get an apartment near Max, help him out if he eventually had kids . . . have an uneventful but decent life. She could swim every morning in the ocean, then one day, when she tired of it all, she could just let herself float out to sea, or swim with an open cut to increase the chances that a shark might attack her—no, that would be a far too gruesome and painful death.

She was almost at the other end of the pool when she saw a pair of hairy legs, followed by a loose, hairy belly, lower into the water. *The Turtle.* How to make a bad day worse. Frances was just two strokes away from the end—surely he would wait, and let her go ahead.

But no. The Turtle pushed off a hair's breadth ahead of her. *Inconsiderate, bloated turd!* Frances stopped. She gave him a good twenty metres' head start, then pushed off.

The head start wasn't enough. She caught up to his lumbering form in no time. She moved to the left and started to swim past, but The Turtle was taking up a lot of space.

Smack!

Her forehead collided, hard, with a swimmer coming the other way. All three of them stopped: Frances, The Turtle, and Daniel Craig's brother.

"You! What is wrong with you?" The Turtle yelled. He turned

to Daniel Craig's brother. "This woman's a menace. Every time I come here it's a contest, she's gotta pass, pass, pass!"

"Because you're *slow*!" Frances shouted. "You should be in the slow lane!"

"No, *you* should be in the fast lane! Am I right or am I right?" He posed this query to Daniel Craig's brother.

"Oh, you definitely belong in the slow lane, sir. I thought you were a corpse the first time I saw you in the water. I was this close to calling 911."

The Turtle puffed up his chest, outraged. "Guard! Lifeguard!" He waded through the water towards the pool's edge.

Frances clutched her forehead. Daniel Craig's brother looked at her with concern. "Are you all right? You got it worse than me."

"I'm not sure. I'm seeing spots."

"Let's get you checked out." He took her by the elbow and guided her slowly towards a ladder. The Turtle was now out of the water, gesticulating madly at a lifeguard.

"Are you hurt?" she asked.

"Nah, I'm fine. My skull is like granite."

"I'm truly sorry."

"Don't be. That guy's a cunt." Frances's eyebrows shot up in alarm. "Sorry, sorry, I keep forgetting the power that word has here. In the UK, it's like calling someone a jerk." Frances was only half listening, because she was mesmerized by the water, which was now ribboned with red. "Oh, my," he said.

Her nose was gushing blood.

Moments later the lifeguards evacuated the pool.

Frances sat on a chair in the first aid office, towel wrapped around her waist, head tilted back, gazing up at a pimply faced, bored-looking young lifeguard. He held a cloth to her nose. Daniel

Craig's brother peered down at her. The Turtle, thank god, had left. "Is it broken?" asked Frances.

"Nah, it's just a gusher," said the lifeguard. "And I don't see any signs of concussion."

"So I'm okay to drive home?"

"Might be better if you could call someone to pick you up. Just to be on the safe side."

"I can drive you home," said Daniel Craig's brother.

"I couldn't put you through the trouble."

"It's no trouble."

Even with her head tilted back, she had enough peripheral vision to note that he looked awfully good in his jammers. *Oh, sweet Jesus, I must be concussed.*

The lifeguard handed her a tampon.

"Um, thank you, but I haven't needed one of these in years."

"For your nose. Unless you want to gush all over this guy's car."

Frances inserted the tampon. The string dangled freely. Daniel Craig's brother tried not to laugh. He was unsuccessful.

She stood. As she did so, her towel dropped to the floor. "Lordy," said Daniel Craig's brother, the laughter dying in his throat.

The lifeguard's gaze drifted downward, and his eyes widened in alarm.

Frances followed his gaze.

The waxing, combined with the chlorine, had turned her inner thighs into a sea of angry red welts.

It was horror-movie hideous.

Frances grabbed her towel and covered herself. She could feel a hot flash coming on as she hurried to the door. "See you outside the main entrance in ten?" said Daniel Craig's brother.

"Let's make it fifteen." Frances scurried into the women's change room. She grabbed her things from her locker. Still in her swimsuit and flip-flops, her towel wrapped around her waist to hide her legs, she hurried out the side entrance, past pedestrians who looked at her in alarm because a) it was cold outside and b) she had a tampon dangling from her nose.

She found her car, climbed inside, and peeled out of the parking lot.

From now on she would swim at UBC pool. She would never come back here, ever again.

32

By Monday morning Frances had a lump on her forehead the size of a goose egg and a faint greenish-yellow eye. But it was a lovely spring day, so she hauled her mint-green bike out of the garage, pumped the tires, and rode to Kits Point for their next garbage-picking session.

When Geraint and Parker saw her, their eyes widened. Geraint threw his claw to the ground. "Tell me where he lives. NOW. I am going to drive there and kill him with my bare hands!" Then he burst into tears. "*How could he do this to you?*"

Frances patted his back. "Geraint, it's okay. I can explain." She told them most of what had happened, leaving out the more intimate details. This was the third time she'd told the story. First Daisy on Saturday, then Jules and Carmen over dinner at their place on Sunday (including the more intimate details). Thanks to the retelling, the worst of the sting was already dissipating. Some of it, Frances could see, was actually funny. She was a storyteller, after all, and she was beginning to hone the material, playing it for laughs. The cologne, the *thwunk* of the manuscript, the Vegas Eiffel Tower, the tampon up her nose, her inflamed thighs—she'd worked out when and how to tell those bits for maximum impact, and she could see that Geraint and Parker were reacting in all the right places. She didn't know what it said about her that it gave her an immense amount of pleasure.

"I'm so sorry, Frances," said Parker when she was done. "I really thought he seemed okay."

"And please let me assure you, there is no way on earth it was a"—Geraint's face curdled at the expression—"a *pity eff*, as you called it."

"Hundred percent," said Parker.

"I guarantee that he simply thought he'd won the lottery on two counts instead of one."

"You are beautiful. You are brave. You are loved," Parker quoted some of her favourite affirmations. "And there will be other fish in the sea."

"Perhaps," said Frances. "But I'm going to hang up my rod for the time being." Before they could protest she added, "I'm not saying never, just not now." They started to amble along the path by the Maritime Museum. A group of kayakers paddled just offshore. Frances picked up a beer can with her claw.

"I've got my court hearing," said Geraint. "It's in a couple of weeks. I've been doing a lot of reading in the evenings. I may need to gather some—some affiedaffies—"

"I think you mean *affidavits*," said Frances, experiencing a now-familiar pang of guilt.

"It's a steep learning curve, let me tell you. No wonder lawyers go to school for so long!" He picked up a muddied ball cap with his claw and studied it. Frances was relieved when he put the cap into his trash bag. A man in a business suit was walking briskly towards them from the parking lot, and for a moment Frances thought it was Jeremy.

It was. "Frances." He stopped in front of her, forcing her to stop, too.

"Jeremy." At the sound of his name, Parker and Geraint audibly gasped. "How did you know where I was?"

"I still have you on Find My Friends."

"You're stalking me?" Her phone started to buzz.

"I think perhaps Parker and I will continue down the path a bit, just out of hearing distance," said Geraint. But they didn't budge.

"You left me no choice," Jeremy said. "You've been completely ignoring me."

Her phone kept buzzing. She glanced at the screen—*Shady Pines.*

"Do you really want all of this to play out through our lawyers? We can drag it out for years through the courts if that's what you want, but it will drain our savings—"

"I have to take this," she said as she answered the call. "Hello, this is Frances."

"Frances, it's Jamal." His voice sounded strained. "I don't know how to tell you this."

Fear ran like an electrical current up her spine. "What's happened? Is Cordelia okay?"

"We took a field trip to the salmon hatchery in Capilano Park. Cordelia was right there with us."

"Why are you using past tense, Jamal?"

". . . I'm afraid she's wandered off."

"My mother is missing. Is that what you're telling me?" *On the North Shore. In the forest. Next to a canyon. Surrounded by wilderness.*

"We're doing everything we can to locate her. The police are on their way, and we've called North Shore search and rescue—"

Frances didn't hear the last bit because her knees gave out and she sank to the ground.

33

She'll be fine, Frances. Everything is going to be fine." Jeremy drove the two of them towards the North Shore. She'd joined him without a second thought because his Tesla had been steps away. Now, though, in spite of her frantic worry, she wished she'd gone with Geraint, who together with Parker had hurried back to his Subaru to follow them. It was agony being in such close proximity to a man she'd loved so deeply, so effortlessly, but whom she now loathed. She had cultivated that loathing over the past number of months, nurtured it and fed it every single day. And now, here she was, inches from its subject. She had a strong urge to leap from the moving car.

"You don't know that," she replied, her voice tight.

"There are lots of people looking for her."

"What on earth were they thinking? Who takes a bunch of dementia patients into a potential death trap?"

"It's a salmon hatchery, Frances."

"In the forest! Surrounded by wilderness! Regular, everyday people go missing on the North Shore all the time. They take a wrong turn, fall down a cliff, get attacked by a bear."

"Frances, you're catastrophizing—"

"*Jesus Christ, why aren't we moving?*" They were inching their way over the Lions Gate Bridge in bumper-to-bumper traffic, only one lane open in their direction.

"Let's take a few deep breaths, okay? We'll do it together." He breathed in deeply. She did the same. They breathed out together. They did it five more times.

And it helped. She had always been prone to "future fucking," as Jules liked to call it. She would play out worst-case scenarios in her head if, say, Daisy or Max or Jeremy were late coming home; her imagination always worked overtime, which was good for her writing but terrible for her well-being. Jeremy had talked her off the cliff on a regular basis during their marriage. He'd always known how to put things into perspective. It was yet another thing she missed about him.

Big, fat tears started to roll, unbidden, down her face. She turned away, but not before Jeremy saw.

"I'm so sorry, Francy." His pet name for her. "For everything."

Frances didn't—couldn't—respond. She just stared out the window, the landscape blurry through her tears. A second lane opened going northbound and Jeremy darted into it; finally, they were moving. She kept her gaze on the neon-yellow piles of sulphur on the far side of the bridge.

"I know you think I was lying to you all those years. But I wasn't, not intentionally. I didn't even know I was lying to myself. Not for years and years. You met my parents." She had. They were God-fearing Lutherans without an ounce of humour. "I was taught my entire life that homosexuality was a sin, so I pushed any 'sinful' thoughts right out of my head. If I thought about it at all, I wondered if perhaps I was bisexual."

"You couldn't have told me that?"

They were off the bridge now, driving northeast towards the park. "To what end? I never intended to act on the feelings. I became an expert at tamping them down."

She turned to look at him. "Then why didn't you just keep tamping them down?"

"Because it was slowly killing me."

Frances took a moment to absorb that. "So what you're saying is, being married to me was a slow death."

"That is not what I'm saying, and you know it."

She did know it. But she wasn't ready to say so.

"Do you remember how, in the last few years of our marriage, I had all sorts of ailments and doctors couldn't pinpoint the cause? Stomach pains, exhaustion, general fogginess?" She remembered all of it. Vividly. She'd put on a calm face around him, then lie awake at night, worried that he had some form of incurable disease. "My therapist said it was like I was suffocating a key part of myself. Trapping it in an airless room. Then I met Kelly and that part of myself made a break for it."

"Can you understand how wounding these words are, Jeremy? You're telling me I was someone you couldn't be your whole self with. Then along came your knight in dentist's armour."

Jeremy took a deep breath. "I need you to hear this. I was just as much 'me' when I was with you as I am with Kelly. He helped release that part of me, a big part, but—I don't expect your sympathy, believe me—"

"Well, thank god for that—"

"But you will never know just how much I miss you. I miss so much about us."

". . . So do I."

"But I couldn't do it any longer, Francy. I couldn't do it to me, and I couldn't do it to you."

Frances could feel a small bit of her hatred evaporating, and it irritated her. Hatred was straightforward. Hatred was easy. But now some of it was being replaced with something more complicated: a profound sense of sadness and loss. "I wish we'd never met."

Jeremy pulled into the hatchery parking lot. "You don't mean that."

"I do."

Frances opened her car door before he'd come to a complete stop. Geraint and Parker pulled up next to them. The Shady Pines minibus was at the curb, residents seated inside, including Alfred, who was near the front. He banged on the window when he saw Frances. Frances motioned to the driver to open the door, and he did so reluctantly, clearly not wanting to lose anyone else. "She was right beside me," Alfred began. "I don't know what happened. And they won't let me look for her—"

"It's okay, Alfred. We're going to find her," said Frances with an assurance she didn't feel. The doors to the bus closed, just as Jamal hurried up to them.

"Frances, Jeremy, I'm so sorry—"

"Do you have any idea which way she went?" asked Jeremy.

Jamal shook his head. "North Shore search and rescue have been notified, and the police are on their way."

"How long has she been missing?" asked Jeremy as Geraint and Parker hurried up.

Jamal glanced at his watch. "Close to an hour."

Frances groaned. "We can't just stand here. We need to do something."

"Why don't Parker and I head down the path to the east?" Geraint said. "You and Jeremy can take the path to the west."

Frances nodded, and the four of them set off.

34

"*om!*"

"*Cordy!*"

She and Jeremy walked down the dark, forested path. They'd been searching for almost half an hour, not talking except to shout out Cordelia's name.

Suddenly Jeremy asked, "Did you really mean it?"

"Mean what?"

"That you wish we'd never met."

"Yes. No." She sighed. "I don't know."

"Look at our beautiful kids."

"I would have had beautiful kids with someone else."

"Maybe. But none of them would have been Daisy and Max."

"Maybe I'd have had a better version of Daisy. One who didn't act like the Thought Police." Jeremy smiled. "Sorry," said Frances. "I love Daisy just as she is. That was tasteless."

"But also funny. You've always been the queen of tasteless and funny. *Cordy!*"

They walked in silence for a few moments. "I think I knew, you know," Frances said after a while. "Deep down."

"That I was gay?"

"No. But I knew our marriage was in trouble. For at least a year before you left. You just seemed so sad. Your parents had both died a few months earlier . . . the kids were grown up . . . it was all a big transition. So I chalked it up to a mid-life crisis. I told myself you were just mildly depressed." Frances looked straight ahead as she spoke. "You tried to talk to me one night. Do you remember?"

"I do."

"And I think I could sense it was something I didn't want to hear, and I somehow managed to shut it down."

Jeremy spontaneously grabbed her hand. She didn't pull away. "I miss you, Francy."

"I miss you, too."

"I'm going to tell you something. But you have to promise not to laugh."

"I'm not prone to laughter, under the circumstances."

"Kelly has a Royal Doulton collection."

"No."

"Yup. A large one."

"But you *hate* knick-knacks. And you especially hate—"

"Royal Doulton. They're everywhere, Frances, and I mean everywhere—"

Frances's phone started ringing. She grabbed it from her pocket. "Parker?"

The reception was poor. "We . . . she's . . ."

"I can't hear you. Have you found her?"

"Yes."

Frances's phone pinged—Parker had pinned her location.

"Is she okay?"

But the line went dead.

Frances and Jeremy jogged back to where they'd started. Two police cars had arrived, and an officer was speaking with Jamal. "They've found her," she shouted as they veered onto the trail Geraint and Parker had taken. Jamal and the officer followed.

A few minutes later Frances spotted Parker, waving her arms in the air. Geraint was behind her.

It took Frances a moment to piece together what she was seeing. Geraint's arms were wrapped around Cordelia. He was holding her in one of her favourite bear hugs. Cordelia beamed up at him.

"Is she okay?" she asked Parker.

"She's fine. Her shoes are soaked through; she wandered off the path and into a creek. Geraint spotted her and lifted her out."

Frances's heart swelled with gratitude. She turned to Jeremy. "I need to ask you a favour."

"Anything. Anything at all. Whatever you need, I'll do it."

She looked towards Geraint. "It's not for me. It's for a friend."

35

J eremy is amazing," Geraint gushed as he and Frances entered their second-last anger management class a few days later. Instead of one of his track suits, he wore grey trousers with a checkered button-up shirt, because he'd met with Jeremy that very afternoon. "He knows so much more about family law than I do."

"Perhaps that's because he's an actual family lawyer," said Frances.

"And he's such a great guy! So down-to-earth and friendly." He took in Frances's expression. "I mean. He's not *that* great. Good lawyer, but as a human being? Meh."

"It's okay, Geraint. What does he think your chances are in court?"

"Good, apparently. He says judges only take a child away from a parent as a last resort."

She looked at his outfit again. "Geraint—I have to ask, your trousers. They're not—"

"They are!" He turned from side to side like a runway model. "I *told* you they were worth salvaging!" They took their seats. "How's our Cordy?"

"She's doing okay," said Frances. Parker had told her that when she and Geraint first found her, she'd been disoriented and frightened, and said something about trying to escape evil men in the woods. But she'd recognized Geraint. "You're the Grizzly Bear," she'd said when he'd approached her—and she'd accepted his help out of the creek, and his hug, which seemed to calm her down. Instead of putting her in the minibus, Frances and Jeremy had driven Cordelia back to Shady Pines, along with Alfred, who'd held her hand tightly in the back seat. Once they'd settled her in her room, Cordelia had turned to Frances and said, "Thank you, Janet." Janet was her long-dead sister.

Frances had been oddly relieved that Jeremy was with her. He'd driven her back to her bike while she'd wept with the knowledge that she was losing her mom, too.

Frances and Geraint took their seats, just as Parker slipped in, wearing a white crocheted vest over a black turtleneck, jeans, and a magnificent pair of bedazzled Converse shoes. When Dennis arrived a moment later, Frances noted that he'd also upped his wardrobe; he had a new grey suit jacket that actually fit his lanky frame, and he seemed generally more at ease. "Welcome to our penultimate class. I'm so proud of all of you and the journeys you've taken so far." His eyes glimmered with excitement. "Tonight we're going even deeper. We're going to do what's called an exposure scenario." He wrote, as they all knew he would, EXPOSURE SCENARIO on the board and underlined it. "I want you to break into your groups. Then, as best you can, *re-enact* the moment that ultimately led you here. Role-play, if you will. Dust off those acting skills! But this time, instead of responding in anger, I want you to use the techniques you've been working on in this class to see if you can respond in a different way."

Geraint raised his hand. "Yes, Geraint?"

"Um, it's just that . . . my moment involved my wife—*you know*—with my boss. I don't feel comfortable asking anyone to role-play that."

Dennis blushed. "Good point. Perhaps you can just talk through what you might have done differently, then."

"Who would like to start?" asked Geraint once they'd broken into their groups.

Frances stood. "I'll go."

"Ooh, can I play the twelve-year-old boy?" asked Geraint.

"You can, minus the spitballs."

"I'll be the girl who recorded it all on her phone," said Parker.

They moved to the far end of the room, away from Byron and Wayson, who were attempting to re-enact Wayson's road rage incident without the rage. Geraint whispered, "If you ask me, Wayson's performance is rather wooden."

Frances regurgitated part of her presentation, which she knew by heart because she'd done it hundreds of times. "Why does someone become a writer? In my case I believe it had a lot to do with my upbringing. I was an only child, and my mother was a single parent who had to work to support us—"

"Yawn, boring," Geraint said at volume.

"We didn't have a lot of money for extras. But she was a big reader, so we went to the library once a week and I would bring home stacks of books—"

Brap. Geraint belched loudly.

"I was what they call a 'latchkey kid.' I walked myself to school and back, and spent hours on my own before my mother got home, reading and playing elaborate imaginary games—"

"Boo! You stink! Boring old lady! Get a real job!" Geraint was now yelling, a huge grin on his face. He was, Frances observed with irritation, enjoying himself a bit too much.

But she remained calm. She took a deep breath. In . . . out. "Okay, here's what we're going to do. When you're done talking—"

Geraint blew a loud razzberry.

"When you are done talking," she repeated, slowly, with steel in her voice, "I'll continue. And if that isn't possible, we'll just call it quits, okay? I'll go home and you can all go back to class. Because I don't tolerate this sort of behaviour and neither, frankly, should your teachers."

Geraint gave Frances a thumbs-up, impressed.

Then he belched again, loud, long, and defiant. Parker, holding up her phone, started to laugh, her shoulders shaking.

Frances felt her blood pressure rise. But all she said was, "Okay, thanks very much for having me, I'm calling it a day." Then she turned and walked away.

Dennis, who had been watching nearby, started to clap. "Frances, well done!"

Parker high-fived her. "And you still showed that little turd who's boss!"

"I wanted to punch you in the face," Frances said to Geraint.

"Ah, but you didn't," said Dennis. "That's progress!" Then he sauntered to the other side of the room to watch Byron's re-enactment of the confrontation with his boss.

"Okay, Parker, you're next," said Frances. Parker looked at them with trepidation. "You don't have to do this. We can tell Dennis it's too triggering."

Parker shook her head. "No. It's okay. I want to do it."

"Only if you're sure. And we can stop any time." She turned to Geraint. "Since you seem to love acting so much, you can play the creepy guy who followed Parker in the mall."

They began. Parker walked back and forth on their side of the room. Geraint followed close behind. "Hello, young miss. How has your day been so far? Might I compliment you on your pretty outfit?"

"Geraint, that is awful," said Frances.

"How do you know? You weren't there."

"She's right," said Parker. "I told you the guy was a pig."

They started again. "Hello, pretty girl. I would very much like to . . . get to know you better. In the biblical sense."

Frances groaned. "Geraint!"

Geraint gave them both a pained look. "*Please* don't make me do this. I can't say anything untoward to Parker, even if it is just acting. It's too icky."

"Fine," said Frances. "I'll do it."

They started over. Frances followed Parker so closely, she was almost touching her. "Hey, baby, how's it going? Wanna go for a ride in my monster truck?" Because in Frances's mind the guy definitely drove a monster truck.

"No, I don't. Please leave me alone," said Parker calmly.

"C'mon, baby, don't be a cock tease."

"Frances, good heavens!" Geraint interjected. "Maybe you should tone down the language."

"That was tame compared to what he actually said. Am I right?"

Parker nodded.

"But . . . how did you know that?"

"How do you think?"

"This has happened to you, too?" Geraint looked like he might cry.

"Geraint—do you know how many women on this planet have *not* had creepy men say creepy things to them during their lifetime? None, that's how many. Literally none."

Geraint shook his head, dismayed. "On behalf of my entire gender, I apologize."

They resumed the exercise. Frances kept murmuring one disgusting thing after another in Parker's ear. Geraint stood with his mouth agape, absolutely appalled at what he was hearing.

"Back off or I'll call security," said Parker, her voice shaky.

"Call them, they can join in. I can tell you're a dirty slut—"

"LEAVE ME THE FUCK ALONE!" Parker roared, pushing Frances as hard as she could. Geraint reached out a beefy arm and grabbed her just before she hit the floor.

Stunned silence. They both stared at Parker, alarmed. Parker clamped a hand over her mouth. "I'm sorry," she cried. "I'm so sorry." Then she bolted from the room.

Dennis was over in a flash. "What happened?"

"My fault," Frances said shakily. "I lost my balance."

"No, Parker pushed you," Dennis started.

"No. She didn't," Frances said firmly. "I fell."

"Frances is a klutz," added Geraint.

Dennis turned to Byron and Wayson.

"I didn't see nothing," said Byron.

"Me neither," said Wayson.

Dennis knew he was being stonewalled. "I'd like to speak to Parker when she comes back."

But Parker did not come back.

When class was over, Dennis beckoned to Frances and Geraint. "Please let Parker know I need to speak with her. Passing this course depends on good attendance."

"Actually I had a text from her," said Frances. "She started menstruating heavily and wasn't prepared, so she headed home early." As she suspected, at the words *menstruating heavily*, Dennis looked squeamish and immediately backed off.

Geraint spoke to Frances in a whisper as they gathered up their things. "Do you think Parker's okay?"

"Honestly, Geraint, I don't think she is. But we can't let Dennis know that. If she fails this course, things will be so much worse for her." She grabbed her purse off the back of her chair. As she did so, she saw Parker's sparkly purple notebook poking out of the adjoining desk.

Frances grabbed it. She was about to drop it into her purse

when curiosity got the better of her; she flipped it open to a random page.

"Holy shit on a stick," she murmured.

"What?" asked Geraint.

Frances glanced towards Dennis, who was erasing the chalkboards. "Not here," she whispered. She slipped the notebook into her purse and the two of them scuttled out.

"She's got talent, I'll give her that," said Geraint a few minutes later. They sat in Frances's car with the interior light on, hunched over Parker's notebook.

Some of the pages were full of notes from class. Other pages had sketches of dresses that Parker had designed. They were wildly creative and bold. A few pages were filled with positive affirmations, all of them followed by multiple exclamation marks.

But deeper into the notebook, most of the pages were reserved for graphic, violent drawings. On one page, a man was impaled on a spike held aloft by a triumphant red-headed woman. On another, a man's body was riddled with bullet holes; the same woman held a smoking gun, a grin on her face. On another, a man was being disemboweled with a knife—by the same woman.

"The woman looks a lot like—" Geraint began.

"Yes. She does."

"And the man—"

"Is the same, too. He has a distinct kestrel insignia on his chest in every drawing."

Geraint gasped. "No."

"What?"

"The kestrel. It's Sir Godfrey's insignia. Sir Godfrey, from *Knights of the Castle.* Played by Sebastian Trevor." They looked at each other with the same dawning realization. "This is ever so disappointing. He's my favourite part of the show." Geraint sighed. "*Was. Was* my favourite part of the show." They sat in silence for a moment. "What should we do?"

Frances exhaled. "Until now, I've been trying to respect Parker's wishes. So I haven't pried."

"And now?"

Frances pulled out her phone. "Now, I pry."

36

Parker hadn't gone directly home. She hadn't wanted Alexei to be suspicious if she got back before him, so instead she'd gone to a multiplex and watched a movie. She could barely remember a thing about it. Something with superheroes and lots of special effects. She figured she could fake the bare bones of a plot if she needed to, since they all seemed to follow a similar arc.

At their apartment door, she took a moment. *Be cheerful. Smile.* She entered. "Hi, my Sweet Souvlaki, I'm home." There was no answer. "Alexei?" She glanced at her phone; maybe he was still at night school. Except all the lights were on. She walked into their tiny living room and found him sitting on their tiny couch. Unsmiling.

". . . What's going on?" she asked, even though she was quite certain she knew exactly what was going on. Alexei was about to break up with her.

"I've been so worried about you, Parker."

"I know. And I'm sorry for that."

"I've tried to respect your decisions, I really have. But I can't do it anymore."

There it was. Parker's knees felt weak.

"Frances called."

"Alexei, you have to believe me, I didn't mean to push her like that."

"What? What are you talking about?"

". . . That's not why she called?"

"She said you left class halfway through and didn't come back."

"I didn't feel well."

"She found your notebook. Told me what was in it."

"She looked at my book?" Now she thought she might faint. "It's just drawings."

"It's not just drawings! You know it's not just drawings!" He took a deep breath, trying to calm himself. "I can't live like this any longer. I've made a decision. You're not going to like it."

"Just get it over with, Alexei. Just break up with me."

He looked confused. "I'm not breaking up with you."

What Alexei didn't say was that he'd been thinking about it recently. The idea would pop into his head. *I could just leave.* Then he would feel lousy for having the idea and push it away. But it was there, lurking, because his life with Parker had gone from being the best thing that had ever happened to him, to a daily chore. All he wanted was to help her get better, but nothing he did made a difference. He felt useless. He lay awake at night sometimes, feeling desperate, stuck.

"Then what is it?" she asked.

There was a knock at the door. He got up to answer it. "I told them, Parker. Frances and Geraint know everything."

37

In that moment—not in any other moment in their long life together, because they would have a very long life together, complete with an outdoor wedding on the shores of Okanagan Lake (where Frances, Geraint, Jules, Carmen, and Sharon and Daisy and their latest partners, no one could remember either of their names, would be in attendance, and where Geraint would sob buckets of happy tears), fulfilling careers in the TV industry and Clark and Anderson Accounting, respectively (and the day would come when the name would change to Clark, Anderson and Papadopoulos), three children almost back-to-back (only one of whom would cause them terrible anxiety as a teenager but who thankfully came out the other side) and many wonderful grandchildren . . .

But in *that very moment*—Parker felt like the walls were closing in on her, and she wished with all her heart that Alexei had told her he was breaking up with her, instead.

38

When Frances and Geraint left over an hour later, Parker sat very still on their loveseat while Alexei busied himself making tea. She knew he was postponing what he believed would be their inevitable confrontation. In their almost-year living together, *confrontation* was not a word that had entered their lexicon. They almost always got along. When they did disagree, it was on a "should we watch reruns of *Never Have I Ever* or *Heartstopper*" level—they just talked it out.

Alexei finally made his way back into the living room and put down their mugs. He sat down beside her and looked her in the eye. "I know you're angry with me, Parker. But I honestly felt I had no other choice."

To his surprise, Parker threw her arms around him. She started to cry, sobs wracking her body. He held her close and rubbed her back. "Oh, my Shining Star. I'm so sorry. It'll be okay."

But what she couldn't explain until she had the tears under control was that she wasn't crying from sadness; rather, the tears were a release of months of tension and anxiety, and for the first time in ages, knowing that others knew the burden she was carrying—just being able to *share her story* with people who cared about her—made her feel just a little bit lighter.

39

Frances and Geraint did not feel lighter. They felt weighted with sadness for what Parker had kept locked inside her for all these months.

When they left Parker and Alexei's apartment, they went to the closest bar and ordered themselves a drink.

"With the exception of Keith when I thought he'd hit you," Geraint said, "I've never wanted to actually kill someone until now."

"I know," said Frances.

"I am feeling rather disembodied and light-headed," said Geraint. "Could I possibly hold your hand for just a moment?"

"Of course." Geraint's gigantic fingers swallowed hers. "In lieu of murder," Frances said, "I think there may be other ways we can try to help."

"Like what?"

"I'm not entirely sure. But first and foremost, I'd like to get Parker's permission to talk to Jules."

40

I t was a beautiful Saturday afternoon. The crocuses, tulips, daffo-dils, and azaleas were in full bloom in Frances's backyard. It was warm enough that they could sit under the awning, Alexei beside Parker on one outdoor couch, Frances, Geraint, and Jules across from them on the other.

"What do you make of it, Jules?" asked Frances.

"First and foremost, I want his head on a spike."

"Which is exactly what his character did to Lord Whitcombe in season one. Oh, and also exactly what you did to Sebastian in one of your drawings, Parker!" said Geraint. Parker's face turned pink.

Jules tented her fingers and leaned forward, looking Parker in the eye. "You signed an NDA. If he has endless resources—and it sounds like he might—he could make your life hell in many ways if you were to break it. It is a legally binding document." The others absorbed this. "However, what you describe is sexual assault, not harassment, so—please understand I'm speaking from a strictly le-gal perspective—that's helpful. Have you heard of procedural un-conscionability?" Parker shook her head. "It basically means, in layperson's terms, was there something unscrupulous in the way your NDA came about? Were you coerced in some way? Was there a power imbalance? Were you threatened with personal or profes-sional consequences if you didn't sign?"

"All of the above," Alexei blurted, then stopped himself. "Sorry. This is Parker's story to tell."

248

"Alexei's right," said Parker. She told them about the young female lawyer who was in the room when she signed, and how later she'd felt certain they'd had her there for optics. "There was also a vague threat about how hard it would be for me to find work in the industry again if I didn't sign."

Jules nodded her head. "Good, this is all good." She stopped herself. "And again, you know what I mean by *good*."

"I know. It's fine. I really appreciate your help."

"Did they give you an opportunity to seek a lawyer?"

"No. They told me I had to sign it in the room or it would all go away."

"Okay, also good, because that means you were essentially told you couldn't negotiate the terms of the settlement agreement. You were told to take it or leave it." Jules stood and started to pace. Frances knew this was a sign that her mind was going a mile a minute. "Better still, lawyers in Canada voted in favour recently to disallow NDAs to be used as a tool to silence people who've been assaulted or discriminated against. It's not law yet, but—all of these things combined will make it much harder for Sebastian's people to do you any harm if you do decide to break the NDA."

"I don't even know what that would look like," said Parker.

"I do think it's important to point out that even though things are changing for the better, if you go to the police, it will still very much be a 'he said, she said' situation."

"Except *she* is Parker, and we know she wouldn't lie," said Geraint.

"Yes," Jules said patiently, "but *we* are not the people who would need convincing. If you were to try to lay charges, you can bet Sebastian's team would either argue it was consensual, or that nothing at all happened: you were just another crazed fan, and when he rebuffed you, you sought revenge, so they paid you money to make you go away."

Parker closed her eyes. "Two of the grips made fun of me one day because they said I was making googly eyes at Sebastian."

Jules nodded. "And that is the sort of stuff his team will dig up and use against you. That, and worse, I guarantee it."

"And who are they going to believe, a beloved celebrity or a nobody like me?"

"You are *not* a nobody!" Geraint exclaimed; he was finding the entire conversation deeply upsetting.

"What helps in these situations is numbers," Jules continued. "Look at Rose McGowan shouting into the void for years. It took more women coming forward to bring Weinstein down."

"There's no way it was just me," said Parker. "Of course there were others. There *are* others. And the thing that keeps me awake at night is knowing there will be *more* others if he isn't stopped."

"Is there anyone you're still in contact with from the production?" Frances asked. "Someone you trust?"

"I really liked my boss, Wanda. The costume designer. But the way I left—she must think I'm a total flake. And I haven't spoken to her in months."

"Would you feel comfortable contacting her?" asked Jules. "She might have at least heard rumours."

Parker wrapped a piece of her long red hair around her finger. "I don't know. Maybe?"

"These are your decisions to make," Frances said to her gently. "We'll stand by you, whatever you choose to do."

Parker looked at Alexei. "What do you think?"

Alexei's brow furrowed with worry. "You have to think about what the impacts might be on you and your mental health. I just don't want this man to make you feel even worse than he already has."

"Alexei's got a point. It's okay to be selfish in this situation," said Jules.

Parker was quiet for a moment. "I've felt like I've had a personality disorder ever since he did what he did. Like, one moment
I'm fine and the next moment I'm just . . ." She closed her eyes
for a moment. "I kept thinking I'd get past it, but I haven't. So
doing nothing doesn't feel like an option." She leaned forward and
grabbed a brownie from a plate on the table. "I'll reach out to
Wanda. See if she'd be willing to meet up."

41

Geraint was having trouble breathing. He felt claustrophobic. His suit—the same one he'd worn to his mean great-aunt's funeral some fifteen years earlier, when he was a good twenty pounds lighter—was so tight he was worried it might rip at the seams. He could already feel sweat stains forming under his arms. His stomach was making worrisome sounds, and he couldn't tell if he was constipated or minutes away from explosive diarrhea. "I feel like my entire body has been squeezed into a sausage casing," he said, tugging at his tie.

Frances, in a black pencil skirt and a burgundy blouse that looked gorgeous with her salt-and-pepper hair, slapped his hand away. "Leave it. It took me twenty minutes to get that knot right." They stood outside the family court chambers in the downtown law courts. Even though it meant she'd have to see Jeremy again, Frances wanted to be on hand to support Geraint.

The truth was, after her talk with Jeremy—well, she wouldn't say she didn't still feel betrayed or heartbroken, because that would be a lie. But she felt less bitter. She had worked so hard to convince herself that she hated him. But she just couldn't summon up the energy for such a powerful emotion anymore.

And now he was striding towards them, looking calm and confident in his bespoke suit. It hurt her heart to see how good he looked. She'd barely registered his appearance during their last encounter because she'd been so worried about her mom. But now she noticed that he looked a little leaner, a little more muscular. His hair, which had veered towards mad scientist during their marriage, was neatly trimmed. He had a pocket square. That was also new.

Being with Kelly made him take better care of himself. She felt a little wobbly all of a sudden.

Jeremy and Geraint shook hands. "Frances, you look lovely."

"Fuck off," she said, but without feeling. "And thanks. You look good, too."

Geraint tugged nervously at his suit jacket. "How will this work?"

"It's rather like a cattle call. The judge will be making her way through anywhere from ten to forty applications. We just have to be patient and wait our turn—"

"Oh, sweet Jesus Murphy, here they come," Geraint interrupted. He nudged Frances. "I told you she was gorgeous."

Frances followed his gaze. A tall, distinguished-looking woman walked in between Ron and a woman who, she realized, must be Darlene. Darlene wore layers of garish makeup and was—rather like her ex—squeezed into a leopard-print dress that was one size too small. Her dark hair was sprayed so heavily it didn't even move on her head. It looked more like helmet than hair. *Beauty is in the eye of the beholder*, Frances thought.

The air became ripe with a rotten egg smell. "Ooooh, excuse me, I need the bathroom," said Geraint. He scurried down the hall, just as Ron, Darlene, and the woman who was clearly their lawyer stopped in front of them. They wrinkled their noses, picking up the last vestiges of Geraint's fart.

"Jeremy," said the other lawyer.

"Philomena." They shook hands.

Philomena ushered Ron and Darlene into the courtroom. Ron glared at Frances as he passed, but she just smiled sweetly back.

"Interesting," said Jeremy once they were gone.

"What?"

"They've hired an expensive attorney. Philomena Biko." He opened the door to the chambers. ". . . aka The Pit Bull."

As Frances followed Jeremy inside, she was glad Geraint wasn't there to hear.

Parker joined them shortly afterwards, wearing a dress made entirely of tea towels. Frances wasn't sure what to make of it, but Geraint exclaimed, "Parker, you look magnificent."

"So do you," she beamed. "Very pro."

They settled onto a bench in the third row, listening to one application after another. Almost all of them had to do with parenting time or child support. Three deadbeat dads and one deadbeat mom were told to pay what they owed. One estranged couple argued over custody of their shih tzu. The judge, a woman whose nameplate read Justice Fabbro, listened with varying degrees of patience.

After a couple of hours, *Blevins v. Simpson* was called. Frances, on the other side of Geraint, squeezed his hand. He and Jeremy stood and took their places at a table up front, on the left. Ron and Darlene took their places at the table on the right. Philomena Biko stood before the judge. "I'm here to request immediate interim sole parenting for Darlene Blevins, née Simpson, in the matter of her son, Keanu Blevins."

"What are your reasons, Counsel?" asked Justice Fabbro.

"The boy's father, Geraint Blevins"—Philomena gestured towards Geraint—"is currently in a court-mandated anger management class because of his violent behaviour towards Ms. Simpson's new partner, Ron Neumann. One could argue that this in itself is already damning proof that he has issues controlling his volatile temper."

"Objection, my colleague is getting carried away with her overblown adjectives and speculation," Jeremy said.

"Sustained. Stick to the facts, Ms. Biko."

"All right, the facts: Mr. Blevins vandalized Mr. Neumann's car and committed an *indecent act*, for which he was arrested and charged. He also has a restraining order against him because Mr. Neumann fears for his personal safety."

From their seats, Frances and Parker saw Geraint sink lower in his. "But the pièce de résistance is that Mr. Blevins knowingly hosted their five-year-old son's birthday party in the home of a woman who is also in his anger management class—a woman who has been charged with *assaulting a minor*." She turned and pointed at Frances. Everyone else in the courtroom—and there were many of them—swivelled their heads to stare. Now it was Frances's turn to sink lower in her seat. Parker patted her knee and glared at some of the looky-loos. Frances willed Jeremy to stand and object—over what, she wasn't sure—but he had his head down, madly scribbling notes.

Philomena continued. "That this man would expose his son to a known child abuser shows an incredible lack of judgment on his part. It is our belief that he may, in fact, be in a *relationship* with this woman—" Frances almost jumped up to shout *objection* but fortunately Jeremy beat her to it.

"Objection, speculative fiction!"

"Sustained. Ms. Biko, I know you love spinning yarns, but I warn you again to stick to the facts."

"I'm wrapping up, Justice Fabbro. We've sought this emergency hearing to ask for interim sole parenting until this goes before the trial judge, who will decide on permanent parenting rights. We do so out of genuine concern for the physical and emotional safety of the child. Those are my submissions. Thank you."

Frances and Parker shared worried looks. Poor Geraint, she saw, had wriggled out of his suit jacket, and the back of his shirt was soaked through with sweat.

"Mr. Stewart?" said the judge.

Jeremy stood. He smoothed his jacket. Cleared his throat. For a moment, Frances was worried. Had he forgotten what he wanted to say? Had Philomena thrown him for a loop?

"Ms. Biko has done a bang-up job of giving you the click-bait-style headlines. While it's entertaining, it's lacking any form of context and has only shreds of truth. Allow me to briefly take you through the events that led to my client's unfortunate circumstances. On the day he was charged with mischief—"

"And indecent exposure," interjected Philomena.

"—he'd walked in on his wife and her new partner, Ron Neumann, who at the time was also his boss, in flagrante delicto." Now everyone in the courtroom turned to look at Ron and Darlene, and it was Darlene's turn to sink in her seat. Ron, however, merely puffed up like a peacock. "He was understandably upset. He did not react with violence towards another human being. He did, however, vandalize Mr. Neumann's car." He handed the judge a photo.

"*Man whore*," read Justice Fabbro, and Frances swore she saw her suppress a grin.

"As for the 'indecent act,' Mr. Blevins urinated in Mr. Neumann's fountain, which, unbeknownst to him, a neighbour witnessed—hence the added charge. Mr. Blevins has nothing but remorse for these actions, and the Crown clearly did not think he was a risk of any sorts, which is why they recommended my client for the alternative measures program."

Philomena leapt out of her seat. "Mr. Neumann succeeded in getting a restraining order against this man, which suggests he was genuinely worried for his safety."

"Thank you, Ms. Biko, for bringing that up," Jeremy continued. "I was rather puzzled that the police had issued a restraining order against my client, so I did a bit of my own digging. The officer who issued the order went to high school with Mr. Neumann and can often be found in Mr. Neumann's suite at Rogers Arena during Canucks games—"

"Objection, we aren't here to cast aspersions on our men and women in blue."

"Overruled." Frances noticed Geraint was now sitting a bit taller in his seat.

"I have also spoken with his diversion officer, Carol Jansen, who says he is progressing well through the program. I have no doubt that once he has completed alternative measures, his record, such as it is, will be wiped clean."

"This is all well and good, but there remains the matter of the company Mr. Blevins keeps," said Philomena.

"Of course. I must again thank my esteemed colleague for getting me back on track. Full disclosure—because I'm sure if I don't tell you, Ms. Biko will—the woman who hosted Keanu's birthday party is my soon-to-be ex-wife, Frances Partridge. She, too, happened to have one very bad day. I have here the video that went viral and led to the charges against her."

"No need, Counsel, I've seen it," said the judge, and Frances felt her face burn with shame.

"Then let me assure you that in her twenty-five years or so as a children's author, during which time she has done hundreds of school visits, nothing like this has happened before. And I can tell you that as her husband of twenty-five years, I never once saw her get violent. Unless she was battling with our lawn mower, in which case, watch out."

Frances smiled.

Jeremy picked up a folder from his table. "Lastly, I refer you to the submitted affidavits. If I may, I'd like to quote just a few excerpts. Parker Poplawski, a friend of Geraint's, says, *Anyone would be lucky to have Geraint as a father. I wish he was my dad.* His friend and former co-worker Jorge Soledad says, *Geraint is the kindest, most decent person I've ever met. He would never harm his child*. His diversion officer, Carol Jansen, says, *This application is a load of hogwash. Geraint's a great guy*."

"Okay, surely that's enough," Philomena said to the judge.

"I'll be the judge of what's enough, Counsel," said Justice Fabbro. "Since I'm the judge. And I'm enjoying the rare experience of hearing *kind* words spoken in here today. Proceed."

"Just one more. Frances Partridge says, *Geraint is a lovely, gentle, uncomplicated man whose love for his child is patently obvious. He and Keanu adore each other. He is a wonderful male role model who will help his son grow into a fine young man. We need more men like Geraint Blevins*."

Frances noted that Geraint hadn't budged; he remained firmly planted in his seat, facing forward. Then his shoulders started to heave, and she was pretty sure she heard a sob.

Jeremy continued. "This entire proceeding appears to be a vindictive attempt by the plaintiff to hijack parenting time and put my client in an unfavourable light for the trial judge, who will ultimately decide on custody for both parties. Mr. Blevins already has a rotten parenting deal. He currently only sees his son on Wednesday nights and every other weekend."

"Might I remind you, your client readily agreed to those terms," interjected Philomena.

"Only because at that point he still had hopes for a reconciliation. When this formally goes before the courts, we will be arguing for Mr. Blevins to get *equal* parenting time. I urge you to consider temporarily granting him those terms today. Thank you." He sat down.

Justice Fabbro took a few moments before she spoke. "I'm inclined to agree with Mr. Stewart. There is a whiff of spite around this entire proceeding. I'm loath to take away parenting time, particularly when the parent appears, by all accounts, to be a loving,

attentive father. Mr. Blevins's actions were situational. He was reacting to a stressful event. There is no history of family violence
and no evidence before me that would lead me to believe he would
harm his child.

"The application is denied, Ms. Biko. Further to that, I hereby
temporarily grant Geraint Blevins equal parenting time until you go
before the trial judge, who will decide on the permanent arrangement." Justice Fabbro turned her gaze towards Darlene. "As for
you, Ms. Simpson, I hope you'll find it in your heart to realize that
it's in your child's best interest to maintain a positive and healthy
relationship with his father." Darlene looked down at her hands.
From her vantage point, Frances could see that Ron's thick neck
had turned bright red. "Adjourned."

Someone started to slow-clap in the back.

They all turned: it was The Sarge.

42

Outside the family court chambers, Geraint was a heaving mass of tears, snot, and sweat. He threw his arms around Jeremy and squeezed him in a long, suffocating bear hug. When he finally released him, Jeremy had damp patches on his suit and a smear of mucus on his shoulder. "You are the best lawyer ever," Geraint gushed. Then, seeing Frances nearby, he added sternly, "But a lousy husband, in the end. No excuse for it."

"Does this bode well for the trial?" asked Frances.

"There's an expression in family law: *So goes the interim application, so goes the trial*," said Jeremy. "You stand a very good chance of retaining fifty-fifty parenting."

Geraint turned his attention to Frances and Parker. "And all the lovely things you said about me in there." He lumbered towards them, arms outstretched. Frances tried to duck out of the way, but she was too late; he pulled them both into a moist, malodorous hug. When he saw Carol he started to hug her, too, then stopped himself, unsure of the etiquette of hugging his diversion officer. But Carol practically launched herself at him, revelling in his damp hug. "Carol, thank you so much for your words of support."

"I lived through a nightmare like this. Didn't seem right for you to live through it, too." She glanced at her watch. "I've got to get back to the office."

"I need to do the same," said Jeremy. To Frances he said, "Talk soon?"

She nodded. Giving her a small smile, he followed Carol towards the exit.

"Can I take you two out for a celebratory lupper?" asked Geraint. They looked at him, confused. "It's a cross between lunch and supper. Since it's almost three."

"I can't," said Parker. "I'm meeting with my old boss at four."

"And I'm going with her," said Frances. "Jules is coming, too."

"Would you like me to also—" Geraint started.

"No," said Frances, not unkindly.

Geraint nodded. "I will be rooting for you, Parker." He caught sight of Ron, Darlene, and Philomena leaving the chambers. His stomach roiled and he realized he urgently needed the loo again. "Must run. Goodbye, Frances! Goodbye, Parker! Thank you for being here!"

Then off he went, walking as fast as he could towards the washrooms for the second time that day.

Geraint did his business. It was humiliating because it was loud, so he sat waiting until he was sure he was alone before he emerged.

But he was not alone. Ron stood waiting by the sinks. He waved a hand in front of his face. "Ugh, Geraint. It smells like rotting animal carcass in here."

Both men started to wash their hands. Geraint watched Ron warily in the mirrors. "Your restraining order has expired."

"Don't sweat it, Geraint. I mean, it looks like you've sweat enough already. How Darlene ever managed to get naked with you . . ." He shuddered.

Geraint tried to think of the assertiveness exercise they'd done in anger management. He could hear Frances telling him he shouldn't be a pushover. Voice trembling, he replied, "Your words can't hurt me. Best man won in there. I'm referring to me. *I* am the best man."

"Yup. You won this round."

Geraint looked at Ron's reflection. "What do you mean, *this round*?"

"Just that anything can happen between now and the formal divorce proceedings. Like, what if they found nasty images on a thumb drive in your possession?"

"Nasty—I don't have any nasty images. Why would I have nasty images? I don't even have a thumb drive." Ron just grinned again, showing his blinding white teeth. "Why are you doing this? Surely it's not because you want to see more of Keanu."

"Of course not. Kid's a little Geraint Mini-Me. Blech."

"Don't insult my son."

"Why, what are you going to do? Hit me? I would love it if you hit me."

"I'm not going to hit you. I just want to know why you're bothering with all of this."

He sighed. "It all boils down to love."

"For Darlene?"

"No, for my car. You mess with my car, you mess with me." He grabbed a huge wad of paper towels to wipe his hands. "And I play the long game."

Ron tossed the paper towels towards the garbage can and missed. The wad landed on the floor. He gave Geraint one more pearly white grin and left the washroom.

All of Geraint's good feels went away. His stomach started to roil again. He instinctively picked up Ron's litter and chucked it in the bin. Then he rushed back into the stall.

43

O h, Parker. That's awful." Wanda pushed a hand through her silver-dyed hair. She was around Frances's age, wearing stylish tortoise-shell glasses and jean overalls. The four of them—Wanda, Parker, Frances, and Jules—sat huddled around a small table in a coffee shop in Burnaby, close to the *Knights of the Castle* production office. "He really did that?"

Parker nodded.

"I should have asked you more questions. But when you did your disappearing act—I just figured you were one of those unreliable millennials we hear about."

"Did you have any idea Sebastian was . . ." Frances began.

Wanda bristled. "You think I'd put my team in the line of fire if I knew?"

"Sorry. We didn't mean—"

"We're just doing a little bit of intelligence gathering," said Jules, trying to smooth the waters. "To see if we can learn anything that might be useful."

Wanda's expression softened. "No. Of course I didn't know. But—" she stopped.

"But?"

". . . After you left, a few of my girls did comment that he could be a little handsy. So from that moment forward I never let them go to his trailer alone. They travel in pairs."

"And you never thought to tell the producers any of this?"

"It was my first season on the show. I figured, if he was a gen-uine threat, someone would have spoken up long before we came along."

"So you figured it was someone else's problem," said Jules.

Wanda put down her coffee mug. "I didn't come here to be interrogated." She reached for her bag.

"Wanda, please don't go," said Parker. "We appreciate your help, we really do. No one is blaming you, isn't that right, Jules?"

Jules nodded. "Apologies. I'm a criminal defence lawyer. I tend to come in hot."

"When you said you figured someone else would have spoken up," said Frances, hurriedly. "What if someone did, and no one listened?"

"It's possible," said Wanda, considering. "The producers have been with the show from the start. If this is a pattern—you'd think, over six seasons, someone would have said something."

"I've wondered that, too," said Parker.

Wanda looked at Jules. "Maybe you're right. Maybe I should have spoken up. But I've been in this business a long time, and I've seen a *lot* of bad behaviour . . . I just figured Sebastian was one of those actors from another era. You know, maybe a bit lecherous, but ultimately harmless." She drank the last of her coffee. "This show's been a slog from the beginning, and now this—thank god we've only got one week of filming left."

"It's exceedingly unlikely Parker's the only victim. We're trying to get a critical mass, so that hers isn't the only voice," said Jules. "Can you think of anyone else we should talk to?"

"I'm sorry. No." She stood and put on her sweater. "You did good work for the brief time you were with us, Parker. Next show I get, I'll see what I can do about bringing you on."

Parker's face lit up. "Thank you, Wanda. That means a lot."

The bell above the door jingled as Wanda left. Frances, Parker, and Jules sat clutching their empty mugs, discouraged. "Well," said Jules, "it was worth a try."

They got up and pulled on their jackets. The bell above the door jingled again.

Wanda had returned.

"I just thought of something. It may or may not be connected. A young woman on the crew was suddenly replaced about a month after you left, Parker. There one day, gone the next. I remember it was weird because everyone liked her and she seemed to be doing a good job."

"What's her name?" asked Jules, taking out her phone.

Wanda pursed her lips. "I'm not telling you that. I need to contact her first. If she says it's okay, I'll pass on her number."

And with that, Wanda turned and walked out of the café for a second time.

44

Geraint spent a sleepless night tossing and turning on his apart-hotel mattress, listening to strains of Iron Maiden from next door. He was terrified of what Ron might try to pull next. What had he meant by "nasty images"? Geraint was fairly certain he knew, but his mind, which he always tried to fill with pleasant thoughts, did not want to go there. Worse, he was terribly worried for Keanu. What was it like for his sweet boy to spend time with a man who thought he was *blech*?

In the morning, on little to no sleep, he drove to his house—because it was still his house, too, was it not?—to pick up Keanu, as it was his weekend. He prayed Ron wouldn't be there.

Darlene answered the door in her housecoat, looking tired. He expected her to be snippy after their day in court, but to his surprise, she was almost apologetic. "Look, Geraint. About the whole . . . Maybe we overreacted."

"I can't believe you would think I'd ever put our son in harm's way."

"I didn't. I mean, not really. But Ron was legit worried."

"Is he here?"

"No. He doesn't like our house. Says it's for hobbits."

Geraint took a deep breath. "Ron threatened me, Darlene. In the courthouse washroom. Told me he'd find a way to keep me from Keanu."

"That's ridiculous," she said. But he could see a glimmer of doubt in her eyes.

"Why would I make something like that up?"

"If he said anything like that it's because he's thinking of Keanu."

"He doesn't even like Keanu! He told me himself, he thinks he's *blech*! Our beautiful son!"

Her face hardened. "That's not true."

"It is. And I think you know I'm telling the truth because you know I'm the worst liar on the planet." Before he could say anything further, Keanu barrelled through the front door and flung himself at Geraint. "Daddy, Daddy, Daddy! I've missed you so much."

"I've missed you, too, my dear sweet boy." He lifted Keanu into his arms and hugged him tightly, breathing in his slightly sweaty hair and his sweet-smelling skin. "Have you got your backpack?"

"Oops!" said Keanu. He tore back into the house.

Geraint said calmly, "We need to work out a fifty-fifty parenting plan."

"Yeah, I'll get to it soon—"

"Not soon. Now. We start fifty-fifty next week. You can have first pick of days."

Darlene looked at him, startled. And Geraint *felt* startled. It was almost like an out-of-body experience. He had stood up for himself. Calmly, firmly. *With assertiveness.*

Dennis, he thought, would be proud.

Keanu came rushing back out, clutching his Thomas the Tank Engine backpack. This time he launched himself at Darlene, who picked him up and gave him a long hug. "Love you, Kee-Kee."

"Love you, too, Mommy."

"Have a good time with Daddy."

"I will."

Darlene kissed his chubby cheeks and lowered him to the ground. Keanu ran to Geraint's car. "Have him home by seven-thirty tomorrow night," Darlene said coolly. But before she went back inside, she added, "I'll work on the parenting plan."

Geraint and Keanu spent an action-packed thirty-six hours together. They went to Granville Island via the Aquabus and bought a Lee's doughnut. Keanu chased the seagulls and pigeons, and when a seagull grabbed his doughnut and flew away with it, they went back to Lee's and got him another one. They went to the playground near Geraint's apart-hotel, where Keanu spent hours playing an elaborate imaginary game that involved being chased by a monster (Geraint) as he "escaped" via the slide, the swings, and the monkey bars. This was normally Geraint's happy place, but today he found himself continuously gazing at his son with a feeling of dread. *Would Ron do something?* Later, when they were eating pizza and watching *Elf* for the umpteenth time because they both agreed it was the best movie ever and not just at Christmas, Keanu looked at him and said, "Daddy, why are your eyes leaking?" He was finally seeing his son again and he could barely enjoy it.

When he drove to Darlene's on Sunday evening, he had fantasies of driving right past the house and continuing all the way down to Mexico. He could change their names and raise Keanu as, say, Ignacio, on his own. He'd always liked the name Ignacio. Keanu—Ignacio—would quickly become fluent in Spanish. Geraint would find work as a mechanic and take night school courses so he could (much more slowly) learn the language. Perhaps he'd even meet a lovely señorita.

But then his fantasy fast-forwarded to the part where a bounty hunter busted down their motel room door and he was charged with kidnapping and extradited and spent the rest of his life in prison and never saw his son again.

So he pulled into the driveway and dropped his son off as planned, showering him with hugs and kisses. After Keanu had enthusiastically told his mom everything he'd done with his dad, he barrelled inside to feed his turtle. Darlene handed Geraint an Excel spreadsheet. "Here's what I came up with. I have Keanu Thursdays to Saturdays, you have him Sundays to Tuesdays, and we alternate Wednesdays."

"That seems fair."

"We've raised a pretty awesome kid, Ger," she said with what Geraint thought was a hint of nostalgia.

"That we have."

She went inside and closed the door, and Geraint stayed where he was for a moment, gazing at the place that he had poured so much sweat and love and effort into, that had once been his home, too.

As he drove back to his apart-hotel, trying to focus on the parenting plan victory rather than Ron's possible retribution, his phone rang. "Geraint, it's Alexei. I've looked through all of Jorge's invoices from corporate. Can you drop by?"

"I'll be there in ten," said Geraint, then added: "No, make it twenty. I'll see if Frances can join, too."

Sundays were usually the one evening of the week that Daisy deigned to spend with her mother. Frances would cook an elaborate meal, Daisy would devour it, then she'd disappear downstairs with excuses of "needing to prep for the work week" (which, as far as Frances could tell, involved watching episodes of *Love Island*), leaving Frances with all the clean-up. But this particular Sunday, Daisy had been called in to her current temp job at the PR firm to "write some press releases for a brand activation that needs to go live first thing on Monday." Frances wasn't sure what that meant, but she was delighted that Daisy seemed happy with her work situation for once.

When Geraint phoned, she'd just finished making a pot of chili, so she packed up the food and took it with her.

The four of them ate at Parker and Alexei's tiny kitchen table and got each other up to speed. Parker told Geraint about their meeting with Wanda. Geraint told them about his encounter with Ron in the courthouse bathroom.

"That guy is pure evil," said Parker.

"I'd love to hoist the man with his own petard," said Frances, and when everyone looked at her quizzically she added, "Shakespeare. I don't really know what it means, either. I just mean I'd like to kick his ass."

"I don't know if any of this will help," said Alexei as he pulled out a folder. "But some of his monthly charges to the franchisees are really suspect." He ran his finger down a column. "For example, *administration fee*. Five hundred a month per franchise. It's one of those impossibly vague terms that's hard to question or quantify. But if you think about ten franchisees—"

"Eleven," said Geraint.

"Okay, eleven, that's an extra five thousand five hundred a month that goes to corporate."

"*Corporate* meaning *Ron*," said Geraint.

Alexei moved his finger down the page. "Tell me about this item. What's an EDF?"

"It stands for environmental disposal fee," said Geraint. "We have to properly dispose of any used auto body parts. Some of them are considered hazardous waste."

"How does that work?"

"Franchisees deliver used parts once a week to the flagship store. Ron has a contract with a private company. They pick up all the items twice a month and drive them to a hazardous waste disposal depot."

"And Ron charges each franchise a thousand per month for the service?"

"Well, he has to pay the company, and the depot would have its own fees . . ."

"It still sounds inflated."

"You think he could be putting some of it in his own pocket?" asked Frances.

"It's easy enough to find out," said Parker. "What's the name of the disposal company? We can phone them, find out their rates."

"Now that you mention it, I'm not sure I ever knew the name of the company," Geraint admitted.

"Did you see them come to the store to take things away?" asked Frances.

He shook his head. "They always came after hours."

"Did that seem strange to you?" asked Frances.

"I honestly never thought about it. Ron would stay late those nights and send the rest of us home. Which, now that I think of it, was unusual. He hated it if anyone left before him. But the parts were always gone by morning."

"When was the company scheduled to come by?" asked Frances.

"First and third Monday of the month."

"Tomorrow's the third Monday of the month," said Alexei. They all exchanged a look.

"Are the four of us thinking the same thing?" asked Frances.

"We all want seconds because this is the best chili we've ever eaten?" Geraint ventured.

Frances sucked in her breath. "Are the *three* of us thinking the same thing?"

Parker and Alexei nodded. While Geraint served himself more chili, they got him up to speed.

45

B est Christmas movie of all time," Geraint said from the driver's seat of his Subaru. Frances was in the passenger seat. They both wore dark clothing and ball caps. The car was parked down the block from Ron's flagship Quicky Muffler shop, near Main and Terminal.

"*A Christmas Story*," said Alexei from the back seat.

"*Polar Express*," said Parker, beside him. They, too, were dressed head-to-toe in black.

"*Miracle on 34th Street*," said Frances.

"*Bah!* You're all wrong," said Geraint smugly. "It's *Elf*."

"None of us is wrong," said Frances. "Best Christmas movie ever is a matter of opinion."

"Ah, but my opinion is the right one," Geraint said, even more smugly. He had been asking them his version of trivia questions for over an hour.

Initially they'd found their first-ever stakeout exciting, but now, almost two hours in, their enthusiasm was waning. Geraint opened a large bag of ruffle chips, grabbed a handful, and passed it to Frances, who passed a package of Twizzlers into the back seat.

"Guys, look." Alexei pointed out the windshield. They followed his gaze. Ron was exiting through the back door of Quicky Muffler. They watched as he headed to his Huracan, waited for the Batman-style doors to open, climbed inside—and drove away.

The energy in the car deflated. "Well, that was anticlimactic," said Geraint.

"You're sure this is the right night?" asked Parker.

"It was when I worked here. It may have changed."

"None of this makes sense," said Parker. "I called every single hazardous waste disposal company in the Lower Mainland today. Told them I worked for Quicky Muffler, and I wanted to go over our disposal schedule."

"And?" asked Frances.

"Not one of them had Quicky Muffler as a client."

"So odd," said Geraint. "Ow!"

Frances had elbowed him, hard. A plain white cube van was backing into Quicky Muffler, towards the large garage doors. Once it was parked, the driver got out.

Ron.

They all watched as he opened the garage doors and began filling the cube van with heavy industrial garbage bags and boxes. "Those are the used parts," said Geraint.

It took Ron a good twenty minutes to fill the truck. When he was done he locked the garage doors, climbed into the driver's seat, and drove away.

"I don't get it," said Geraint. "Why would Ron be doing this himself when he could just hire someone? It's not like he doesn't have the money—" Again Frances elbowed him, hard. "Ow! Frances, must you do that—"

"Shut up and follow him!"

"Oh. Right." Geraint turned on the ignition. He did a U-turn and, keeping his distance, began to tail the truck.

"This is all rather nerve-wracking and exciting. Like we're in our own spy movie or TV show. Pardon me while I get my shoe phone, ha ha ha ha."

"I don't get it," said Parker.

"Maxwell Smart from *Get Smart*. I used to watch reruns at my nice great-aunt's house." Geraint had kept up a constant stream of nervous chatter like this for well over an hour. They'd been following Ron at a safe distance on well-trafficked roads as he'd travelled east through the city and onto Highway 1, driving deeper and deeper into the Fraser Valley, past Burnaby, Langley, Chilliwack.

"Where on earth is he going?" murmured Frances. "We're almost in Hope."

"And we're well past any of the hazardous waste disposal places I called," said Parker.

"Maybe he drives to one that's further away because they charge him less," said Geraint, "and he gets to pocket more."

"He's put his blinker on," said Alexei.

Sure enough, the truck took the next exit. Geraint took the same exit, staying well behind.

But still Ron kept driving. He drove for at least half an hour longer, into the mountains. Geraint started to whistle tunelessly. Frances cleared her throat. He stopped whistling. "Right. One of your many pet peeves."

Finally, Ron turned onto a logging road. "Don't turn yet," said Frances. "Keep driving." Geraint did as he was told. "Okay, now pull a U-turn and follow him. And kill the lights."

Geraint killed the lights, plunging them into a thick, all-encompassing darkness. "Oh, boy. It is very hard to see."

"Just stay well back and drive as slowly as you need to. Your eyes will adjust."

They drove like this, uphill on a rutted, potholed logging road, for another five minutes. Everyone in the car had gone very quiet—suddenly aware that they could, in fact, be driving into a dangerous situation. "This is feeling less *Get Smart* and more *Breaking Bad*," said Geraint. "What if he's meeting a drug lord? Or a gun runner? Or a human smuggler?"

"With used car batteries and mufflers?" said Frances, but the truth was she felt anxious, too.

"There he is," murmured Parker.

Up ahead they could see the cube van, parked perpendicular to the road, headlights on. Ron opened the door and climbed out. Loud music—was it Nickelback?—blasted from the truck. He got swallowed by darkness. A moment later he reappeared, lit up by the headlights. He was carrying one of the industrial garbage bags.

They watched as he hurled the bag down into what must have been an old quarry or a ravine. He disappeared into the darkness again, coming back with another. Then another.

"This is low even for Ron," murmured Geraint.

When Ron had dumped a number of bags, Parker said: "Um, guys? What are we going to do when Ron is done?" They all stared at each other, the problem coming into focus. When Ron was done, he would drive back down the logging road. The logging road they were currently blocking, with no place to hide.

Geraint's mouth formed a little O of fear. "Fudge."

"We need to turn around carefully and get out of here now," said Frances. "Before he's done."

"But what if he hears us," Geraint began.

"He won't. He's blasting his music."

Geraint started the car. It took forever to turn around because the road was narrow, and it was dark, and they were terrified of getting stuck. It was a twelve-point turn, but he did it.

"Wait," said Alexei before Geraint started to drive back down the logging road. "We don't have proof."

"We have our word for it. And the location of the dumping site," said Frances. "It'll have to be enough, we need to go."

They heard a door open in the back. Then another.

"Drive to the main road," said Parker. "Come get us after he's left." Then she and Alexei closed their doors. A moment later they were both gone, swallowed up by the darkness.

Geraint and Frances parked near the exit to the logging road, tucked behind a large stand of fir trees. They waited. And waited. Geraint started whistling tunelessly again, then stopped mid-whistle when he saw Frances's stony gaze. "If anything happens to either of them . . ." he said, unable to finish the thought.

"I'm sure they're fine," said Frances, with more confidence than she felt.

"I should have been the one to get out of the car."

"But Geraint, you're *driving* the car." They both fell silent after that, consumed by their own anxious thoughts.

A few minutes later, they heard the truck. It turned onto the main road, towards them. They held their collective breath, even though they were well hidden. The truck barrelled past. An awful thought occurred to Geraint as he pulled out and swung onto the logging road. "What if he has Parker and Alexei tied up in the back?"

"You've been watching too many crime shows," Frances replied, even though she'd had the exact same thought. "But if we don't find them, I took down his licence plate. We'll call the police."

They made their way slowly up the logging road for the second time that night. About halfway to Ron's dumping spot they saw, in Geraint's headlights, Parker and Alexei running towards them, Alexei using the flashlight on his phone to guide their way. They climbed into the back seat. Geraint started his twelve-point turn again. "Are you all right? He didn't spot you?"

"He didn't have a clue," Alexei said gleefully. "Parker, show them." Parker leaned in between Frances and Geraint and held up her phone.

She had taken dozens of photos. Some were blurry or too dark. But some, thanks to the truck's headlights, were excellent. There were shots of Ron hurling bags of garbage. There were shots of the ravine filled with garbage—Ron had clearly been using this spot as his dumping ground for a long time. "Alexei has just as many on his phone."

"You two . . . this is amazing," said Geraint. "And very brave."

Frances shook her head in disbelief. "So not only is he illegally dumping hazardous waste, but he's charging his franchisees for a non-existent service, pocketing thousands of extra dollars a month."

"And that's just one line item," said Alexei. "You get a good forensic accountant on this, and I bet they'd discover more fraudulent activity." He started to giggle. "Sorry, I think I'm in the midst of an endorphin rush. That was amazing. If I didn't love accounting so much, I'd become a spy."

"I'd join you," said Parker, throwing her arms around him. "We'd be like the parents in *Spy Kids*."

The mood was boisterous on the drive home. When they got back to Vancouver, Geraint insisted on stopping at DQ, where he bought them all a round of Blizzards. They sat in a booth, having a closer look at the photos.

While they did so, a text message popped up on Parker's screen.

"It's Wanda," she said. "She's given me a phone number." She scanned the message. "I remember this woman. Evelyn. She was a stand-in. She's willing to talk, but strictly off the record." She looked at the others. "Apparently she has a story to tell."

46

He told me his management team had sent him a screenplay for his consideration. He said there was a small part in it that would be perfect for me, and that he could make my involvement one of his stipulations." Evelyn was beautiful, a willowy thing with high cheek bones, no more than a few years older than Parker. "He told me to drop by his trailer after he was done for the day, and he'd show me the script."

She wrapped her arms around herself before she continued. "I should have known better. But I let my ego get the better of me. I wanted it to be true. So I went to his trailer. When I arrived, he was only wearing a robe, nothing underneath. There was no script. He exposed himself and then he tried to"—she started to shake—"he tried to force himself on me. I just went numb. It was only a stroke of luck that the third AD knocked on the door. I bolted out of there as fast as I could."

Parker, Frances, and Jules sat across from Evelyn at a picnic table in a small park near Evelyn's house in North Vancouver. Frances's heart went out to her; she could see the residual fear, and worse, the residual shame, in Evelyn's eyes.

"He's definitely got a pattern," said Parker, then she told Evelyn her story, because she knew that while neither she nor Evelyn would wish this on anyone, there was comfort to be had in knowing you were not alone.

"Did you tell anyone?" asked Jules.

"I told one of the producers. He said he'd look into it. Next thing I knew, I was replaced."

"Were you offered money in exchange for your silence?" asked Frances.

"No."

"You never signed an NDA?" said Jules.

"No."

Jules leaned forward. "Would you be willing to go on record?"

Evelyn looked down at her hands. "I'm really sorry. You can use my story, but I need to remain anonymous. I'd like to help, but—I have a family. A beautiful little boy and a great partner. I've got a great new gig . . . I don't want to get blacklisted. He's got a lot of power." Tears welled up in Evelyn's eyes. "The hardest part is the shame."

Parker nodded. "I feel it every day."

"I ask myself all the time, did I do anything to provoke him? Did I flirt with him? I mean, I *wanted* that non-existent part."

"I let my hair down. Before I went into his trailer," said Parker; it was the small detail that haunted her to this day. "Because I've always been told my hair is my best feature. And I wanted to look good for him." Her eyes filled with tears, too. The two young women gripped hands across the table.

"Neither of you did anything wrong," said Frances, her own eyes welling up.

"We know that, on an intellectual level," Parker responded. "But it doesn't stop the spiralling thoughts."

Evelyn stood, wiping her eyes. "I have to go. My son gets out of preschool soon."

"Thank you for meeting us, Evelyn," said Jules.

Evelyn nodded, then she hurried away.

Parker and Frances both looked at Jules, who shook her head. "I'm sorry, Parker. But I don't think it's enough, not yet. Police will be reluctant to press charges without more concrete evidence. And sometimes concrete evidence can simply mean more women who are willing to go on record." Jules stood. "We'll keep talking. But right now I have to get back to the office."

She left. Frances and Parker rose from the picnic table and started the walk back to their cars.

"I know where he stays during production," said Parker. "The Wellington on Georgia."

"So?"

"So he's still here. Wanda said they had one more week of shooting."

"So?"

Parker stopped. So did Frances. "I'm just thinking . . . What if *he* went on record?"

"Sebastian Trevor?" said Frances. "He would never do that."

"Not on purpose."

"I'm not following."

"Just—hear me out."

Frances listened, wide-eyed, while Parker outlined her plan.

47

While Parker was sharing her idea with Frances, Geraint was being ushered into Ron's office at the flagship Quicky Muffler shop. Ron sat behind his desk in the same tan leather office chair that he and Darlene had been . . .

Geraint shook the image from his head. He was wearing his grey trousers with the checkered button-up shirt, wanting to look somewhat professional. Ron gestured for him to sit, so he sat across from the desk in a chair that he knew for a fact had had two inches cut off the legs, so that no matter who sat there, Ron would tower over them. "You've got a lot of nerve, showing up here," said Ron. "Although I guess it's better than sending crazy ladies on your behalf."

Geraint maintained his calm. "Your restraining order has officially expired."

"So you keep saying. Let's cut to the chase, Geraint. To what do I owe this displeasure?"

"Two things: I want my money back . . ."

Ron barked out a laugh.

"And more important, I want you to stop interfering in my custody proceedings with Darlene. You've said it yourself, you don't even like Keanu."

"No, I don't. But I like to *win*, so the answer is no on all fronts."

Geraint held up his phone. Ron leaned forward, squinting. "What's that?"

"Please have a good look. Then we'll see if you'd like to reconsider."

Ron kept a poker face as he scrolled through the photos, but Geraint could see his eyelid start to twitch. When he was done, Geraint reached for the phone but Ron held onto it. "I could destroy this. I could run over it like your psycho friend did to my phone."

"You could. But do you honestly think those are the only copies?"

Ron reluctantly handed back the phone. "What do you want?"

"A cheque for fifty grand."

"Fine."

"And I want you to stop cheating your franchisees out of their hard-earned profits; they're struggling enough as it is. My accountant friend has outlined your worst transgressions." He handed Ron a sheet of paper.

Ron's face was getting red. "Fine."

"And last but not least: I simply want equal parenting time. If you try any of your dirty tricks, I'll send the photos to the authorities." Ron was about to speak, but Geraint held up a hand. "And might I suggest that you do your best to see Darlene when I have Keanu. Because if I hear that you have done anything to hurt my son—said so much as an unkind word—I will end you, Ron. It is that simple."

Ron sat back in his chair and put his hands behind his head. "Never took you for a blackmailer, Geraint." Geraint realized with alarm that Ron was looking at him with respect for the first time in . . . well, ever. "But okay. Less time I spend with that kid is no skin off my ass."

"So we have an agreement."

"I do these things, you make the photos disappear. And you tell no one."

"Exactly. Once the cheque has cleared, and once Darlene and I have finalized our parenting agreement—the photos will be deleted off all of my devices."

"How will I know you've actually gotten rid of them?"

"Ron. Look at me. Haven't you always said I'm the worst liar? Haven't you always been able to trust me one hundred percent?"

"I have."

The two men shook.

A few days later, Geraint received a cheque for fifty thousand dollars. A few days after that, he and Darlene went before the trial judge and signed a new, fifty-fifty parenting agreement.

That evening, Geraint double-checked to make sure the cheque had cleared. He opened a cold tall can of Yellow Dog hazy pale ale to celebrate.

Then he sent the photos to the Ministry of Natural Resources, the police, several dozen media outlets—and every single Quicky Muffler franchise owner in the Lower Mainland.

Local Businessman Faces Charges for Illegal Dumping

Lars Devlin, *Vancouver Post*

Ron Neumann, owner and operator of the flagship Quicky Muffler Shop on Vancouver's west side, has been charged with illegal dumping of hazardous wastes at a remote location near Hope, BC.

"Based on the scale of what we've discovered, it looks like it's been going on for years," said a bylaw officer who was sent to investigate. "This is in direct violation of the Canadian Environmental Protection Act."

"I'm stunned," said Jorge Soledad, one of eleven Quicky Muffler franchise operators in the Lower Mainland. "Mr. Neumann charged us a steep environmental disposal fee every month. To find out that money was going into his pocket . . . It's terrible. For the environment, and for guys like us who are trying to run an honest business. He's tarnished the Quicky Muffler name."

Based on franchisees' claims, this may just be the tip of the iceberg for Mr. Neumann. A police officer who spoke on the condition of anonymity added, "I suspect we'll be adding fraud and theft charges in the near future—and I'm quite sure the CRA will be interested in some of his 'accounting practices.'"

The illegal dumping came to light when police received an anonymous tip from a concerned citizen.

48

P arker tried to emanate far more confidence than she felt as she strode into the opulent Wellington hotel lobby, with its chandeliers, gold-patterned wallpaper, and dark mahogany wood. Her hair cascaded around her shoulders. She was wearing a shimmery silver dress. It had been bought in a moment of madness at a second-hand store called Turnabout, when she and Alexei were first dating and he'd invited her to a fancy restaurant. She'd spent the entire night shivering, and later Alexei admitted that he'd spent the entire night worrying that he was using the wrong piece of cutlery. They'd both decided then and there that they far preferred a night out at their neighbourhood pub, eating bangers and mash. The silver sheath had gone right to the back of their tiny closet, not to be worn again until tonight.

When they picked her up, Geraint had taken one look at her and shaken his head. "I just want to cover you up with a parka." He was not at all on board with Parker's plan, not in the slightest. Frances wasn't on board with it either and had tried strenuously to talk Parker out of it. But Parker had told them she was doing it, with or without their help, and there was no way either of them were letting her do this alone.

"I still think we should wait until Alexei can join us," Frances had said as they'd left the apartment.

"Alexei has night school."

"But he knows what you're doing, right?" asked Geraint. "He'll join us when he can?"

Parker had grabbed her clutch purse, not looking Geraint in the eye. "Of course." This was a bald-faced lie, and Parker felt rather guilty deceiving these two old people who'd become her good friends. But it was necessary. Alexei had no idea what she was up to, because if she'd told him, he'd have tried to talk her out of it or insisted on coming. And if he laid eyes on Sebastian, she didn't think he'd be able to stop himself from confronting him, which would almost certainly ruin everything.

Now, as she strode towards the bar, she tried to pretend she was a model on a catwalk. *Own the look*, she told herself. She strode past two people sitting in the lobby, scrolling through their phones. The woman was well dressed, fitting in well with the opulence of the Wellington. The man was wearing a red track suit and stood out like a sore thumb. Parker did her best not to make eye contact, but their presence gave her comfort.

Wanda, bless her, had done some more digging for Parker. She'd found out through a friend in the production office that Sebastian had a nightly routine: he sat at the bar and ate a steak and salad for dinner, along with one or two vodka martinis, before heading to his room. She knew she was taking a chance; he might have other plans tonight. But as she'd told Frances, "If he isn't there, I'll come back tomorrow night."

The lounge was dimly lit, the music rather loud. She scanned the room. It was early enough that there were just a handful of people. Only one elderly man sat at the bar. Parker felt a pang of disappointment, until she realized that the elderly man was Sebastian.

She started to shake. *It's okay*, she told herself. *He can't hurt you here.* She slid her phone out of her clutch purse. Her plan, such as it was, was to try to get him to admit what he'd done to her and get it on tape. She pressed record. Then she took a deep breath and forced herself to put one foot in front of the other.

He didn't look up from his meal when she slid onto the stool next to his. He was reading an article on his phone, which, Parker saw, was an article about him. *Ugh, how did I ever think he was good-looking?* she thought. *He has a wrinkly neck. He has hairs growing out of his ears!* "Cranberry and soda, please," she said to the bartender.

At the sound of her voice, Sebastian glanced up. Her heart started to race. Every fibre in her body was telling her to flee. She hadn't thought this through very clearly: What would happen when he recognized her? Would he be furious? Would he get up and leave? Would he go to his room and immediately contact his lawyers?

"Cran and soda," he said. "Aren't we being puritanical."

That was it. No anger, no fear. She tried to give him her best flirtatious smile, even though bile was rising in her throat. "It's a school night."

"Even schoolgirls are allowed to be naughty once in a while." He graced her with an oily grin. "Allow me to order you a real drink. You look like a cosmopolitan girl." He called the bartender over. "Steve, another martini, and a cosmopolitan for the lady." Parker thought she saw the slightest look of disapproval cross Steve's face, but whether it was directed towards her or Sebastian, she didn't know.

None of this was going quite the way she'd thought it would. For one thing, the music in the bar was quite loud. What if it drowned out his voice on her phone? And for another, it was like he'd forgotten what had happened between them in his trailer, what he'd done to her . . .

"What's your name, darling?"

The realization hit Parker like a ton of bricks.

He didn't recognize her.

The entitled asshole who had ruined her life in under five minutes *did not even recognize her.*

Suddenly Parker's fear was gone, replaced with a blood-boiling rage. Now, more than ever, she was determined to follow through with her plan, but she couldn't do it here. She needed to get him somewhere quieter.

"Darling? Your name?"

Parker took a deep breath. *Focus on your goal.* Then she turned to him and gave him her best dazzling smile. "Victoria," she said. "My name is Victoria."

Sebastian held out his hand. Parker took it, even though touching his skin made her want to puke. "Well, Victoria. It's lovely to meet you. I'm Sebastian. Sebastian Trevor." The bartender put their drinks in front of them.

"Oh," said Parker as she raised her glass, "I know who you are."

They stayed for two more drinks. Whenever Sebastian wasn't looking, Parker—with silent apologies to the cleaners—poured hers onto the carpet beneath her bar stool.

She barely remembered what they talked about, except that he did most of the talking, telling her stories of his "humble beginnings," his childhood in the Cotswolds, and anecdotes from various movies he'd done over the years that involved a lot of name-dropping and making him look like the hero. She swore he played up his posh British accent. She barely said a word, just oohed and aahed and giggled in all the right places.

Finally, after an hour or so, when he was very liquored up and she was stone-cold sober, he settled the bill. Parker waited with bated breath.

"Well, Virginia. It was very nice to meet you."

"Victoria. And the pleasure was all mine." As he slid off his bar stool, Parker saw her opportunity sliding away with him.

"Would you care to join me in my room, Victoria?"

Bingo. She smiled demurely. "I would love that." She hopped off her bar stool and pretended to stumble. "Oh my. Those cosmopolitans have made me a bit loopy." She made sure to hold her phone in her hand.

"Steady, sweetheart," he murmured. "Take my arm." Parker linked her arm through his and allowed him to guide her out of the bar.

Frances and Geraint tried to occupy themselves. Geraint played *Candy Crush* on his phone. Frances had opened *Mindful of Murder*, a page-turner of a book she'd picked up just the other day, but she was so nervous she couldn't absorb a word. "She's on the move," Frances murmured without looking at Geraint. "My two o'clock. She's with Sebastian."

Geraint glanced over, trying to be subtle.

"She can barely stand," said Geraint with concern. "She said she wouldn't drink."

"Why is she heading towards the elevators with him?" asked Frances. "We agreed: public spaces only."

"And where is Alexei? Shouldn't he be here by now?"

The elevator doors opened.

"Maybe she's just saying a final goodbye before he heads to his room," said Frances.

Sebastian stepped into the elevator, followed by Parker.

The elevator doors closed.

The two of them stared at each other. An icy dread crept up Frances's spine.

"This. Is NOT. The plan!" said Geraint, his pitch going up at least an octave.

"Oh god," said Frances. "What if he slipped something into her drink?"

Geraint emitted a strangled sound. He leapt to his feet. "Find out what floor he's on and text it to me."

"You think someone's just going to hand me that information?"

But Geraint was already sprinting across the lobby towards the stairs.

As it turned out, someone *did* just hand her that information.

Miguel was drying glasses behind the bar and thinking about Sebastian Trevor. He loathed that man. Even though he'd told him his name countless times, he still insisted on calling him Steve.

Miguel knew Sebastian's type. Guys like him came into his bar all the time. Men who traded on their celebrity and/or their money to lure in women half their age. But in a sea of boorish men, Sebastian was the worst. The things he said to Miguel about the women he'd bedded, when it was just the two of them in the bar—it made Miguel's hair curl. He never engaged, but he also knew, if he wanted to keep his job, he couldn't tell him to shut the fuck up.

He was ruminating on all of this when an attractive older woman hurried up to the bar. She grabbed a hundred-dollar bill from her wallet and held it out to him. "Hi, look, I realize how crazy this sounds but I need your help. Our friend was just in here with Sebastian Trevor, and she's gone back to his room, and I fear she's in physical danger. I know it breaks all the rules but please, if you know his room number—"

"Twenty-twelve."

"I'm begging you, there's no time to lose—"

"Twenty-twelve. His room number is twenty-twelve."

Frances stopped. She gazed at Miguel in disbelief. Then she quickly texted the number to Geraint. "Thank you," she said, sliding the hundred-dollar bill towards him. "Thank you so much."

He slid the money back. "Keep your money. Just—don't tell anyone I told you, okay? I like my job. I just don't like Mr. Trevor."

Geraint had sprinted up the first five flights of stairs when his phone pinged. "Jesus Murphy, the *twentieth* floor?"

He jogged up the next three, then walked up the next two. After that, he had to drag one leg after the other up each stair. His lungs were on fire. Sweat ran liberally from his pores, soaking the T-shirt under his track suit. He wasn't getting enough oxygen. His breathing was laboured and short. He was starting to see spots. He worried he might collapse. But then the thought would enter his head, *If that creep hurts Parker again*—and he would manage another step, and another.

Finally he reached the twentieth floor. He pushed open the fire door with a *clang* and limped towards room twenty-twelve. He pounded on the door. "Open up, you monster! I know you're in there! If you dare lay one finger on my friend I will pulverize you! You will be nothing but a pile of bones and goo!" A few doors along the corridor opened and people peered out, alarmed. "Call security!" he shouted at them. "A crime may be underway at this very moment!"

"Geraint?" Geraint turned. He was perplexed by what he saw. It was Parker. She had just stepped off the elevator, and she was followed by Sebastian. He looked cowed. He was rubbing his wrist.

Parker beckoned urgently to Geraint from the elevator doors. "Time for us to go." She stepped back inside, holding the doors for him.

Sebastian tried to push past Geraint to get to his room. He was, like so many actors, shorter than he appeared onscreen. Geraint stepped in front, towering over him. Sebastian gazed up at him, fear in his eyes. "You're lucky I don't believe in violence," said Geraint, "because I really ought to bop you in the nose."

"Geraint!" Parker said anxiously.

"Whatever she tells you," Sebastian said, pointing a trembling finger towards the elevator, "it's all lies. She is a lying, crazy bitch."

Geraint gave a disappointed sigh. "Well, now you've left me with no choice."

He bopped Sebastian in the nose.

Then he joined Parker in the elevator. The doors closed just as the second elevator doors opened and two security guards stepped out.

"What the hell were you thinking?" Frances said ten minutes later. They'd decamped to a coffee shop a few blocks from the hotel, figuring it was wise to put some distance between them and the Wellington. "That was unbelievably dangerous."

"YOU HAD US SO WORRIED!" said Geraint in his high-pitched voice. He sat clutching a Snapple, looking miserable in his sweat-soaked track suit.

"I know," said Parker. "And I'm sorry. But it was noisy in the bar. And I just had to get him to admit what he'd done, especially when I realized he didn't even recognize me. And I'm okay. I'm really okay."

"What did you say to him?" asked Frances.

Parker smiled. She pulled out her phone, placed it on the table and hit play.

"You don't remember me, do you?"

"Sorry, darling. Refresh my memory, why don't you."

"I worked on this season of Knights of the Castle.*"*

"You did? Were you background?"

"*No, I was a wardrobe assistant. Brand new. You asked me to come to your trailer one day. Then you tried to sexually assault me.*"

There was a long pause on the recording.

"*I don't know what you're talking about.*"

"*I think you do.*"

"*Look, you—*"

There was another pause on the recording, and a gasp, followed by a whimper. "He grabbed my arm at that point," Parker explained calmly. "But I've taken self-defence classes, so I used a wrist lock. He wasn't going anywhere." The recording continued, Sebastian now sounding breathless and in pain, and Parker in firm control:

"*You were naked under your robe. You tried to force me to give you a blow job. I whacked your balls with a cudgel.*"

"*That was you? You bloody well hurt me. You completely overreacted—*"

"*To sexual assault?*"

"*Oh, for—it wasn't sexual assault. I was just having a little fun. Don't tell me you weren't enjoying it—*"

"*What gave you the idea that I enjoyed it? Was it the fact that I tried to make excuses to get out of there? Or the fact that I struggled? Or that there was fear in my eyes? In my voice? Does any of that scream 'enjoy' to you? Or consent?*"

"*Look, you little bitch*"—here, Frances and Geraint drew in sharp breaths—"*you signed an NDA, and if you say anything to anyone, I will destroy you.*"

"*Oh, Sebastian. You've already destroyed me. I have nothing left to lose. You're the one who should be scared.*"

"Then we arrived on the twentieth floor, and I released his wrist," Parker said.

"Wow," said Frances. "That is exceedingly damning."

"And you held it together so well," said Geraint.

"Assertiveness without anger," Parker said with a smile, quoting Dennis.

"But you still should not have done that," said Frances sternly. "It was very dangerous."

"I thought I'd have a heart attack running up twenty flights of stairs," Geraint added.

Frances looked at him, puzzled. "Where were you when I texted the room number?"

"Fifth floor."

"So, why didn't you just take the elevator from the fifth floor?"

Geraint blinked. It was clear the idea had not occurred to him. Parker came to his rescue, saying with kindness, "The Wellington still has an old-school elevator, but you didn't know that. You probably assumed you'd need a key card."

"Y-y-yes. Yes, that's it," said Geraint. "It must also be a very slow elevator. Because how on earth did I get to the twentieth floor before you?" Then his eyes widened. "Unless—you know those stories about toddlers who get pinned under a vehicle, and the mother's adrenaline kicks in, and she lifts the car with superhuman strength? Did I find superhuman strength and somehow beat you there?"

"That must have been it," said Parker.

Geraint leaned back in his chair, grinning in amazement. "Well, I'll be. Who knew I had that in me?" He drained his Snapple. "If you'll excuse me, ladies, I'm going to try to freshen up a bit." He walked away, whistling as he went.

Once he was out of earshot Frances asked, "Okay, what really happened?"

"I'll tell you if you promise to never tell Geraint."

"Promise."

"You know how he loves the movie *Elf*?" Frances nodded. "Alexei and I finally watched it the other night. There's a scene where Buddy steps onto an elevator for the first time in his life, and he presses all the buttons so it lights up like a Christmas tree. So I did that. We stopped on a bunch of floors on the way up. It was my safety plan. I figured if he tried anything, I'd have an escape route every twenty seconds or so."

"But he also had an escape route every twenty seconds or so."

Parker grinned. "Not with my wrist lock, he didn't."

The women kept their promise from that day forward. They never breathed a word. And the story about the day he beat an elevator to the twentieth floor to help a friend became one of Geraint's go-to tales. He trotted it out at dinner parties. He told Keanu when he was old enough to understand. He told his grandchildren when they were old enough, too. And even though it wasn't exactly true, Geraint had absolutely behaved heroically, and it was a great story, and perhaps in the end these were the things that mattered.

Perhaps it wasn't the truth, but it was *a* truth.

49

The next day was sunny but blustery, and Geraint decided to speed-walk around the seawall. He was due at Frances's later that afternoon for a meeting with Parker, Alexei, and Jules. Because Frances wasn't with him, he whistled tunelessly and happily throughout most of his walk. Jorge had called him just last night to tell him he'd heard Ron's Lamborghini Huracan had been repoed, right in front of all his employees at the flagship store. "Apparently he's been in over his head for years, spending money he didn't have, trying to recoup some of it from us. They're going after everything he owns."

Geraint almost felt bad for Ron.

Almost.

He whistled "Blue Skies" as he approached his building. A woman was pacing out front.

It was Darlene.

"What are you doing here?" he asked, immediately concerned. "Is Keanu okay?"

"Keanu's fine. I've left him with his favourite sitter. Remember Isabelle?"

"Sure. She's terrific. Can play with Lego for hours."

Darlene pushed her hair behind her ears. "I was hoping we could talk."

Geraint didn't want her to see his sad little apartment, so he took her to a nearby coffee shop instead. He bought them both a decaf and a rather stale Danish to share.

"I'm not seeing Ron anymore," she said.

"Oh. Well, probably for the best," said Geraint as nonchalantly as possible. "I hear he's in a spot of trouble."

"He sure is. But I was thinking of ending it before any of that happened."

"Really?"

She nodded. "I was a fool, Geraint. He never liked Keanu. He turned me against you . . ." She started shredding her napkin. "I don't know why I did it. I think I was just bored. Looking for something more. When the truth was, I had everything I needed, all along."

Geraint looked at her, puzzled.

"*You*, Geraint. *You* were all I needed. A simple man with simple needs who loves me exactly as I am." She gripped his hands. "I want to get back together."

"But . . . we're in the midst of a divorce."

"I know. But maybe second time's the charm. Look at Elizabeth Taylor and Richard Burton. Melanie Griffith and Don Johnson. They married twice."

"And divorced twice."

"We could have a simple ceremony, just the two of us and Keanu, on a beach in Cabo San Lucas. Where we spent our honeymoon." She leaned across the table. "Think about it. We can be a family again."

Geraint gazed at her across the table. God, she was beautiful, with her thick hair and blue eyeshadow and false eyelashes; like a young Tammy Faye Bakker (the object of Geraint's first, guilty masturbation sessions when he was a lad). And now she was saying the words he'd wanted to hear for months.

So it was hard for him to say what he said next. "I will always love you, Darlene." He extricated his hands from hers. "But no. I'm sorry. I do not want to get back together."

Darlene blinked in surprise. "I understand you're still hurting, and you have every right to be," she said. "But you don't mean it—"

"Oh, but I do." He sat up straighter in his chair. "I loved you so much, Darlene. But I think I always knew, deep down, that you didn't love me."

"I didn't mean what I said. It was a stupid thing to say—"

"Come, now." He smiled sadly at her. "You did mean it. And that's okay. You've always wanted more than I can give you. But I'm happy with my life. And I don't want to be someone's consolation prize. You deserve more than that."

And then he had a revelation, a sensation that was new to him, because all his life he'd been made to feel—from his drunk pa, his cold ma, his mean great-aunt, his boss, and yes, his ex-wife—that he wasn't good enough, wasn't handsome enough, wasn't smart enough, wasn't enough of anything. So he voiced that revelation with a kind of wonder and awe:

"*I* deserve more than that," he said.

50

S o let me get this straight." Jules stood in the middle of Frances's living room later that same afternoon, gazing down at Frances and Geraint, who sat across from Parker and Alexei. "With your express knowledge, Parker ambushed Sebastian Trevor at his hotel." They all cowered under her fierce lawyerly gaze. "*And* you let her put herself in the line of danger—"

Geraint leapt to his feet. "Objection! We had no idea she was going to get into the elevator with him."

Jules rubbed her forehead. "I can't decide if what you did was incredibly brave or incredibly stupid."

"If it's helpful," said Alexei, "I've landed on a combination of both." Alexei had gone through a gamut of emotions the night before when Parker told him what she had done, but in the end, it was impossible for him to be angry with her for not including him in her plan because she'd been so euphoric. It seemed like a part of her had been freed. For the moment at least, it felt like a victory. Plus, she'd practically dragged him into the bedroom for two rounds of passionate sex.

"Would the recording be admissible in a court of law?" asked Frances.

"Yes," said Jules. "In Canada we have something called one-party consent. It allows private citizens to record confessions." She turned to Parker. "But if you go to the police, and the Crown finds there's enough evidence to meet the charge approval

300

standard—which is still a big *if*—it could be a long, painful, frankly nasty road for you, because you are still only one voice."

"I've been thinking about that, too," said Frances, "and I have another idea. Have any of you heard of Caroline Beresford?"

"Of course. Investigative reporter. Her path is littered with the men, and the odd woman, she's destroyed. Thorn in my side during a few of my cases," said Jules. "And excellent at what she does." She pulled out her phone and gave Frances, then Parker, a small smile. "I might even have her contact info."

Frances left a message for Caroline that very afternoon. Within hours, Caroline called back. Frances put her on to Parker, who agreed to a meeting. At that meeting, Caroline told her that rumours had swirled around Sebastian Trevor for years, and that Parker's tape, along with the anonymous source and a few other incriminating stories Caroline had dug up, might be enough for her to convince her editors to run an initial article. It would help, she said, if she could meet Evelyn and corroborate the story for herself; Evelyn could retain her anonymity.

Evelyn agreed to meet with her.

A couple of weeks later, after her paper's legal team vetted it, Caroline published her first article, "The Trouble with Trevor." She didn't use Parker's name, but within hours, the story blew up internationally. Within days, Sebastian Trevor's lawyers sent Parker a registered letter threatening to sue her for breaching her NDA, and another letter to Caroline's newspaper, threatening to sue for libel.

Over the next few months six other women came forward, two on the record, four anonymously. Sebastian Trevor's PR firm issued a statement on behalf of the actor, vehemently denying all of the charges and vowing to fight to clear his name.

Then another woman came forward, on the record: Analise Olsen—aka Lady Charlotte, Sebastian's co-star in *Knights of the Castle*.

The floodgates were opened.

The same PR firm that had helped craft Sebastian's denial dropped him like a hot potato. So did his agent and his management team.

When Sharon finally found out the truth, she rallied behind Parker in her own way, telling anyone who listened that she'd always gotten a bad vibe from Sebastian and that her daughter had clearly inherited Sharon's ability to speak truth to power.

A while later, Parker heard from Wanda that the writers of *Knights of the Castle*, who were deep into working on the seventh season of the show, had been asked by one of the new producers (the old ones had, unsurprisingly, been fired) to write Sir Godfrey out of the show in the first episode, without ever having to use the actor in the flesh.

When the season eventually aired a year and a half later, Sebastian's body double fell overboard and was torn to bloody shreds by a sea monster.

51

What would you rather: Be circled by sharks while swimming in the ocean or charged by a grizzly bear on a hike?" Geraint asked. The three of them walked side by side through Trout Lake Park, windbreakers unzipped, sun hats on.

"Definitely the bear," said Frances. "At least I'd be able to stand, and I could try to throw things or punch it in the nose."

"Same," said Parker.

They'd had their final anger management class a couple of weeks earlier. Everyone was there except Wayson. "Unfortunately he got into another road rage incident," said Dennis. "Still, I figure my success rate is rather good for my first kick at the can." Frances decided not to point out that his success rate was four out of seven, or just over half.

He'd bought them a Safeway cake to celebrate. "*Happy Retirement Bettina?*" Byron asked.

"It never got claimed," Dennis explained. "So it was half price."

They all had a big slice, and Dennis poured them glasses of sparkling apple juice. "I want to congratulate you all on your hard work in this class. I hope you've gained some valuable insights and learned some strategies to use moving forward."

"I can't believe I'm saying this," Frances replied, "but I think we all did."

"Job well done, Dennis," said Geraint, raising his glass.

Dennis had positively beamed.

And now it was their last garbage-picking session, too. Frances saw something tucked under a bush and retrieved it with her claw. It was, she hoped, the last poopy diaper she would ever have to handle, at least until Max or Daisy gave her grandkids.

"I have some news," said Parker. "Wanda called me. She's starting a new show in a couple of weeks and she's going to bring me on."

"Parker, that is fabulous," said Geraint, high-fiving her. "I have news on the work front, too. Jorge and I have decided to go into business together. We're changing the name of his Quicky Muffler shop to The Muffler Magicians."

"Catchy," said Frances.

"We're going to go halfsies. Means we'll both be gainfully employed while also getting to spend more time with our kids."

"That's fantastic, Geraint," said Parker.

Geraint picked up a discarded umbrella from the path. He tried to open it. Half of it sprung to life; the other half hung limply, the spokes broken. He shrugged and tucked it into his backpack. Frances laughed. "Why, Geraint? Why?"

"Well, say you're half-protected by an awning, or by trees, in a rainstorm. Really all you need is half an umbrella."

"That is certainly a unique perspective."

They were approaching the end of their route. Geraint started to drag his feet, walking more and more slowly. "What's wrong?" asked Parker.

He sighed heavily. "Just, I'm going to miss this."

"Seriously?" asked Frances.

"It's less the garbage picking, and more the time spent with you two."

"We'll still see each other," said Frances. But there was a hint of doubt in her voice. They were very different people, after all, travelling in very different circles. People thrown together under unlikely circumstances. Chances were high that they would drift apart, and she was surprised that the thought filled her with melancholy.

A familiar white pickup truck was parked up ahead. Carol Jansen leaned against the truck bed, reading a tattered *Hello!* magazine. Frances noted she was wearing makeup again. "Good day, Carol," said Geraint. "Come to congratulate us for completing our community service, have you?"

"Yup, that's it. Your medals are in the truck."

"Ooh, really?" Geraint's eyes lit up before he clued in. "Oh. Sarcasm."

"I have to collect your stuff. But I did bring some Timbits to celebrate." She pulled a box out of the passenger seat and passed it around, along with a bottle of hand sanitizer. Frances was just popping a second chocolate-flavoured one into her mouth when Carol said, "Frances, if I could have a private word."

Geraint and Parker raised their eyebrows. "Of course." Frances was suddenly nervous. Had she messed something up, so her charges wouldn't be diverted? She followed Carol to a private spot under a tree. "What is it?"

"I think you know."

"I can assure you, I do not. Have I done something wrong?"

Carol gave her a hard stare, like she was trying to figure out if Frances was toying with her. "I'm just gonna lay my cards on the table. I'm pretty good at intuiting a lot of the undercurrents of human emotion. The what-do-you-call-thems—the *nuances.*"

"Are you, now."

"So I know you're in love with Geraint."

Frances's eyebrows shot up.

"I see the way you look at him. You are crushing, hard. Don't even try to deny it."

Frances opened her mouth to do exactly that, but Carol didn't wait for a response.

"Thing is," she continued, "I would never encroach on another woman's territory. Not like that bitch Pam did with my ex. So you tell me to back off, I'll back off."

A lot of comebacks were racing through Frances's head. But she decided to try a different tack. "I appreciate that, Carol, I really do. But alas, much as I may wish he did, Geraint has no romantic feelings for me whatsoever."

She brightened. "You're sure?"

"Very. What can I say. If you are interested in Geraint, I will not stand in your way."

Carol grabbed Frances's hand and shook it, hard. Her grip was painfully strong. "You're a gracious loser, Frances Partridge." Then Carol did something Frances had never seen her do before: She smiled. A big, genuine, toothy grin.

A while later, Frances punched in home on Google Maps, even though she knew the way. "Continue straight on West King Edward Avenue for three kilometres," said the AI voice.

"Sorry I've been so absent, Siobhan," Frances said. "But . . . well, I've had a lot going on."

"There's a two-minute slow-down ahead. You are still on the fastest route."

As she drove, she felt a pang of sadness, already missing Geraint and Parker and the hours they had spent together. It had helped fill her days, but it was more than that. She liked them. A lot.

As she neared Yukon Street, she felt the pull. Not as powerful as in the past . . . but still, a pull.

She turned right. "Don't judge me, Siobhan. I just need to see how it feels."

"Recalculating," Siobhan replied.

Frances parked outside the sky-blue Arts and Crafts house.

The days were getting longer, and it was hours until the sun would go down, so it was harder to see through the windows. She wasn't even sure anyone was home, but that wasn't the point. What did she feel this time, gazing at her ex-husband's new home, his new life?

It still made her mourn for the past, a past that she had fully imagined would be her present and her future.

But it didn't hurt as much. The pain was less acute.

A tap at her window made her jump.

Kelly was peering in through the passenger window. He gave her a small smile and a wave.

Reluctantly, Frances opened the window.

"Hi, Frances. Haven't seen you here for a while."

Ugh. She did her best to look puzzled. "Who? Me? I'm not sure what you mean."

"Jeremy's not here. He's at a conference till Friday."

"Ah."

"I'm very sorry, Frances. For the pain I've caused."

"Well, you didn't make him gay, Kelly. And *he's* the one who caused me pain."

"Yes, but . . . I never, ever thought I'd be a homewrecker—"

"Now, now, do not put me in a position where *I* feel the need to comfort *you*."

"Right. Of course." She could see that he was definitely balding and trying to hide the fact. And while Jeremy had trimmed down, Kelly had added a bit of padding around the middle. Guilt padding, perhaps? She was trying to figure out whether or not it made her feel better, or worse, that she been left for a man who was average-looking at best—because it obviously meant that there were so many other, non-surfacy ways that Kelly was fabulous—when he said, "Would you like to come in for a drink?"

"No. No, I most definitely would not—"

"I could show you my Royal Doulton figurines."

She tried to keep her tone disinterested. "Jeremy may have mentioned you had a collection."

"I have over one hundred. My favourite is the one with William and Kate, holding baby George."

That sealed it. Frances made her decision. "I will have one drink." She opened her car door and climbed out. "And I would *love* to see your Royal Doulton collection."

Three Months Later

I t was a gorgeous early July day. Frances's garden was an explosion of colour. Her guests mingled among blue and pink hydrangeas, gladioli, day lilies, brown-eyed Susans, and foxgloves. Chickadees and nuthatches flitted in and out of the three new colourful birdhouses Geraint had built for her. She couldn't have asked for a more perfect afternoon for Daisy's send-off party.

Over breakfast four weeks earlier, Daisy had told her mom she had some news. "Good Buzz has offered me a full-time job. The PR firm. As their media relations person."

"Daisy, that's amazing."

"They're super happy with the work I've been doing." Her eyes were bright with excitement.

"Of course they are. I'm so proud of you."

"The only thing is . . . it's in Calgary. They're opening a satellite office there."

"Ah." It had been a small punch to her solar plexus, but Frances had managed to keep the smile on her face.

"I don't need to go, Mom. I can turn them down."

Frances knew the subtext: *You, and my worry for you, would be my reason to stay.* "Daisy. You must go. This is absolutely the best news. I promise you, I will be fine." Then she'd embraced her in a hug. "Kwame will be sad."

"Kwame's old news, Mom. I'm seeing Fabiola now."

Frances smiled. Her dear little monster was finding her footing and leaving the nest. She was heartbroken and over the moon all at once.

While she waited for the oven timer to go off, she looked through the kitchen window at her guests. Jules and Carmen were deep in conversation with Parker and Alexei. Parker was wearing the most incredible sundress, which she'd designed herself, white cotton printed with large red and yellow flowers. Amita and Nabil were chatting with Cheryl Underwood. Meera and Rishi had found the bocce set and were attempting a game on the lawn. Daisy and Max were huddled together, talking non-stop and occasionally bursting into laughter.

Frances had to stop herself from running outside and throwing her arms around Max again; the poor kid had been home for just forty-eight hours of his three-week visit, and she had barely given him a moment's respite. "Stop pawing him, Mom, he's your own flesh and blood!" said Daisy. "It's creepy!" So Frances was trying to give him some space. She knew how important it was for him to have some alone-time with his sister and, hopefully, his father.

Speaking of his father: Jeremy stood in another corner of the garden, chatting with Cordelia and Alfred. Cordelia was fast deteriorating; more regularly confusing Frances with her long-dead sister Janet, no longer able to play her beloved bingo, and sometimes having wild hallucinations, seeing people who weren't there. But Frances was relieved that, for the most part, her mother did not seem to be in too much distress. And Alfred was still devoted to her. Frances had learned to be deeply grateful for that.

She saw Jeremy look longingly towards Max. So far Max had said no more than a frosty hello to him.

Norah and Maryam entered the yard through the side gate. Frances had recently resumed her weekly coffee date with them, because after a few weeks of embarrassed silence, they had become dogged in their persistence. She wasn't sure she would ever feel quite as close to them as she had in the past. But it didn't matter, because she had new friends. Completely unexpected, who'd-have-thunk-it friends.

She had also started to write again. For the first time in almost a year, words were actually pushing and jostling to come out of her head and onto the page. She was working on something completely different now, a total departure from her other books, and for the first time in a long while she was experiencing joy when she wrote. Maybe no one would publish it, but that was a bridge she would cross. For now, she simply revelled in the act of being creative again.

The timer went off. Frances took out a tray of mini-quiches and transferred them to a plate. She carried them outside. She was trying to find space for them on a table already laden with food when Cheryl approached. Frances steeled herself for a backhanded compliment or an onslaught of negativity. "Your garden looks beautiful."

Frances looked at her, pleasantly surprised. "Thank you, Cheryl."

"Guess it's another thing you'll miss when you have to sell."

There it was. "I'm not selling. Jeremy and I have worked it out. Once Daisy moves I'm going to have a tenant in the granny suite." She and Jeremy had sat down and done the math one night; the rent would go directly to Jeremy, so that slowly—very, very slowly—he'd be bought out of his half of the house. When Frances started earning again—either through writing or working as a greeter at a Walmart, who could say—she'd pay him from her income as well.

Cheryl wrinkled her nose. "A tenant, huh? No kids, I hope. It was bad enough having to listen to your two for all those years."

"Oh, there will definitely be a kid," Frances replied brightly.

As if on cue, Keanu rushed up to her and threw his chubby arms around her legs. "Frances, Daddy showed me my bedroom."

"Do you like it?"

"I love it! He's getting me a race car bed!" He dashed off to join Meera and Rishi in their game of bocce.

Geraint approached, dressed in khaki shorts and a loud Hawaiian shirt. "It is a great suite, Frances. Not a water stain or cigarette burn in sight!"

The idea had seemed so obvious once Frances knew that Daisy would be moving out. Geraint couldn't stay forever in that dreadful apart-hotel, and Frances had a lovely, about-to-be-empty two-bedroom suite. Geraint had almost burst into tears when she'd proposed the idea. "Yes, yes, a thousand times yes," he'd said. A mere half an hour later, his questions had begun: "Will Keanu and I be able to use the yard whenever we want?"

And "How would you feel if we put up a trampoline?"

And "Can I set up a small woodworking shop in your garage?"

And "Would you be averse to a treehouse?"

And "What if we got a small dog? Ooh, or a large dog. I love Bernese mountain dogs."

And "What do you think about planning joint meals? Personally, I think we should plan at least three or four a week, don't you?"

Frances had said yes to using the yard anytime, yes to the trampoline, yes to the woodworking, no to the treehouse, no to the dog ("But Mr. Pickles can visit whenever you like"), and yes to a maximum of two joint dinners a week. If she was honest, Daisy's imminent departure had been eating her up inside. And this—having her new, annoyingly cheerful and sometimes downright irritating friend move in downstairs, along with, half-time, his adorable young son—took away some of the sting. Yes, it meant she could keep the house, but it also meant she wouldn't be alone. Besides, she reckoned that Daisy had driven her crazy in her own way; now Geraint would drive her crazy in his own way.

Life moved on.

Cheryl scowled and filled her wine glass to the rim. She was about to walk away when Frances said, "Maybe you could join Geraint and Keanu and me for dinner one night."

Cheryl blinked, startled.

"Oh, please say yes, we'd love to have you," added Geraint.

Cheryl stood rigidly still, like she was trying to decipher the meaning of their words. "I'll think about it," she finally said. Then she took her full glass of wine and disappeared back into her own yard.

Geraint checked a message on his phone. "Carol's on her way."

"How is that going?"

"Fabulous," he gushed. "Frances, she thinks I'm the sexiest man alive. Me! She can't get enough of me. And good lord, she is on fire in the boudoir, if you catch my drift . . ."

"I'm catching it, and I would ask you to stop—"

"She has these *toys*—"

"Please, I beg you . . ."

"It's the grizzly bear!" Cordelia called from her corner of the garden. Geraint stepped away to give Cordelia a hug and Frances was relieved to be spared any more intimate details.

Jeremy sidled up beside her and handed her a glass of prosecco. "You looked thirsty."

She smiled. "You always were good at knowing what I needed, even before I did." They clinked glasses and she had a sip. "How's Kelly?"

"He's fine." None of them—not Frances, not Jeremy, not Kelly—had been ready for Kelly to join the party.

"I had no idea he was such a monarchist. I guess that's why William and Kate and baby George are his favourite figurine. Personally, mine would have to be the balloon seller."

"This will never get tired for you, will it?"

"No, it will not."

Jeremy gazed past her, a wistful look on his face, and Frances knew he was looking at Max.

"Give it time. If I can stand to be in the same room with you now and then, he'll get there, too."

Jeremy smiled. "We've done well by them, Frances."

"We have, haven't we? Better than we perhaps anticipated." They stood in silence for a moment. "I'm not *not* glad that you're happy, Jeremy," she said.

He smiled. "I thought you hated double negatives."

"I do. But it felt right in this case."

He took her hand. "Well, thank you. I'm not *not* glad to hear that."

As they stood there, side by side in the yard of the house they had bought together all those years ago, Frances suddenly choked up. She excused herself before Jeremy could notice. "I should go and prep the cake."

On the kitchen counter was another of Alexei's magnificent creations, this one in the shape of an airplane. *Congratulations, Daisy!* it read. Frances rooted in the drawer for candles, then remembered they'd used the last of them for Keanu's birthday months earlier.

Candles were hardly an imperative. But on the other hand, there was a corner store just three blocks away, and her emotions were getting the better of her. She could clear her head, be back in ten or fifteen minutes, and no one would even notice she was gone.

Frances slipped out the front door. Her favourite blue sundress billowed in the wind, and the warm breeze felt good on her bare legs. Where her own family was concerned, she was about to become a true empty nester; her children *and* her husband, gone. Her mother was rapidly drifting away. She thought of a line she had read somewhere, that life was a series of losses. She'd had more than her share this past while. But even though she knew she couldn't ignore it, even though she knew she had to acknowledge those feelings of loss and sadness, she was also done with dwelling in a place of bitterness and regret. *Be happy for what you have*, she told herself, quoting a meditation app she'd recently started using, *instead of dwelling on what you lack.*

Bells jingled above the door as she entered the mom-and-pop store on West 4th Avenue that had been a mainstay and a lifesaver over the years. She greeted the owner and wandered down the cluttered, narrow aisles.

"Tampon Nose," said a voice behind her.

A Scottish voice.

She turned. "Daniel Craig's brother."

"I definitely have the better nickname."

"That you do."

"Although I did feel Tampon Nose sounded better than Angry Rash on Thighs."

She smiled. "Agreed. Why not call me Frances?"

"Frances. I'm Owen." He held out his hand, and they shook. "Are you still swimming? I haven't seen you at the pool for months."

"I started going to UBC instead. No Turtle."

"Definite bonus."

An awkward silence. He was wearing light blue shorts and a navy polo shirt, and Frances couldn't help but notice he had nice pecs.

"Do you live around here?"

She nodded. "A few blocks away. You?"

"Just moved into the neighbourhood. I've only been in Vancouver for a year. Just bought a condo, so I guess I'm staying for a while."

"What brought you here?"

"I needed a change from Glasgow, so when my company opened an office here, I asked for a transfer."

"Why did you need a change?"

"I got divorced two years ago."

"Ah. I'm in the process of that myself. A divorce, that is. Not a transfer."

"I figured."

"Do you like it here?"

"I'm starting to. Takes a long time to make friends. Vancouverites are friendly but flaky. Hard to pin down."

"That is a fair assessment."

Another awkward silence. "Well, nice to see you again, Frances."

"You too, Owen."

He left.

And Frances immediately felt a pang of regret.

She found her candles, paid for them, and left the store.

Owen stood on the sidewalk, hands shoved into his pockets. "I tried to find you, you know. First I just wanted to see if you were okay, then I just really wanted to see you again, but it was like you'd vanished off the face of the earth."

"Oh."

"So now that I've found you, I'm just going to ask. Could I perhaps have your phone number?"

"Yes. You could." He smiled, and she noted he was awfully handsome when he smiled. He handed her his phone, and she added her number. He took his phone back and immediately sent her his. "Ah," she said. "*Eion*." Why was Owen, when spelled Eion, so much sexier?

"Perhaps this is too forward, but—what are you doing right now?" he asked. "We could go for a walk. Or a stand-up paddle board. I just joined the Jericho Sailing Centre."

"Sorry. I have a household full of guests. I really should head back."

"Ah, of course. Well, nice to run into you, Frances." He gave her a small wave, then walked away.

Frances stood on the sidewalk, watching him go.

He was a bit bowlegged.

She called out to him. "Eion?"

He turned.

"Why don't you join me? My friends would be delighted to meet you."

Acknowledgements

This is my first "grown-up" novel. The idea first came to me because, as the author of seven middle-grade/YA novels and a handful of picture books, I've done a lot of school visits over the years. The vast majority are wonderful and inspiring. But very early on in my novel-writing career, I had a mortifying experience at a middle school. A seventh grader said something completely inappropriate to me. I saw the shock on a teacher's face. Afterwards she beelined up to me, and I assumed it was to address the incident. Instead she asked, "You said you worked on *Degrassi*. Did you meet Drake?"

I'm laughing as I write this, but at the time I was furious. I guess you could say I snapped. I chased the boy down and gave him an earful. I remember thinking, "Who is this person who's taken over my body?" and also "I wonder who's going to be in more trouble—the boy, or me?"

But by the time I left the school, the voice in my head was also saying, "This could be a hilarious scene in a novel." It took me over ten more years to begin what became *SNAP*.

This is a new endeavour for me, writing for grown-ups instead of kids, and it was equal parts daunting, challenging, and fun. I owe a huge thanks to my very first readers: Linda Bailey and Susan Juby, two exceptional writers who graciously took time from their own projects to give me terrific suggestions on how to improve the manuscript. Linda also deserves full credit for the title. I told her I was grappling with what to call it and gave her the

321

one-liner—"It's about three people who snap"—and she said, "That's your title." I felt a little sheepish, to be honest—why hadn't I thought of it already?

My dear agent, Hilary McMahon, put on a good show of being pleased that I was trying something new, even though it was not a slam dunk. She believed in the novel and worked tirelessly on finding the book a good home.

And boy, did she find it a good home! Jennifer Lambert, editor in chief at HarperCollins Canada, immediately championed the manuscript. Thank you, Jennifer, for believing in this book, and to Iris Tupholme for believing in Jennifer. Jennifer's editorial letter resulted in a couple of substantial changes (not to mention many smaller ones), and the book is so much stronger because of it. I love my HarperCollins family.

My husband, Göran Fernlund, read a more polished version and had some helpful notes along with undying encouragement. My good friends David D. Clarke and Dr. Fraser Norrie agreed to be beta readers, and I got excellent suggestions from them as well, especially around digging deeper into Frances and Jeremy's relationship. Thanks also to my beautiful son, Oskar Fernlund, for help with the paragraphs about rugby.

Stephanie Fabbro was a lifesaver when it came to all things family law in the novel, as was Claire Hatcher for all things criminal law. They both carefully read the manuscript and spared me from looking like a total idiot. Any mistakes are my own. If I ever get divorced or commit murder, I will know who to call. Thanks, too, to Richard Hamilton, another excellent family lawyer, for his help early on.

An additional shout-out goes to Karen Hardie, one of the many brilliant women in the Magic Lake Swim Club on Pender Island, for her helpful sewing machine advice. Ditto to Sarah Dodd and Sloane Kinney for their help with the correct terminology for Dungeons & Dragons campaigns (I may have just used the wrong terminology again).

Last but definitely not least, I want to thank my incredible team of writers on *Family Law*, the TV show I created and was showrunner on for four successful, laugh-filled, creatively fulfilling seasons. These talented folks are the best in the biz and they gave me four of the most fun years of my professional career. There are many elements from the show that have crept their way into my novel in some form or other. To Sarah Dodd, Ken Craw, Sonja Bennett, Corey Liu, Kaylyn Johnson, Scott Button, Damon Vignale, Jordan Hall, and Qaseem Fazal—I love you all and I hope we get to work together on something else soon.